SWING AND A KISS

Carolina Waves Series Book Four

TINA GALLAGHER

Galsalla Press

Swing and a Kiss: Carolina Waves Series Book 4

By: Tina Gallagher

Published by Galsalla Press

Copyright © 2020

Cover Design: Qamber Designs

Editor: Jeannine Luby

A big thank you to Maura for giving me the perfect title for Dale and Karen's story.

And as always, for my Family

Chapter One

DALE

I TURNED into the crowded parking lot and pulled into a spot toward the back. I'm late. I hate being late. Especially to events like this. It makes me feel like people think I'm trying to make a grand entrance or something. Which I'm definitely not.

Grabbing my cell off its mount, I texted Jack to let him know I'm here then opened the door and stepped out of the car. I'd planned on arriving before everything started, but my flight was delayed. According to the schedule I was given, dinner started a half-hour ago. At least it's a buffet so I won't be tiptoeing through tables during a formal dinner service.

Laughter and an occasional screech breached the sound of the surf so the event must be as casual as Jack said. Then again, it is a beach bash. It'd be kind of difficult to make it too serious.

I walked through the parking lot and spotted Mrs.

Garrett sitting behind the registration desk at the entrance. She heads the Citizens Against Drunk Driving committee that hosts this annual event. I've met her and some of the other volunteers when they attended spring training games.

"Mrs. Garrett, it's nice to see you again," I said as I approached the table.

She stood and shook my hand.

"Thank you so much for coming," she said. "It's been wonderful having Jack these past couple years and we're thrilled you're able to make it this year."

"I'm happy to be here and I'm sorry I'm late. There was an issue with the plane so they had to bring in another one and that took a few hours."

"Thankfully they figured out there was an issue before you took off," she said and I nodded in agreement. "We're not very formal here. I've already given my speech so you can be thankful you missed that." She chuckled. "The buffet will be out for the next couple hours." Picking up a neon orange band, she removed the tab covering the adhesive, wrapped it around my wrist, and secured it in place. "This gets you in and all you can eat. You can help yourself when you're ready."

"Thank you." I walked toward the festivities but stopped when I spotted the crowd in front of me. Stepping back to Mrs. Garrett, I asked, "Do you by any chance know which direction Jack is in?"

"He's sitting over toward the buffet area."

"Thanks. You just saved me from wandering around for an hour."

Stepping into the sand, I took a minute to admire the jumbo slide, bouncy house, and assorted games to the right. Most of the attendees were seated but a few die-hards took advantage of dinnertime to get in a few extra runs. Jack volunteered to sit in a dunk tank and he'd also mentioned a speed throw so I figured there were more activities hiding behind the slide. It's definitely a great setup.

I turned left and walked toward the buffet and spotted Jack and Hannah seated directly across from it, three tables in. Hannah saw me and waved as I wove through the tables and walked toward them.

"Glad you made it," Jack said as I approached.

"Can't let you have all the fun."

He smirked. "If that's the case, then I'll tell Mrs. Garrett you volunteered to sit in the dunk tank."

"You know I would but I didn't bring a change of clothes." I rested my hand against my stomach. "But I did bring a huge appetite. I haven't eaten since breakfast so I'm gonna hit the buffet before I sit."

I glanced around as I walked to the buffet, telling myself I wasn't looking for anyone in particular. Just taking in the sights.

Grabbing a plate, I made my way down the line filling it as I went along, making small talk with the man in front of me. If he recognized me, he didn't say and I sure as hell didn't introduce myself. I wasn't lying when I said I was hungry, so I was hoping to get some food in my stomach before I had to put on my game face. I've been lucky so far. Everyone seems to be too busy eating to pay attention to me.

I backtracked to the bar and got two glasses of water before heading to the table. I sat next to Jack, and Hannah introduced me to the others sitting with us. I'm pretty good with faces, but none of them looked familiar. Maybe they didn't attend the games with the rest of the volunteers the past couple of years.

Mr. Hanover, the owner of the Waves, is very community-oriented and he likes his players to have a lot of fan contact. Which my friends and I enjoy and we tend to do more than is expected. Case in point, this event tonight. This beach bash fundraiser is one of Jack's pet projects. I'm just along for the ride.

A few years ago, one of Jack's ex-girlfriends wrote a tell-all book about him. It was relatively tame as far as that kind of thing goes, but Mr. Hanover decided Jack needed to improve his image to combat any bad publicity. So he had him work with Hannah Adams from the public relations department and she set up a variety of events like this for him to attend.

Even though the book is long forgotten, Jack still attends the events and holds meet-and-greets at the stadiums both here in St. Pete and at home in Myrtle Beach for people he's met along the way. Besides the fact that he really enjoys meeting fans, he also credits the whole PR blitz for the fact that he fell in love with Hannah and she's changed his whole life.

They got married last year so I'm the last man standing in my small friend group. Dan tied the knot the year before that and Cal just took the plunge last week down in the Keys.

"How were your extra days in the Keys?" Jack asked.

"Good. Relaxing." I took a bite of swordfish, eager to change the subject. "Mmm, this is really good."

"Yeah, Mrs. Garrett does it right." He stood. "In fact, I'm gonna go get seconds." He looked at Hannah. "I'll grab you another drink. Do you want anything else?"

"Some of that fried shrimp would be great."

"You got it." He leaned down and gave her a quick kiss before heading to the buffet.

I continued to eat, looking around between bites.

"Looking for anyone in particular?" Hannah asked.

I winced at her all-knowing smile.

"No." I shook my head. "Just taking it all in."

I focused on my plate as I shoveled food into my mouth. I felt her still watching me and glanced over and raised my brow.

"You doing okay?"

I nodded and swallowed. "Sure."

Hannah looked like she was about to say more but Jack returned and sat between us.

"Here you go," he said, handing her a virgin strawberry daiquiri with an insane amount of whipped cream on top.

She took it from him and rolled her eyes, but then they shared an intimate smile. I've seen something similar between the two of them dozens of times since they've gotten together. Dan and Sabrina have the same type of secret language and now Cal and Barbara do, too. Not to mention my sister Penny and Kenny Hanover.

I've never had a deep enough relationship with a woman to share anything so special. Lord knows I didn't live like a monk for most of my career. I had women to spend time with wherever I happened to be in the country, but things were always pretty superficial.

Then a couple years ago, I decided I wanted more than casual encounters. I'm sure watching my friends settle down had something to do with that. Especially Jack. Before Hannah, his relationships were as shallow as mine. But now he's head over heels in love and so happy it's almost shocking.

Jack pulled me from my thoughts, bringing me into the conversation he was having with two men across the table. Apparently they'd asked about the upcoming season and I was happy for the distraction.

We answered the usual questions about the health of

our teammates and what we think our chances are of winning the series this year with our standard answers. Everyone feels great after winter break and if we all stay healthy and the baseball gods smile down on us, we believe we can win it all.

Jack's phone buzzed and he silenced the alarm then stood.

"It's time for me to get to the dunk tank," he said.

Hannah and the woman next to her had just finished a conversation so she decided to join him.

"I want to get some pictures for the Waves website," she said.

"I'm coming too," I said. "I don't want to miss this."

We excused ourselves from the table and walked across the beach toward the dunk tank. Thankfully Jack had given us enough time to chat with people who approached us along the way. Hannah had a never-ending bag of Waves swag with her and we handed that out as well.

"Hey Jeremy," Jack said as we walked toward the speed throw.

The two met and bonded when Jack first attended this fundraiser two years ago. Jack has made it a point to stay in touch with the boy since then and Jeremy and his mom Karen are regulars at spring training games and whenever we play Tampa.

Jeremy introduced his two friends, Mark and Tyler. At first, their mouths hung open as they stared at Jack and me, but then they relaxed and started talking. We chatted for a few minutes and it took all my willpower to stay focused on the boys instead of looking around for Jeremy's mother. There are a lot of people here, but it's inevitable I'll run into Karen sooner or later.

"They're waving me over to the tank," Jack said and we followed him over.

The previous volunteer was climbing out as we approached. He shook Jack's hand and warned him about the cold water in the tank.

"I'm going over to the other side to take pictures and video," Hannah said.

"Do you want me to take some from this side?" I asked.

"That'd be great. Thanks Dale."

She walked through the people standing in line who were ready to pay for the opportunity to dunk Jack.

"Did you want to get in line?" I asked Jeremy, Mark, and Tyler as I reached for my wallet.

"No, I think I'd rather just watch," Jeremy said, but the other boys took me up on my offer. I handed each some cash and they ran over to the back of the line.

I pulled out my phone and took a few pictures as Jack climbed the ladder, stepped into the tank, and sat on the board, dangling his feet over the water. Then I switched to video and taped as person after person stepped up to the line and threw their ball toward the target.

Jack talked smack to the people wearing Tampa jerseys and they teased him back, but it was all good-natured.

"It doesn't seem like that target would be so hard to hit," Jeremy said.

"They're aiming too much and most are throwing too hard."

Just after I said that, a man stepped up to the line and wound up then sent the ball sailing over the target and into the tarp hanging behind it.

The next person hit the edge of the target, but it wasn't enough to trigger the mechanism. Jack hammed it up, pinching his nose closed and dramatically holding his breath.

Two more people were unsuccessful and I started

thinking about getting in line myself if this didn't end soon. At least it's raising money for a good cause.

Mark and Tyler each took a shot and missed.

A teenage girl stepped up to the line and after studying the target, stepped back then forward in a windmill windup, throwing a perfect strike. The ball hit the center of the target, sending Jack splashing into the water. The crowd cheered and Jack laughed as he came up for air, slicking his hair back.

I turned off my video and looked at Jeremy.

"See, she relaxed and studied her target then made a natural throw. Nothing crazy."

"That makes sense."

"Are you coming to the game next week?" I asked.

"Yeah and I can't wait. I love spring training games. I mean, regular season is awesome but spring training is so chill."

"Yeah, it's nice down here. Different for sure." We watched two people climb the ropes to the top of the big slide. "Hey, want to race?"

He blinked then nodded. "Sure."

"Let's go."

We ran to the line, which surprisingly wasn't too long.

"So, did your season start yet?" I asked while we waited.

"Travel ball has. We had our first tournament two weeks ago."

"How's it going?"

"Good. I'm getting a lot of playing time and I really like my coach." He smiled up at me. "He's even been having me practice pitching. Since there's only fourteen of us on the team, he wants me ready just in case."

"That's great. I loved pitching."

"You didn't always play first base?"

I shook my head. "When I was your age I played short-stop and pitched. In high school, they moved me to first base on the days I wasn't pitching and those are the positions I played in college. When I got drafted, it was for first base and I've been there since. I like it because I get to play more, plus I get to bat. But I do miss being on the mound."

He was about to ask another question but it was our turn. When the attendant told us to go, we both ran toward the huge slide and I grabbed at the ropes and climbed, letting Jeremy stay a half a step ahead of me. We reached the top and sat then I waited until he pushed himself down before shifting forward to start my own descent. He stood just as I reached the bottom.

I know I must look like an idiot laughing with a huge smile on my face, but that had been awesome. What a great ride.

"It's been a while since I did anything like that. Thank you," I said to him.

"No, thank you," he said in one breath and in the next said, "Hey mom."

I glanced over my shoulder and saw Karen Walsh, looking just as beautiful as she had the last time I'd seen her, if not more so. My stomach tightened and flipped more than it had when I was coming down the slide.

Damn, it's like getting hit in the gut with a bat.

KAREN

"HI KAREN."

"Hi Dale," I stuttered, feeling like an idiot. How hard can it be to say two words?

But in my defense, I'm shocked that he's here. He's never attended before.

I tucked a stray piece of hair behind my ear, wishing I'd taken some extra time with my appearance instead of coming straight from work. Why? I have no idea. Sure he's asked me out in the past, but last time we'd seen each other, he basically ignored me. Although I guess that's to be expected since I've never agreed to a date.

Being turned down would be a blow to any man's ego, and Dale Montgomery isn't just any man. He's a professional athlete, sexy as hell, and a nice guy. Talk about a hotness trifecta. I'm probably the only woman crazy enough to say no to him about anything.

But I'm not stupid. Life isn't like a romance novel. If it was, I would have had my happily-ever-after with Jason. Instead he was killed by a drunk driver and now I'm a single mother trying to keep it together for my son. I like my life orderly and something tells me letting Dale into it would make it anything but, even if it was just for one date.

"Is it okay if I go find the guys?" Jeremy asked.

As much as I don't want to be alone with Dale, I can't expect Jeremy to stay by my side the entire night. He's getting too old for that.

"Sure. Just make sure your phone is on."

"Thanks mom. See you later, Monte."

I watched him run off then turned to look at Dale. He scratched his chin with the back of his hand drawing my eyes to his mouth. His bottom lip is slightly plumper than the top and from the moment I saw him, I've wondered what it would feel like to kiss him. The last time I had thoughts like that about anyone was back in middle school when I first met Jason.

"He's getting tall."

It took me a moment to refocus and realize he was referring to Jeremy.

"Yeah, he had a growth spurt this past fall. He'll be passing me out soon."

"And by next year I won't have to slow down so he can beat me on the slide."

He chuckled, a deep rumble that vibrated through my body making my nipples perk up. I crossed my arms over my chest hoping he wouldn't notice.

"I'm surprised to see you here."

"Jack asked me to come last year but I needed to be in Aspen and couldn't make it. This year worked out well. Cal's wedding was last week in the Keys and we don't have to report until Tuesday. So here I am."

His biceps bulged when he held his arms out to the side.

I cleared my throat. "So you live in Aspen off season?" I asked, as if I didn't know the answer. Just because I won't date him doesn't mean I didn't do some cyber stalking.

He nodded. "I have a small ranch there. Have you ever been?"

"No, but I hear it's beautiful."

"It is, especially in the fall. But I'm fortunate that my job takes me all over the country so I get to see a lot of cool places." He glanced at me. "What?"

"What?"

"You looked surprised or something."

"It just sounded strange to hear baseball referred to as a job, even though that's what it is at the level you're playing." I glanced around. "In fact, I'm surprised we've been speaking this long without someone interrupting."

"The key is to not make eye contact."

I'd managed to get my nipples under control but his sexy smirk and bobbing eyebrows had them standing at attention again. I looked around, in the hope that taking my eyes off him would help and I noticed a young boy approaching with a man I assumed to be his father.

"Looks like I spoke too soon," I said, nodding my head in their direction.

Dale looked at them and smiled, which gave them the courage to approach. He stooped down, putting him at the boy's level and introduced himself, as if that was necessary. The boy handed him a ball to sign and they carried on a conversation. Their interaction didn't go unnoticed and soon a small crowd gathered.

I was about to excuse myself when Jack and Hannah joined us. After that, even more people approached.

"Come on," Hannah said. "Let's go get a drink and let these guys do their thing." She handed Jack the tote bag she'd been carrying. "I expect this to be empty next time I see you."

"Yes ma'am." He gave her a kiss and smiled and I couldn't help but feel a pang of jealousy for the pure love flowing between them.

We wove through the crowd toward the tables and the buffet. Thank God because I haven't eaten yet and I'm starving.

"I've stayed with Jack the past couple years but I think he and Dale can handle things together."

"They're both so good with fans. The Waves must do some heavy-duty PR training."

"The players do receive training, but there are some things you just can't teach. Jack, Dale, Cal, and Dan are all amazing with fans. They make my job easy."

We walked up to the bar and Hannah ordered a virgin strawberry daiquiri. I opted for an orange creamsicle slushie.

Hannah took a sip of her drink. "This is my third one but I can't help it, they're so good."

"I'm jealous. I love strawberries but I'm allergic." We walked by the buffet and my stomach growled at the amazing smells. "Thank God the buffet is still out. I'm so hungry."

"Here, give me your drink and go grab a plate. I'll meet you at the table."

I did as I was told and joined her at the table with a full plate in my hand.

"The food is always so good here." I forced myself to take human bites.

"You and Jeremy are definitely coming to the first game, right?"

"MmmHmm," I muttered around a mouthful, then swallowed and added, "Jeremy really looks forward to it. Thank you so much. You and Jack have been so good to him, to us."

"He's a great kid." She smiled. "And you're a great mom."

I smiled at her compliment and continued eating.

"There they go," she said, looking toward the slide.

I spotted Jack sliding down about a foot behind the boy on the other side.

"Poor Jack. How many times did he do that slide last year?"

"I don't know, but he was feeling it the next day," she said. "At least this year he has Dale to split the runs with."

Sure enough, Dale was the next one down, across from a young girl.

And so it went with the two guys alternately appearing on the slide. I eventually lost count of how many times they each slid down.

"I'm getting exhausted just watching them."

"It looks like they're slowing down now," she said when the next three runs were people we didn't know.

Dale appeared at the top again but when he reached the bottom, instead of disappearing around the back, he walked toward us.

"Holy hell, that's a workout." He plopped into the chair next to me.

"You were warned," Hannah said.

"That I was, but it was fun. I'm glad I was able to make it this year."

"Me too." Hannah stood. "I'm going to grab some dessert."

"That sounds great," I said and started to stand.

She placed her hand on my shoulder, holding me in my seat. This isn't the first time I've gotten the feeling she's playing matchmaker.

"I'll get a variety we can share," she said then shifted her eyes to Dale. "And I'll grab a pitcher of water for you and Jack."

"That would be appreciated," Dale said then looked at me. "Jack is taking one last run with Jeremy and then they'll be over."

I caught a glimpse of rock-hard abs when he lifted the bottom of his shirt and used it to wipe his face.

Take a deep breath, girl.

I did as my inner voice directed but it only filled my lungs with the mouth-watering scent of Dale Montgomery. How he could smell so clean, like fresh air and sandalwood, after the workout he just had is beyond me.

Thankfully I spotted Jack and Jeremy on the slide reminding me that my job is to focus on my son, not the insanely attractive man sitting next to me.

Now I just have to convince my libido to let go of the first man who's piqued its interest in years.

Chapter Two

DALE

BENNIE JARVIS STOOD over by second base with a bucket of balls and hurled them at me, one throw worse than the next. I picked the balls out of the dirt, stretched left, right, and center for short throws, and jumped for balls over my head.

"You better make sure you catch those," Jack said from behind me. "I don't want to get hit."

"Me neither," Dan said.

With Bennie still assaulting me from his bottomless bucket, I didn't have time to look at them, but I know exactly where they're positioned and what they're doing. We've had pretty much the same stretching routine for years. I came out early today because Bennie has to leave and he's the best at feeding me shitty throws.

"No worries," I said, continuing to take what Bennie was dishing out. "With Jack at short, I'm used to bad throws like this."

"Yeah right," Jack said. "All my throws are frozen ropes right to the middle of your chest."

"I'm working here. Don't make me laugh, I need to concentrate."

Bennie held up his hands, showing three balls in each. Only six more to go. And of course, he didn't make them easy. He alternated the throws from side to side and instead of bouncing, the last ball skipped across the dirt and came at me at a weird angle. Thankfully I snatched it before it got past me. If it went anywhere near Jack and Dan, they'd bust my ass about it for the rest of the season.

"Thanks Bennie. You're the best bad thrower around."

He laughed and watched me refill the bucket. He's in better shape than a lot of seventy-year-olds, but as a former ballplayer, he's also riddled with arthritis in his back and knees and has a hard time bending and stooping. Along with a lot of the retired Waves, he comes to help out at spring training every year. I've learned so much from those guys through the years and they continue to help me more than a decade into my career.

We agreed to meet an hour later for the rest of the week and he walked toward the dugout to grab a drink. I joined my friends who were still stretching along the first base line.

Sitting next to Jack, I put my legs out in front of me and folded forward grabbing onto the bottom of my feet. Sweat dripped down my nose and plopped onto my pants.

I sat up straight and wiped my face with the hem of my shirt then spread my legs wide and moved from side to side, before walking my hands forward as far as I could go. My hips and hamstrings protested, but I took in a deep breath and slowly let it out settling into the stretch. After a minute, I walked my hands back, pulled my legs together and folded forward again.

"What's up for dinner tonight?" Dan asked.

"I know Hannah and I have to either go somewhere or get takeout because the cupboards at Chez Reagan are bare."

"Mine too," I said. "If you guys weren't doing anything, I was just gonna grab a pizza on my way home."

Finishing my stretch, I rested back against my elbows.

"We can do something. I'm sure we'll have enough pizza nights once the games start. How about *The Battered Bluefin*?" Dan asked, referring to our favorite seafood spot. "I could go for their calamari."

I was just about to respond when I caught a flash of copper out of the corner of my eye. Looking up, I spotted my sister Penny and Kenny Hanover leaning against the railing up on the concourse. The fact that they're a couple is still a shock to my system.

"We can go somewhere else if you don't want to go to *The Battered Bluefin*," Dan said.

"No, it's fine."

"It doesn't look fine," Jack chimed in. "You look pissed."

"Not about dinner." I sat up and nudged my chin toward the stands. "And not pissed exactly. Just still getting used to it."

They both looked over at Penny and Kenny and nodded.

"He's not a bad guy," Dan said.

"Yeah, he's an okay guy, just not someone I'd pick for my little sister."

"And who would you pick for her?"

I smirked at Dan. "Wait until Lexi starts dating then answer that same question."

"I don't have to worry about that for a while. Lexi isn't allowed to date until she's at least thirty."

"Yeah well Penny is almost thirty and it doesn't make me feel better." Dragging the back of my hand against my forehead, I wiped away lingering sweat then rested my arm on my bent knee. "And I know she's my sister not my daughter, but it's always been the two of us, so it's weird."

What I didn't add is how bizarre it is to have my three best friends get married and my little sister find love in such a short timeframe. I'm glad they're all happy, but I definitely feel like the odd man out sometimes.

Dan looked up at them then shifted his eyes back to me.

"Well, thankfully it's time for batting practice. You can take out your stress on the ball." We all stood and he patted me on the back. "Then maybe you'll be in a better mood."

"There's nothing wrong with my mood."

I rolled my eyes and walked toward the dugout. I need a drink and to get away from those two hens for a minute. They're two of my best friends, but since they've found love, they think everyone else should, too. Or at least Cal and me. And of course, Cal has, so it's just me now.

They know my history with women and they also know that I've changed my habits the past couple years. As I got older, having a different woman in every city stopped being fun and started feeling a little stereotypical and a whole lot pathetic. So I made a decision to not date—or do anything else with—women I don't feel connected to.

The thing is, Karen Walsh is the only woman who's met that requirement in almost two years. And despite the fact she's turned me down the multiple times I've asked her out, that connection hasn't gone away.

After downing two cups of water, I grabbed my bat and walked back onto the field ready to pound some balls with one question running through my head.

Why is it that once I decided I want to find *the one* and settle down, the only woman I'm interested in won't even give me a chance?

KAREN

BUTTERFLIES FILLED my stomach as Jeremy walked out to the mound. I'm usually pretty relaxed when he plays, but this is the first time he's pitching so I'm a little nervous.

"Relax, he's going to do great," my sister-in-law Chloe said. "He didn't seem nervous when I was driving him over. More like excited."

My job as a real estate agent gives me the flexibility to work around Jeremy's schedule but this game was rescheduled because of rain. Chloe travels a lot for work but when she is in town, she helps me out when I need it. So today instead of me having to cancel a showing, she picked Jeremy up from school and got him to the field in time for pre-game practice.

Jason and I started dating in seventh grade and since Chloe is only a year older, we basically grew up together. She truly is my sister from another mister. We've always been close and she even lived with Jeremy and me for a while right after Jason died.

"Here we go," Chloe said and I watched Jeremy focus intently on the batter who just stepped into the box.

His first two pitches were high but the next one was called a strike. The batter hit the next pitch. A high fly ball that thankfully the center fielder caught.

"One down, two to go," I muttered, more to myself than Chloe.

The next guy hit a line drive over the third baseman's head. Thankfully the left fielder got the ball in fast enough to hold him to a single. Jeremy looked toward the dugout and nodded at whatever his coach was telling him.

He stepped back onto the mound and kept looking over his shoulder to hold the runner close to first base. The batter swung at the first pitch and hit a ground ball just to the left of second base. The shortstop scooped it up and stepped on the bag then threw the ball to first base for a double play.

I clapped so hard, my hands hurt. I also felt much more relaxed than I had before the game started.

"Not bad," Chloe said. She took a sip of iced coffee, then looked at me with a small smirk. "So Dale Montgomery was at the fundraiser last week, huh?" I nodded, not sure what to say. "I just find it strange I had to hear that from Jeremy when you and I talk almost every day."

"I didn't think it was that important." A laugh was her only answer. "I don't know what's so funny."

"Sure you do. You knew I'd be interested, which is why you didn't tell me."

The game had started again and Chloe and I both remained silent as our first two batters went deep into the count before being walked.

"Did he ask you out again?" she asked.

"No and I don't think he's going to, thank God."

"You must be insane."

"Why do you say that?"

Our next batter hit the ball over the left fielder's head allowing one run to score.

"I say that because he's good looking, sexy as hell, and from what both you and Jeremy say, a nice guy. I'd jump at the chance to go out with 'the full Monte.'"

"Maybe you can pretend you're me. People always mistake us for sisters. "

Jason and I had been what our friends called a "brother/sister couple." With our blond hair and blue eyes, we could have passed for siblings. And since Chloe looks a lot like him, the same goes for the two of us.

"Not that much alike," she said. "Seriously Kar, why won't you go out with him?"

"I need to focus on Jeremy, not the hot ballplayer who comes to town a few times a year."

"First of all, Jeremy isn't a toddler anymore. I think you could go out on one date without scarring him for life. And second, isn't a guy who won't be around all the time perfect since you say you don't want to get involved?"

"As Jason's sister, shouldn't you be against me dating someone new?"

"*As Jason's sister*, I know he wouldn't want you pining away for him for the rest of your life. He'd want you to be happy." She placed her hand over mine and squeezed. "It's been five years."

Again, I didn't know what to say. I shook my head and focused on the game. I'm not sure what happened while we were talking, but our team had scored four runs and was still batting. Jeremy's coach uses a designated hitter for the pitcher, so at least I didn't miss my son batting.

"I'm sorry," Chloe said. "I didn't mean for things to get so serious, I just planned on teasing you a little."

"It's fine. I just don't know how to handle all this. Dating in general. Dale specifically." I chuckled. "Not that he's interested anymore. The man can have his pick of women. Why would he keep chasing after the one who keeps turning him down?"

"Because he obviously likes you, and if you like him too, you should give it a shot." She crossed her right leg over the left and shifted her body to face me. "As far as the rest, you just take it one day at a time. Or one date at a time as the case may be. When are you going to see him again?"

"At the game next week. But I'm not sure if we'll interact at all."

"Well if you do, just give the guy a chance."

Out of the corner of my eye, I saw Jeremy running out to the mound again.

"Okay," I said, turning my attention back to the game.

Chloe held up her hand with her pinky out. "Pinky swear?"

I turned my head toward her and frowned.

"How old are you?"

She held her hand in front of my face until I relented and linked my pinky with hers.

"Pinky swear."

Chapter Three

DALE

I STEPPED into the on-deck circle watching the new pitcher take the mound. New York's starting pitcher had walked two then gave up a home run to John Kasprzyk to start the inning so they yanked him here in the fourth. Meanwhile, our starting pitcher, Chris "Rusty" Russell, is doing a stellar job. He had some control issues in the first half of last year, but ended strong and looks great so far.

Holding the bat at both ends, I folded forward and touched it against my toes then straightened and arched back holding it over my head. I leaned down and grabbed the doughnut then slipped it on and, holding the bat in my right hand, swung my arm in big circles to loosen my shoulder then repeated the process with the left.

As I moved through the rest of my routine, I scanned the stands. There's a decent-sized crowd tonight which is pretty common. Fans are usually starving for baseball after a long winter and it's a perfect night for a game.

I banged the handle of the bat on the dirt and dislodged the doughnut then took a few practice swings, careful not to look behind me. As I knew they would be, Karen and Jeremy are here. I'd spoken to him before the game but I've made it a point to avoid looking where I knew they'd be sitting.

The umpire signaled that the pitcher was on his last warm-up pitch so I took one last swing and rested the bat against my shoulder. My attention was pulled to that taboo section and as I walked toward the plate, I gave in to my urge to look, figuring a peek couldn't hurt. Trying not to be too obvious, I glanced over my shoulder and met Karen Walsh's gaze. The netting and distance between us did nothing to lessen the impact of her cornflower blue eyes on mine.

Taking in a deep breath to combat the weird twisty-flippy thing going on in my stomach, I turned back toward the field and walked to the plate. Stepping into the batter's box, I took in another deep breath and slowly let it out as I settled into my stance. But neither the job I had to do nor the cleansing breath stopped me from relishing in the fact that Karen had been watching me.

A fast ball to my sweet spot pulled all my focus back to the task at hand. Stepping forward with my left leg, I shifted my hips and extended my arms, swinging the bat around with quick hands. The satisfying crack of the ball hitting the wood vibrated up through my shoulders as I watched a line drive sail over the shortstop's head into the gap between left and center. The first base coach waved me on to second and I ended up with a stand-up double.

Jimmy Chavez stepped up to the plate and I took my lead. After getting to a full count, he hit a ground ball to Noah Shepard at third base. I stayed a few steps off the bag waiting for the throw so I could advance. But instead of just looking me back and throwing to first to get the out, Shepard turned toward me and started to throw then stopped. He couldn't throw because no one covered the bag behind me.

Realizing his mistake, he turned and rushed the throw to first. The ball went sailing over the first baseman's head. I rounded third as the right fielder picked up the ball and threw it home, sliding across the plate a split second before the catcher caught it and slapped the tag down.

Jumping up, I ran toward the dugout and caught Karen's eye again and smiled, feeling all warm inside when her smile widened. I have no idea what it is about this woman, but she makes me feel things I've never felt before.

Stepping down into the dugout, I grabbed a cup and filled it with water then settled onto the bench next to Jack and Dan. We have a six run lead now so I doubt I'll be going back out for the fifth inning, but I won't get too comfortable until the coach officially tells me that.

"What's the matter, old man? You winded from running?"

I swallowed the last of my water and looked at Jack. "You should know since you're a year older than me."

"Speaking of running," Dan said. "I wish I had a picture of the look on your face when Shepard turned your way instead of to first. You looked like a deer caught in headlights."

"That's exactly what I felt like." I stood and refilled my cup. "I mean come on, that's a Little League play. Look the runner back then throw to first. It's not like I was that far off the bag."

"But your reputation precedes you. Everyone knows you usually end up running," Dan said as he stood and grabbed his helmet, bat, and batting gloves.

"Still, no one has ever done that to me." I shrugged. "That I remember anyway."

"There's a first time for everything." After imparting those words of wisdom, Dan jogged up the steps and out to the on-deck circle.

Oskar Marquez hit a little blooper to short right, scoring Leo Marakis.

Dan worked the count full and fouled off four pitches before launching a high fly ball right at the center fielder for the third out. As I'd predicted, I was told not to head back out to the field and watched as the spring training invite jogged out to first. Dan, Jack, and the rest of the starters were also joining me on the bench.

My first few years in the Majors I'd get pissed during spring training whenever I didn't play or when they yanked me when we were ahead. But now I know it's all just part of the game. I don't need to prove myself anymore and besides that it's a long season. I need to take breaks whenever I can.

I grabbed a bag of dill pickle sunflower seeds and settled onto the bench to watch the game. Jack sat next to me and held out his hand, as if there weren't boxes of the things right behind his head.

"Did Hannah talk to you about Sunday?" he asked then shoved a handful of seeds into his mouth.

"She did." I cracked a shell open with my teeth and spit it out then chewed the seed. "And I told her that I don't need a birthday party."

"Despite that fact, it seems you're having one," Jack said around a chuckle. "You know how my wife loves to plan things."

The guys and I have always spent a good amount of time together, even off season, but that's definitely increased since Hannah has been in the picture.

"Doesn't she organize enough things at work?"

"Guess not."

I finished the seeds in my mouth and took a drink, then watched all the young guys out on the field.

"It's just us, right?"

Jack nodded. "And Penny and Kenny."

I grunted in response and continued to eat my seeds.

Kenny Hanover really is a good guy, but since his father owns the Waves, it's like having my boss around and definitely changes the dynamic. But Penny seems head over heels for him and he treats her like a princess so I'll just have to deal.

I'll also have to deal with the fact that I'm turning thirty-five. Which I know isn't old for normal people, but it's bordering on ancient for professional athletes.

Thankfully the Waves just signed me on for another four years, so at least I still have my career for now. As long as I stay healthy that is. I saw how lost Cal was when he got hurt and had to retire. At least now he has Barbara and his new venture.

I bought the ranch in Aspen shortly after I started playing for the Waves and have been renovating with the intention of retiring there. The thing is that the closer that day comes, the less I'm sure it's where I want to be.

Thankfully I have another four years to figure it all out.

KAREN

I WATCHED someone who is not Dale run to first base and start warming up the infield. The Waves are winning by seven runs so I guess they're giving the newbies a chance to show what they can do.

"Mom, can I get another drink?" Jeremy asked.

"Sure honey." I pulled my purse onto my lap and reached in for my wallet. "Would either of you like anything?" I asked Hannah and Ivy Sherman, who is dating the pitcher, Rusty Russell.

"No thanks," they said in unison.

I handed Jeremy a twenty as he stood and handed me the bag of swag Jack had given him. I watched him make his way down the aisle then turned my attention back to the game. Although I have to admit, it's less interesting now.

"Missing anyone in particular out there?" Hannah asked.

I looked at her and rolled my eyes. "You're not very subtle."

She laughed then nudged her glasses back into place.

"Neither are the two of you," she said. "There were sparks flying between you at the fundraiser last week and you've been staring at him the entire game."

I shook my head, not sure what to say. Thankfully there was some action on the field to offer a distraction.

"What's going on?" Hannah asked Ivy.

"The bat shattered and a piece of it hit Rusty in the leg," Ivy said.

I turned my attention to the pitcher, who was shaking his head at the hovering manager and trainer. A spot of blood was visible on his shin but he seemed to be insisting he's okay. They had him throw a couple practice pitches before heading back to the dugout.

Ivy took in a deep breath and let it out.

"I'm gonna have to start taking Valium when Rusty pitches," she said. "Talk about nerve-wracking."

"I totally understand," Hannah said. "I watched these games for years but after Jack and I got together, it became a whole new experience. I'm always nervous he's going to get hurt." She turned to me. "You must feel the same way." I widened my eyes, not sure how to respond and she took mercy on me and clarified. "You must be nervous when you watch Jeremy play."

"It's funny, I never really was, but he pitched for the first time the other night and I was so nervous I was afraid I'd throw up. I was so tense throughout the whole game, my whole body hurt later that night."

"I hardly knew anything about the game until I got involved with Rusty last year," Ivy said. "Now I can tell the difference between a slider and a curveball." Her eyes shifted back to the field and a sappy smile crossed her face. "That was a curveball," she said as Rusty threw one across the plate, striking out the batter for the third out of the inning. Holding up her iPad, she added, "Time to get back to work."

She'd told us earlier that she's going to school for graphic arts and is working on an assignment. Somehow she manages to focus on her task while the Waves are batting.

My phone buzzed and I pulled it from my purse and checked the text.

> Mom, I ran into Johnny. We're hanging out behind you at the railing watching the game.

I turned around and spotted him and his friend leaning against the railing and waved, then gave him a thumbs up. It's amazing how independent he's becoming. The first few years after Jason died, he rarely left my side. But he's officially a teenager now, so it's to be expected. Thankfully he's not at the point where he's gone out all the time. The house is way too quiet when he's not around. I don't even want to think about what it will be like when he goes away to college or moves out for good. It's too depressing to contemplate, but I refuse to be one of those clingy mothers who doesn't let her child grow up.

"I guess Jeremy found a friend," Hannah said.

"Yeah, he's at that age," I said, echoing my thoughts.

"He's grown so much since last year and he looks more mature."

"I know. He just turned thirteen. It's still a shock to say that."

"Well he's a great kid. Jack really likes seeing him and so do the other guys."

As the Waves got up to bat, Jack, Dale, and Dan stepped out of the dugout and stood at the railing. Jack looked over his shoulder and offered a sexy smirk when he spotted Hannah. I shifted my eyes toward her and watched a blush spread up her neck to her cheeks.

"So I take it you two have settled into marriage," I said.

She looked at me and her smile widened. "It's amazing. I mean, we lived together before we got married so it shouldn't have mattered, but it does feel different."

"You guys are great together."

We both looked back down at the guys, although I'm sure Hannah's attention was on Jack while I focused on Dale. He slipped off his hat and scratched his forehead. The sun brought out the chestnut highlights in his brown hair and I watched as he dragged his long fingers through the thick strands before sliding his cap back on.

While I should have directed my attention back to the game, I couldn't help but let my eyes take a slow tour down his broad shoulders to his amazing ass.

"Can I ask you something?"

I'd been so focused on Dale's amazing backside I jumped at Hannah's voice.

"Sure."

"Are you interested in Dale?"

"Oh, uh–"

She held up her hand to halt whatever pathetic words were going to come out of my mouth.

"I only ask because I know he's interested in you. He wouldn't have asked you out if he wasn't," she said, looking me directly in the eye. "And if you're interested in him at all, you should give him a chance. He really is a great guy."

I blinked, absorbing her words, not sure how to respond.

"Unless you're involved with someone."

She raised her voice slightly on the last word turning her sentence into a question.

"No." I cleared my throat. "No, I'm not involved with anyone."

"Then you really should give him a chance. And I realize this is none of my business but you know how it is, once you fall in love you want everyone to be in love."

I looked down at Dale and felt my stomach flip, the same way it does every time I see him.

"Can I be honest with you?" I asked, turning my attention back to Hannah.

"If you mean you're wondering if I'll keep whatever you're thinking of telling me to myself, the answer is yes."

"Yes, I'm attracted to Dale. Besides the fact he's hot and good-looking, he does seem really nice and in another life, I'd definitely go out with him."

"But…"

"But I haven't dated anyone since Jason died. A few

guys have asked and I've turned them all down because I just didn't feel ready."

"And now?"

"Jason's been gone five years and I'm getting there." I shrugged. "I'm more attracted to Dale than I have been to any of the other guys, I just don't think he's someone I should date."

"Did I ever tell you that I had a crush on Jack for years before we got together?"

I shook my head, trying to figure out what her question had to do with what I'd just told her.

"I spent my days surrounded by not only the players but a lot of the male staff who are often just as hot and nothing. But Jack made my heart pound and my palms sweat."

"Did you ever tell him?"

"God no! First of all, I figured I wasn't his type and second, I swore to myself I'd never get involved with an athlete or an actor."

"So what happened?"

"Jack's ex wrote a tell-all book and Mr. Hanover approached me and asked what we could do to up his image. I suggested a PR blitz, which Jack turned around on me by insisting I attend all the events with him."

Her face practically glowed with love as she spoke about her husband.

"Somewhere along the line, he noticed me as some-thing more than a coworker and my crush turned into something much deeper. And it's been amazing." She smiled. "I understand you have more to consider than I did, but as your friend and his, I'm saying you should give him a chance."

I opened my mouth and closed it, but the right words didn't come. Shifting my gaze back to Dale, I struggled to remember why I was so reluctant about going out with him. At least on one date.

"I'm not sure that he's even interested anymore," I said, looking at her again.

She chuckled at my words.

"Dale's birthday is Sunday," Hannah said. "We're having a small party at Rudy's Place down on the water at six o'clock. It's just Jack and me, Dan, and Dale's sister Penny and her boyfriend. Why don't you come have some good food, a drink or two, and just hang out?"

"To his birthday party?" I shook my head. "I don't know."

"It's more a regular get-together than anything and I planned it so I can invite whoever I want," Hannah said. When I continued to shake my head, she added, "Just promise me you'll think about it."

Since Jeremy is on a school break, my parents are picking him up tomorrow and taking him to Orlando until Wednesday. They're meeting up with some of their friends and their grandchildren and hitting Disney World and Universal Studios.

I looked back down toward the field and was sad to see Dale had gone back inside the dugout.

"Okay, I'll think about it."

Chapter Four

DALE

JACK WALKED Hannah to the door and kissed her goodbye while Dan and I continued to stuff our faces with Chinese food. Based on the number of containers scattered across the table, it seems like Jack ordered one of everything on the menu. I mentally chuckled figuring most of them would be empty by the end of the night.

"See you guys later," Hannah said as she left to meet Penny. Kenny has to attend a business dinner with his father so they decided to have a girls' night.

Jack settled back at the table and dug into his dinner. I reached for the General Tso's chicken and flinched then pulled my right hand back and grabbed it with the left instead. I scooped a few pieces onto my plate then realized the guys had stopped eating and were looking at me.

"What?"

"You okay?" Dan asked.

"Yeah. That wild hop dinged me right in the collar

bone and it's a little sore." I pulled the neck of my shirt over to reveal part of the purple bruise.

"Shit, I didn't think it hit you that hard."

Jack whistled. "Wow, that really got you. You know it's a good one when you can see the seams."

I put my shirt back into place and shrugged.

"I'll ice it again later, pop some Advil, and be good to go in the morning."

Jack snorted. "More like, it'll still hurt like hell but you'll play through it tomorrow."

"Either way, I'll be on the field tomorrow."

"Can't show physical weakness to the young guys."

"Speaking of, what is up with that Moss kid?" Dan directed the question to Jack.

"No clue, but he's a cocky little prick. I can't believe Mr. Hanover didn't trade him after that stunt last year."

Derek Moss is the shortstop for the Fayetteville Waves. So chances are if he keeps doing well, he'll end up being Jack's replacement in a few years. Last year, Jack got put on the injured list after a collision with a runner resulted in a slight concussion. Normally when he gets a day off Oskar Marquez shifts over from second to short. But since Jack was going to be out for an extended time, they called up Moss.

The kid did all right but he's too much of a hot dog at shortstop to be effective long-term. He also talks a lot of smack to the opposing team and gets into fights, which is a big no-no as far as Mr. Hanover is concerned. And, as if those two things weren't enough reason for him to be at the top of the trade list, when he got sent back down after Jack came back, he didn't go quietly. He plastered his social media with pictures of himself sitting outside the Triple A stadium with the caption, "Stuck in Fayetteville."

"It's a shame. He has a lot of potential. If he'd listen and pay attention, he could be great," Dan said.

"I tried with him the first year he was down here, but after that pretty much ignored him unless he approached me." Jack took a long drink of beer then smirked as he swallowed. "And I might have mentioned that I have my agent negotiating for an eight-year contract when he was nearby."

"He must have lost his shit when he heard that," I said.

"He definitely didn't look happy. I think he's expecting me to leave when my contract is up at the end of the year and that's definitely not happening. You guys done?" he asked, pointing at the containers.

Dan and I nodded, easily following his change in topic. But since he'd brought up his contract renewal, I asked, "So what kind of contract are you looking for?"

"Another three or four years. Whatever works out better." He stacked the empty containers on top of one another and closed the others. "If he wants to stay with the Waves and has half a brain, he'd talk about shifting over to second so he can move up and take over Oskar's spot when he retires after next season."

"He's cocky enough to think he's gonna bump you out," Dan said.

"Well, that's not happening for a few years." He stood and collected the stack of empty containers and walked to the kitchen and dropped them in the trash. "Hell, he's lucky I found Hannah or I'd probably hang on forever." He chuckled.

"It's weird, isn't it?" Dan asked.

"What?" Jack and I said in unison.

"Talking about the end." We nodded, looking so solemn you'd think we're at a funeral. "You watch guys play their last game all through your career and somehow block it out, thinking it'll never be your turn. But then you blink and it's right there."

"We are damn lucky though," Jack said. "Making a living playing the best game in the world."

"Yeah, and we were fortunate to have played our whole career with the Waves," Dan added. "Mr. Hanover can be tough but he's fair and he values experience. As long as you can perform, he'll keep signing you no matter your age."

And thank God for that.

Maybe Jack and Dan have moved toward planning their exit from the game but I'm still in the *hang on forever* category. I'll play as long as the Waves will have me. What else am I going to do with my time? Hang out by myself at the ranch? I mentally shrugged. Maybe Penny and Kenny will get married and give me a bunch of nieces and nephews I can spoil because right now, a family isn't on my horizon.

KAREN

CHLOE FILLED the blender with ice then added heavy pours of tequila and triple sec and topped the mixture off with lime juice. She pushed the button on the small appliance and the sound of the whirring machine and crunching ice drowned out everything else in the kitchen.

I finished rimming three glasses with salt as the noise of the blender stopped.

"Just in time." She popped the jar off the blender and filled the three glasses with her famous margaritas then stashed the rest in the freezer. "How are the nachos coming?"

Glancing over my shoulder, I watched our friend Hope sprinkle cheese over tortilla chips she'd topped with seasoned meat, lettuce, tomato, and guacamole. My stomach growled at the sight.

"Voila!" She held up the platter for us to admire before bringing it into the living room and setting it on the coffee table.

I picked up two of the margaritas and three plates and followed her, then handed her a drink before plopping onto the couch. She settled into the chair across from me and licked at the salty rim before taking a sip.

"Mmm Chlo, amazing as always."

"Thank you," Chloe said, as she sat on the other end of the couch, her own drink in hand, which she held up and waited for us to do the same. "To good friends and the perfect storm."

Hope and I echoed her toast before we each took a drink.

I placed my glass on the table and handed out the plates, which we each filled with loaded nachos.

"I still can't believe you're both here," I said.

When Chloe toasted to "the perfect storm" she was referring to the fact that both she and Hope are in town at the same time. I've been friends with them since junior high but they go back further than that. Once I started dating Jason, they took me into their fold and we've been inseparable since. That is until Chloe started traveling regularly for her job and Hope moved to Manhattan to work as a makeup artist at a swanky salon.

Hope comes to visit her parents whenever she can, but that usually ends up being when Chloe is away for work. So anytime the three of us are in town at the same time, we make the most of it. And since my parents whisked Jeremy off to Orlando this afternoon, we can have a true girls' night. In fact, the ladies are spending the night so they don't have to worry about getting home.

"Okay ladies, spill. What's been going on since I was here last?" Hope asked.

She already filled us in on her fancy-schmancy life and the pseudo-celebrities she runs with in the city. Not to mention the hot guy she's been dating for the past six months. If they're still together the next time she comes to town, she promises to bring him along so we can meet. Things must be feeling serious if she's even thinking about that.

Chloe jumped in, sharing the news she'd told me earlier in the week.

"I got a promotion at work. In addition to working with regions throughout the country, I'll also be handling some of the international sites as well. I'm going to Switzerland next month and I'm so excited."

Hope finished chewing a chip and swallowed, then took a drink.

"You know, I feel like you're the Chandler Bing of this group. You know, like from *Friends*."

"I know who Chandler Bing is, I just don't know why I'm him," Chloe said.

"Because I know you make big bucks but I don't have a clue what it is you do for a living, even though you've told me a million times."

"I'm a market research analyst. How hard can that be to remember?"

Hope shrugged and took another sip of her drink before setting the empty glass on the table. "That went down too fast." She stood and smiled. "Let's see if I can take my time with the next one."

That said, she skipped into the kitchen and retrieved the rest of the margaritas from the freezer. She refilled each of our glasses before settling back onto the chair with her legs tucked beneath her.

"Any men worth discussing?" The question was directed at Chloe of course. Hope knows I never have anything to share in that department.

Chloe shrugged. "Not really. I met a guy on one of my trips to Chicago and we spent some time together the last few times I was there. He's left me a couple messages, but I haven't called him back yet."

"Why not?" I asked.

"What's the point? He's divorced and has two kids so if we did get involved, it's not like it can go anywhere. He wouldn't be able to move here and there's no way in hell I'd live in the Windy City." She took a drink and shook her head as she swallowed. "We had fun but it's time to cut ties before any real feelings get involved."

I opened my mouth to ask another question but then caught myself and took another drink. Chloe doesn't do long-term relationships. One lucky guy made it to the six-month mark but that was right when she started traveling for work, so they probably only spent two of those months in the same city.

It seems crazy to me, but that's okay. She finds it bizarre that I've only dated one person my entire life.

"And what about you? How's the world of real estate?" Hope directed her attention to me.

"Good. Busy. It's a seller's market so I feel like I'm always rushing clients from one showing to another. But if I don't the decent properties get snatched up."

She nodded at my answer, then in a semi-related story, told us about her parents' new neighbors. Once she was finished, Chloe smirked and said, "You didn't ask Karen if there are any men in her life."

Hope's eyebrows raised and she shifted her rounded

eyes between my sister-in-law and me trying to figure out if Chloe was being serious.

"Our little girl has an admirer."

Shifting in her chair, Hope wrapped both hands around her glass and looked at me over the rim.

"Do tell," she said before taking a sip.

I shook my head and smiled. What I really want to do is reach over and slap Chloe upside the head, but I'll keep my hands to myself.

"It's nothing," I said.

"It's not nothing." She looked over at Hope. "It's Dale Montgomery. Apparently he's asked her out multiple times since Jeremy started rubbing elbows with the Waves."

"Dale Montgomery?" Hope whispered. I nodded. "Shut the fuck up!" She shifted onto her knees. "When? Where did you go? What happened?"

"See?" Chloe looked at me with a satisfied smirk. "That's the reaction most people have. They don't *turn him down.*"

"You turned him down? Why?" Hope screeched.

"Honestly, I'm not even sure what I said when he first asked me out. I must have just said I was busy or something because he didn't think twice about asking me out again."

I tried to remember why I turned him down, but other than being scared shitless, no good reasons come to mind. I'm thirty-four years old and Jason is the only man I've ever dated. Ever kissed. Ever had sex with. The thought of putting myself out there is terrifying. I've never really been *out there.*

Shaking my head, I said, "I know you both think I should start dating again, but do you really think Dale Montgomery is a good first candidate? That's like skipping a bike with training wheels and hopping right onto a

Harley." I shook my head. "He's not the first man who's asked me out since Jason died, but he's definitely the last I should go with."

They shared a look then turned to me.

"You said yourself he's a nice guy," Chloe said. "What's the worst that can happen?"

I can fall in love with him and get my heart broken.

But instead of sharing that thought, I said, "It doesn't matter because he hasn't asked me out since last season."

"Of course not. You turned him down every time he did," Chloe pointed out. "What?"

"What?" I asked.

Her eyes shifted to Hope. "You see it?"

Hope nodded. "Yep," she said, ending the word with a dramatic pop.

"What are you talking about?"

"There's something you're not telling us," Chloe said.

Sometimes it really sucks when people know you too well.

I rested my head against the back of the couch and stared at the ceiling for a few seconds before answering.

"Hannah invited me to his birthday party tomorrow."

"You're going!" they said in unison.

Letting out a short sigh, I looked between them and said, "I'm not sure I should."

"Why not?" Hope asked.

"First of all, it's his birthday and only his close friends are going to be there. And second, he doesn't know she invited me. What if he doesn't want me there?"

"I'm sure Hannah wouldn't have invited you if she thought that was the case," Chloe pointed out. "You said they're all pretty tight, right?" I nodded. "Then she'd know."

They both looked at me with such hopeful expressions,

I don't know what they'd do if I said I wasn't going. And honestly, I don't want to say that. The invitation has been buzzing through my brain since Hannah issued it.

I admit that Dale makes me feel all mushy inside in a way I haven't since Jason. It might be interesting to explore that even if the thought scares the hell out of me.

Taking in a deep breath I let it out slowly as my friends continued to stare at me.

"Okay, I'll go."

"Yes!" Chloe said as she launched herself across the couch to envelop me in a bear hug.

Not one to be left out, Hope jumped off the chair and wrapped her arms around me from the other side.

"What time is the party?" she asked.

"Six o'clock at Rudy's Place."

"I'll be over at four to do your hair and makeup and figure out an outfit." Hope pulled back and her eyes scanned my face. "I have so many ideas. I'm so excited," she added then squeezed me tighter.

Now that the decision has been made and hair, makeup, and clothes are being planned, I need to figure out what kind of gift to get the man who can buy himself anything he wants.

Chapter Five

KAREN

I SAT on the edge of my bed, eyes closed, and practiced my yoga breathing. Taking in a deep breath through my nose, I exhaled slowly through my mouth with a *haaaaa…* sound. Over and over, I repeated the process, trying to calm my riotous nerves.

Everything was fine while Chloe and Hope were here. It felt like a getting-ready-for-prom party but once they left, the reality of what I'm about to do had me bordering on a panic attack. Hence the breathing.

I opened my eyes and eased into more natural breaths and mentally talked myself down. Honestly, tonight is no big deal. I'm just having dinner with some acquaintances. I have lunch meetings with clients all the time. I can do this. It's not like it's a date or something.

But, what if—

Nope.

I cut off that thought before I could finish it. Jumping

up, I headed toward the bathroom to give myself a quick once-over in the mirror.

Tracing a pinky under my bottom lip, I straightened the line of my lipstick, debating on whether I should wipe it all off. My lips are usually just covered with the slight sheen of *Blistex*, but Hope applied a *Sassy Mauve* stain that makes them look huge. The two coats of dark brown volumizing mascara she added to my short pale lashes make my eyes seem larger too. She even filled in my normally-blonde eyebrows with a light brown pencil so you can actually see them.

As if the makeup wasn't enough, she'd also curled my straight hair then finger-combed and sprayed until it fell in sexy waves over my shoulders. And the turquoise and white maxi dress Chloe brought is a little lower cut in the front than I normally wear, but she insisted it looks great.

Honestly, I barely recognize the woman in the mirror.

"I can't go out looking like this," I said to my reflection as I reached for a makeup wipe.

My cell buzzed as my hand hovered over the package.

> Chloe: You look AMAZING!!! Don't think about changing a thing!!! Go have fun!!!

"Geez Chlo, exclamation point much?" I said to my phone.

It buzzed again. This text was from Hope.

> Hope: Do NOT touch your hair or makeup! You look AMAZING!

The timing of their texts makes me assume they're together somewhere. It also makes me wonder if they're spying on me through my phone's camera.

I dropped my hand, resigned to the fact that I'll be attending the festivities looking like a clown. Because if I did change something, they'd somehow know and I'd never hear the end of it. I picked up my phone and answered their texts with a *thumb's-up* emoji.

Picking up the clear gloss Hope had given me with strict instructions to reapply every couple hours to make my lips shine, I walked back into the bedroom and slipped on a pair of white strappy sandals.

I grabbed the small white clutch off the nightstand and headed for the kitchen. There's no way I'm lugging around my everyday purse with me tonight. Instead, I opened the massive tote and pulled out my wallet, tissues, and tin of cinnamon *Altoids* and stuffed them into the clutch along with the lip gloss.

With nothing left to do, I grabbed the gift bag off the counter, tucked the clutch under my arm and, with keys in hand, headed out to the garage. The restaurant is only about ten miles away but it's through a high-traffic area so I made sure to give myself enough time so I'm not late. I figured if traffic is light, I could always drive around the block or wait in the parking lot so I don't arrive too early either.

But, true to form, the traffic on the way went in starts and stops and I pulled into the parking lot at six o'clock on the dot. I turned off the car and prayed Hannah's already inside. I don't want to arrive before her and have to explain why I'm there.

Grabbing my clutch and Dale's present, I stepped out of the car and walked toward the entrance. Steeling myself, I stepped inside and gave the hostess my name. She waved to a brown-haired waitress who'd just walked out of the door to the kitchen. The woman walked toward us with a smile on her face.

"Carly, this is Karen Walsh. She's with the party on the deck."

"Welcome," Carly said. "Follow me."

I said my thanks to the hostess and did as I was told.

"Is uh, is everyone already here?" I asked.

"We're still waiting on two more," she said. "But I just placed the order for the appetizers and they have pitchers of beer and water at the table. Is there something else you'd like to drink?"

"Club soda with lime would be great," I said.

A cold beer sounds even better but since I'm driving, that's not an option.

"Perfect."

She led me down a short corridor and stood aside gesturing for me to precede her through the sliding doors. I stepped through and there he was.

I can't decide if Dale looks more delectable in his uniform or regular clothes. Both versions are equally yummy. And right now he's wearing a button-down Hawaiian shirt. I can't see what's on the bottom because the table is blocking my view.

"Can I bring you another pitcher?" Carly asked, drawing everyone's attention.

Hannah shared a conspiratorial smile with Jack before turning it toward me. Dan looked a little confused but after seeing Hannah's face, seemed to catch on.

Dale glanced at the almost-empty pitchers on the table. "Sure, another pitcher of each would be great."

Then he looked up and spotted me. His blue eyes widened then he blinked and his face transformed with a huge smile. I felt the edges of my lips curl up, relieved that he seemed happy to see me.

"Hi Dale. Happy Birthday."

DALE

"KAREN. HI." I stood and looked around, trying to remember how to speak in complete sentences. Finding inspiration in the empty chair next to me, I pulled it out. "Have a seat."

"Thank you."

I watched as she walked around the table, keeping my mouth firmly shut so my tongue doesn't roll out onto the floor. Karen is normally beautiful, but tonight she's taken it to a whole other level. Her sweet vanilla scent captivated my senses as she lowered into the chair. I had to fight the urge to bury my nose in her hair and inhale as I pushed it beneath her.

When I first looked up and spotted her, I thought I was hallucinating. But then she spoke. Happy birthday to me, indeed.

"Would you like a beer?" I asked.

"No thank you. Carly is bringing me a club soda."

Jack told me that her husband was killed by a drunk driver so it stands to reason she wouldn't drink if she's driving. I debated on whether or not I should mention that we're all on foot tonight but decided against it. It seems better to not make a big deal out of it.

Thankfully Penny and Kenny arrived, before I had to figure out what else to say. I'm not normally tongue-tied around women, but for whatever reason, Karen is differ-ent. That combined with the fact that I'm shocked as hell to see her here has me at a loss for words. Thankfully my grandmother ingrained manners into me—more like pounded them in—so I did remember to introduce Karen to my sister and her boyfriend.

I'd just done that when Carly reappeared with two

waiters on her heels carrying armfuls of plates. Hannah told them to just set everything down in the middle and once they were finished, the whole table was covered.

"Did you order one of everything?" I asked Hannah.

"No." She flashed a saucy smirk. "There are four orders of calamari because you guys usually end up fighting over it."

She's not wrong.

"So there's one for me and you guys get to share the other three?" Jack asked.

"Hey, it's my birthday. If anyone gets his own, it's me."

"Children behave," Hannah said around a chuckle. "I know you're hungry after your game today but rest assured, there's plenty of food. There are more appetizers coming and you can order whatever entree you want."

"You can tell she handles whiny, overindulged baseball players for a living, can't you?" Penny said to Karen.

"Hey!" Dan, Jack, and I said at the same time, making everyone else at the table laugh.

As everyone helped themselves to appetizers, the smack talk started. Penny has spent enough time with the guys through the years that they treat her like a little sister. Not only that, but they also remember some of her less-than-stellar and bratty moments and they took the opportunity to jog her memory.

"All right, let's settle down and behave," Hannah interjected. "Let's not scare poor Karen away."

"No, this is fun," she said. "It's what my friends and I are like together." Then she turned to Penny. "And I hope you never even think of dying your hair again. It's gorgeous. The color is amazing."

Her comment is in reference to Jack's memory of Penny dying her hair when she was seventeen. She'd adopted a Goth look for a short time. Thankfully it was short because I hated it.

"Thanks," my sister said. "And no more dying my hair. I've come to terms with my ginger goodness. Besides, it's a pain in the ass to maintain color. I get my hair trimmed a couple times a year and worrying about getting my roots done every few weeks was annoying."

"I'm with you. I don't have any desire to dye my hair but every once in a while I think about getting a new style. But this is so easy to deal with and maintain, I haven't done it yet."

Well that answers the *Is she a natural blonde?* question. I kind of figured she is. With her pale blonde hair, light blue eyes, and golden skin she looks like the epitome of a California girl. And it's such a natural look, I'd be surprised if any of it is artificial. In fact, I think tonight is the first time I've seen her with a full face of makeup.

Which definitely makes her different from the other women I've spent time with. Most of them wouldn't have been caught dead with a bare face. To the point where, if we did end up spending the night together, they'd wake before me and fix their hair and makeup before I woke up.

Also, for whatever reason, I've always preferred brunettes. And, since I was looking for a certain type of relationship...if that's even what you'd call those shallow encounters...I attracted a certain type of woman. Some were models, there was an actress or two, and the rest were women so focused on their career they didn't want anything else to intrude. But they were all leggy brunettes who always wanted to see and be seen with someone who could up their profile.

Why the hell was I wasting my time with people like that when someone like Karen was available? Then again, I guess she wasn't...and technically still isn't to me since she hasn't accepted any of my invitations. But she is here tonight so maybe there's hope.

At that thought, I glanced over at her and found her blue eyes trained on me. I offered a small smile that made her blush and in that moment, everyone else faded away. They chattered around us, but it was just background noise.

"Thanks for coming," I said.

She bit her bottom lip and I nearly groaned out loud at the sight. It's been a long time since I've felt such an uncontrollable urge to kiss someone.

"I was afraid you'd be angry that Hannah invited me."

I shook my head. "Not at all. I'm glad you're here."

Normally I'm much more smooth, but this woman has me in knots. Besides she deserves something more than pathetic lines I'd use on just anyone. She's special and should be treated that way. And if she gives me a chance, I will.

Chapter Six

HANNAH HAD PROMISED a simple dinner for my birthday and that's exactly what she delivered. Good food, good friends...and then some, with the addition of Karen...and there's not a banner or balloon in sight.

"Thank you so much for planning this, Hannah. It's perfect."

"You're welcome, but we're not finished yet. There's a cake back at our place. I thought about bringing it here but figured we'd be too full to eat it right away." She stood. "Let me go take care of this and we'll continue the party at the condo."

I reached for my wallet. "I'll pay. You've already gone above and beyond."

"You can't pay for your own birthday party," she said and walked inside before I could say another word.

"What just happened there?" I looked at Jack with raised brows. "Do you ever win a debate with her?"

"Once in a while I do, but I use special tactics." His smile left no doubt what kind of *tactics* he was talking about.

Karen's shoulder brushed my thigh as she reached down and picked up the blue gift bag she'd brought with her. Plunking it on the table, she said, "This is for you. Happy birthday."

I shifted my eyes back and forth between the bag and her. Whatever is in there is heavy.

"You didn't have to get me anything, but thank you."

"It's just a little something," she said, then stood. "Thank you for inviting me. I've had so much fun."

Hannah had returned and Karen's last two sentences were directed at her. Instead of answering, Hannah looked my way. After all, she'd gotten Karen here, the rest is up to me.

"Come back to the condo for cake. I'll open this there." I held up the bag, as if there was any question as to what I was talking about.

"Oh no, I couldn't."

I scrambled for things to say to convince her to come and while a few lines and some bullshit reasons filled my head, I only spoke one word.

"Please?" I looked her in the eye, feeling vulnerable in a way I never have before.

She still looked unsure and I fought the urge to push. If she really doesn't want to come, she'd just say no, not look like she's fighting an inner battle. She nibbled at her bottom lip as her eyes bounced from me to my friends and back again.

"We only live a half a block away. You can park in my extra spot in the garage so you won't have to find something on the street."

"Okay, I can come for a little while."

Everyone had acted like they weren't paying attention to our exchange, but as soon as Karen agreed to accompany us, they stood, ready to leave.

"We can go out the side door so we don't have to walk through the restaurant," Hannah said. "It's really crowded out there now."

"Lead the way," Jack said and slipped his hand to the small of her back as she walked ahead of him.

We all followed behind and Hannah led us through a short hallway and out to the parking lot.

I turned to Karen. "I'll ride with you and show you where to go."

"Oh, okay." She gestured toward a white Subaru Crosstrek two spots away from where we stood. "That's me."

I've pictured her driving a little red convertible à la Christie Brinkley in *Vacation*. She definitely has the look for it. But I suppose this is more practical considering she has Jeremy and Christie's Ferrari didn't even have a back seat.

"You know the code if you get there before us," Jack said.

"Yep."

That said, the rest of the gang walked one way and Karen and I went in the opposite direction toward her car. I followed her to the driver's side then reached around and opened the door before she could do it herself. She looked at me with surprised eyes then lowered into her seat with a small smile.

"Thank you."

"My pleasure."

After closing the door, I jogged around the front of the car and settled into the passenger seat. The Subaru still holds the hint of a new-car smell but it has an underlying note of vanilla.

I settled the bag on the floor between my feet and clicked my seatbelt into place.

"Nice car."

"Thanks." She fastened her own seatbelt then pushed the ignition button. "I got this about three months ago so I'm still getting used to it, especially when I have to parallel park. Which thankfully isn't too often."

She stared straight ahead as she spoke, her hands gripping the wheel. It's pretty obvious she's nervous. I just can't figure out if that's because of me specifically or men in general. I figured I'd continue the conversation so she has something else to focus on besides the attraction arcing between us.

"What did you drive before?"

"A Honda Civic. But it had high mileage and started giving me some trouble so I figured it was time to upgrade. Now that Jeremy is playing travel ball, I wanted to make sure we had something reliable. Plus the extra room is nice." She shifted the car into reverse and slowly backed out of the parking spot. "I'm guessing I'm turning right," she said as our group walked in that direction.

"You guessed right. We're going to that building right there." I pointed to the condo complex down the block and across the intersection. "So where is Jeremy tonight?" I asked, since she mentioned his name.

Her eyes shifted in my direction for just a second before settling back on the road.

"He's actually gone to Orlando with my parents until Wednesday."

Well isn't that interesting? Jeremy is out of town and I have a day game Tuesday, leaving my night free. I swore I wouldn't ask her out again, but I'd be an idiot to pass up this opportunity, give it one last shot. But not right now. No, I'll ask her later, before she heads home.

"See that black gate right there?" She nodded as she spotted the iron gate at the ground floor of my building. "That's where we're going. Just pull up to that yellow box and I'll give you my code to open it."

She pulled into the turning lane and flipped on her blinker.

"You sure you want me to have that?"

"Why, will you come park here all the time?"

Her laughter made my stomach do that weird flipping thing again. It also seemed to release some of her tension and she loosened her grip on the wheel.

"Aren't you worried I'll come here and stalk you?" she asked as she turned and pulled up to the box.

"If only," I muttered under my breath. Karen looked at me and I thought she'd heard what I said, but then realized she was just waiting for my code. "It's 923427. Just key in the numbers. You don't have to hit enter."

She reached over and entered the code and the gate opened.

"Turn left then go straight."

"Do I need to do anything to close the gate?"

"No, it'll close on its own in a second." I'd just finished the sentence when it slowly started to close behind us.

"Convenient."

"Yep." She drove slowly down the aisle. "See that black truck straight ahead?" She nodded. "Pull into the spot right next to that."

She did as I told her then shifted the car into park and turned off the engine. As her seat belt retracted, she asked, "That's your truck?" I nodded. "Nice."

We got out of her car and walked the short distance to the elevator. The doors opened as soon as I pushed the button and I gestured for her to step inside.

"So you all live here?" she asked as the door closed behind us.

I nodded. "Yeah, we're all in this building. Cal even kept his condo after he retired."

This whole complex is only ten stories high and Jack is on the seventh floor but the ride seemed to take forever. I usually feel a connection to Karen, but in enclosed spaces, it's intensified and just buzzes around us. I felt it in the car and it's the same now. She keeps glancing at me out of the corner of her eye and nibbling at her bottom lip so I'm assuming she feels it too. At least I hope she does. I'd hate to think this is all one-sided.

I want nothing more than to push her against the back wall of the elevator and take her mouth in a long, scorching kiss, *Fifty Shades* style. Instead I took shallow breaths to avoid inhaling too much of her vanilla goodness, curled my hands around the handle of the bag, and focused on the numbers changing as we slowly made our way to the seventh floor.

Finally, *finally* the elevator stopped and the doors opened. As Karen preceded me into the hallway, I took in a deep fortifying breath. She seemed to do the same as she briskly walked in front of me down the hallway, which I found amusing since she has no idea which door belongs to Jack and Hannah.

"Karen." Her shoulders tensed as she stopped in her tracks. "This is where we're going."

She turned around and her cheeks colored when she spotted me two lengths behind her.

"Sorry."

"No need to apologize." I punched the code into the keypad and heard the lock disengage just as our gang got off the elevator on the other end of the hallway.

Thank every deity known to man because at least

they'll buffer this...whatever *this* is...between Karen and me. Because the elevator was bad enough. I can't promise to control myself in Jack's condo with a myriad of surfaces I could back Karen against and onto to explore the shy interest I keep seeing in her beautiful blue eyes.

KAREN

"BETWEEN THESE GUYS and my father, Mrs. Button was in heaven," Hannah said, after relaying a story of her former neighbor at her wedding.

It took me a second to decipher her meaning then remembered that Hannah's father is Mac Flynn...I mean Aaran Diskin...world-renowned actor. And yet again, I'm trying to figure out what the hell I'm doing here with these people.

When Jeremy found out Jack Reagan was going to be at that CADD beach bash a couple years ago, he'd been so excited. Jack has always been his favorite player and the chance to meet him was a once-in-a-lifetime thing. Or so I thought. Here we are two years later and not only does Jack still interact with my son at the beach bash, he also still gives us tickets to Waves games, showers him with swag, and he even gave Jeremy his cell phone number so he can text him.

Hannah usually sits with me at the games and we interact regularly through the season to discuss my availability. Jack's friends...mostly Dan, Dale, and Cal...also treat Jeremy like he's one of the guys. And somewhere along the way, Dale Montgomery asked me out. It's all so surreal.

I'm just a regular person who married her junior high sweetheart, had a baby, and ended up a young widow. Stuff like this doesn't happen to people like me.

Directing my attention back to the conversation, I heard Jack say, "Thankfully Cal and Barb got together before the wedding or he and Monte would have been fighting over Mrs. Button."

"And wouldn't she have just loved that?" Hannah asked around a chuckle.

"He has a picture of the two of them at the house in Aspen. When I first saw it, I thought maybe he'd given up baseball to become a gigolo," Penny said.

"In all seriousness, I think that's the most fun I've ever had at a wedding," Dale said.

Oh my heart. Not only is he nice to children, his kindness also extends to the elderly. Well, at least one elderly woman.

Hannah looked at her watch. "It's almost nine-thirty. Are you all ready for cake?"

Honestly, I'm still full from dinner, but the guys seemed eager. Besides it is getting late and the sooner we have cake, the sooner I can remove myself from Dale's magnetic pull. The car was bad enough but when we were in the elevator together, I thought we were going to start a fire with all the sparks flying between us. And I can feel it every time he looks at me, which he's doing right now.

"So what are you doing while Jeremy is away?" he asked when I glanced his way.

"I have work, but other than that, I'm not sure. I'll probably just enjoy staying home instead of running to baseball or whatever activity is happening."

"It's gotta be tough, being a single mom."

I shrugged. "I'm pretty fortunate to have a job that allows me to work around Jeremy's schedule most of the time. When I can't, either my sister-in-law helps out or I make arrangements with other parents. I'm also very lucky that Jeremy is such a great kid and I don't have any issues with behavior or anything."

He was about to ask something else when Hannah announced that the cake was ready to be served. She lit the candles as we all made our way over.

Dale moved to the head of the table and if I'm not mistaken, he's blushing.

"Do you have to sing?" he asked. Almost whined, actually.

Instead of answering, Hannah just started singing *Happy Birthday.* Dale laughed and shook his head while we sang the song out of unison and slightly off-key.

When we were done, Penny said, "Make a wish!"

Dale leaned over but instead of facing the cake, looked at me as he put all the candles out with one blow. Everyone did the obligatory clap and Penny gave him a big hug and a kiss on the cheek. He kissed the top of her head and wrapped his arm around her shoulders and watched as Hannah cut the cake.

Even though I'd asked for a small piece, the plate I was given held a ginormous one. Still, it was delicious and I ate the whole thing. Thankfully I'm wearing a loose dress.

"That was so good," I said. "Where'd you get it?"

"I made it," Hannah said. "It's kind of a hobby of mine."

"Well it was amazing," I added. "Chocolate cake with whipped cream icing is my favorite."

"Mine too," Dale said as he forked the last of his cake into his mouth.

"I'm going to pack slices up for everyone to take home," Hannah said. "The icing is delicious but after a day it's not so great." She looked at Dale. "I'll make a plate for Dan that you can drop off on your way out."

Dan had gone directly to his place right after dinner. He had a call with Sabrina and the kids.

Hannah carried the remaining cake into the kitchen and finished slicing it. "Dale, you have to open your gift from Karen," she said as she worked. "I want to see what it is."

It's really just a silly little gift but I didn't want to show up empty-handed.

We all watched as Dale placed the bag on the table and pulled out the tissue paper with a dramatic flair. Then he reached in and pulled out the six-pack of glasses. He examined them then looked at me.

"You got me glasses with characters from *The Office* painted on them?" It's obviously a rhetorical question but I nodded anyway. "They're awesome." He held them up so everyone could see and read the quotes. "Michael Scott's quote is obviously 'That's what she said.' Dwight Schrute's is 'Would an idiot do that?' Jim Halpert's is 'Congratulations universe, you win.' Pam Beesly's, or Pam Halpert's if you prefer, says 'The ice melts...and then it's like second drink!' Stanley Hudson's says 'Did I stutter?' and Creed Bratton's says 'Let's put a smile on that face.'"

"Those are so cool. Where did you get them?" Penny asked.

"There's a little store in a strip mall near my house named, *Courtney's Craft Corner.* She makes a lot of hand-painted items, including glasses. Some of her stuff is really neat."

"I love them," Dale said. "Thank you."

He went to put them back in the bag and realized there was something else in there. Reaching in, he pulled out the mug that was an impulse buy. A slow smile spread across his face as he read it and started to laugh. My heart had been pounding because I was unsure of how my gift would be received. Now it's pounding for a whole other reason.

Holding it up, Dale said, "This is a Dwight Schrute coffee mug and it says 'Fact. You're a better baseball player than most have ever been or ever will be.'"

Jack looked at me. "You know he's gonna be a pain in the ass with this now, right?"

I couldn't help but laugh. These guys are so great and I love their relationship. It really does remind me of mine with Chloe and Hope.

"Hey, it says it on the mug so it must be true," Dale boasted. Then he looked at me and turned serious. "Thank you again. These really are perfect."

With his denim-blue eyes on mine, I couldn't turn away. Everything and everyone else disappeared into the background and it's just us. And that's when I knew. He's going to ask me out again, I could feel it.

I also knew that attending this party put me smack dab in the middle of a crossroad. In one direction is my old safe life and in the other is a new adventure with Dale. I just hope I pick the right way.

Chapter Seven

DALE

"You're welcome. I wasn't sure what to get you then I saw those and I thought…" Karen trailed off and shrugged. "It wasn't much but I didn't want to show up empty-handed."

I leaned against the wall and shoved my hands in my pockets. That *Fifty Shades* scene is coming to mind again. But I should at least take her out on a date before I pounce on her in an elevator.

"Just you being here tonight was present enough." I stood straight as we reached the ground floor. The doors opened and I waited until Karen stepped out then I followed her to her car. "But I really do appreciate the gift. It's perfect. How did you know I like *The Office?*"

"I heard you quote it a couple times." She looked at her car, at the ground, and pretty much anywhere but at me. "You know, after the games, when Jeremy and I were there."

I smiled at both her shy glance and the fact that she remembered something I'd said, no matter how silly it might have been.

"So does the fact that you recognized the quotes mean that you're also a fan?"

She fiddled with the strap of her purse and finally looked me in the eye, then nodded.

"It's actually one of my favorite shows. And now Jeremy is starting to enjoy it too, which is kind of fun."

Leaning my hip against the side of her car, I asked, "Who's your favorite character?"

"Oh geez, I have no idea. There's something about all of them that I like. I don't think I could pick a favorite. What about you?"

"I kind of feel the same. They all play off each other making them better individually. But if I had to choose, I'd have to say Michael. Just because he's the one who sets the tone for the whole crazy place."

"That makes sense."

"What about your favorite episode?"

"You're really asking the tough questions today." Her laugh echoed through the parking garage making my stomach do that roller coaster thing again.

If she thinks those questions are tough, wait until I spring the one I really want to ask on her.

"Okay, I'll tell you mine first. The one where Jim puts Andy's phone up in the ceiling and Pam keeps calling it so his *Rockin' Robin* ringtone sounds through the office. It's just funny and reminds me of something Dan, Jack, Cal, and I would do."

"Of course, that's when Andy went crazy and punched a hole in the wall."

"Well there is that." I chuckled. "But they had to do something to give him time off to film *The Hangover*."

"That's true," she said, looking much more relaxed. "Mine is Jim and Pam's wedding. It was so sweet, especially when he's talking to the camera toward the end."

"Not to mention that Kevin managed to get six numbers there. One more and he would have had a complete phone number."

"And his tissue box shoes." She rolled her eyes and shook her head. "Poor Kevin."

"Yeah, it's definitely a great show." I could talk about and quote *The Office* all day, but I need to make my move here before she closes up again. "So you mentioned that Jeremy is away. I was wondering if you'd want to go out to dinner with me Tuesday night."

Her eyes rounded and she sucked in a quick breath then started to choke.

I took a step toward her. "Are you okay?"

She nodded, looking embarrassed. "Sorry about that. Two of my talents are falling up steps and choking on air."

"I don't remember ever choking on air, but I've fallen up steps many times. A camera caught me once when I face-planted as I was running out to the on-deck circle. I'm sure you can still find the video on YouTube."

"Then I don't feel so bad. At least no one's ever gotten me on camera so that's something."

"Glad I could point out a bright side." I raised my brow. "So what do you think about Tuesday?"

Karen bit her lip, looking up at me through her lashes.

Rubbing my sweaty palms against my shorts, I held my breath waiting for her answer. I swear I haven't been this nervous asking someone out since middle school. Which seems kind of silly considering the number of women I've dated in my life. Then again, those were all so superficial they didn't really count. This does. For the first time, I'm asking a woman out who has the potential to be really important to me, who can change my life in a major way.

"Dinner sounds nice," she finally said.

"Okay. Great." I cleared my throat, pausing a beat to control my excitement just a bit. "I have an afternoon game that should end around five. Does seven o'clock work for you?"

"Yes."

I pulled my phone out of my pocket and added her name to my contacts then handed it to her.

"Key in your number then I'll text you so you have mine. I'd appreciate it if you give me all seven digits." I flashed a quick smile.

She laughed and quickly typed before handing my phone back to me.

"All seven are there, I promise."

"Perfect." Her phone dinged with my return text. "Now you have my number, too. Can you text me your address as well?"

"Are you sure you don't want me to just meet you wherever?"

"I'm sure."

She didn't look so sure but didn't push. That settled, I opened the car door and shifted to the side so she could sit. Once she got behind the wheel, I leaned forward with one hand resting on the roof and the other on the open door.

"Thanks again for the awesome birthday gift. You have my number if you need me beforehand, but otherwise, I'll pick you up at seven on Tuesday."

"I'll see you then." She clicked her seatbelt into place.

"There's a sensor on this side of the gate so it'll just open as you approach."

Karen nodded, her gaze locked somewhere in the vicinity of my ear.

Bending farther down, I gave her a quick kiss on the cheek before straightening. She held her hand against the spot where my lips had touched and finally looked me in the eye. Slowly her stunned look evaporated and her mouth curled up into a small smile.

"Have a good night," I said and closed the door.

She offered a quick wave before shifting into reverse, backing out of the spot, and driving out of the garage. I just stood there watching the empty space where her car had been, unable to wipe the goofy smile off my face.

KAREN

"GUYS FOCUS! He'll be here in a half hour and I'm a wreck."

Chloe and Hope stopped their mindless chatter and stared at me through my phone screen. I should have taken them up on their offer to come over and help me get ready again but I honestly thought I'd be okay on my own. Seriously, all I need to do is pick out something to wear that isn't too real estate agent or too baseball mom. But apparently everything in my wardrobe falls into one of those two categories.

"What about this?" I held up a pink blouse and slim khaki shirt.

Hope wrinkled her nose. "It's a little better but still too work-ish."

I sat on the floor of my closet clutching the blouse to my chest.

"I should just text and tell him I can't go."

"No!" That single word burst from my phone in stereo.

"You have to go," Hope added.

"This is the first guy you've been interested in," Chloe said. "It's one date. If you don't have fun you don't have to go out with him again."

"You're assuming he's going to ask me out again."

"How many times did this guy ask you out? If he wasn't really interested in *you* he would have stopped when you turned him down the first time."

Logically I know that Hope has a point, but let's face it, my emotions have kind of taken over here.

"Guys, I'm thirty-four years old and have never been on a real first date. Not like this anyway." I rested my head against the wall and stared at the ceiling. "Back in middle school Jason and I hung out with a group for years and by the time we went out alone we were way past this whole awkward thing." I looked back at the phone where my best friends were watching me with wide eyes. "I don't even know how to act. How do you guys do this all the time?"

"Just relax and be yourself," Hope said. "From what you've said, Dale seems like a nice guy."

"He is. I just wish he wasn't…" I trailed off trying to figure out how to put what I mean into words but wasn't successful. So I just said, "*Dale Montgomery.*"

Thankfully they understood.

"He's just a man," Chloe said.

I snorted at that.

"He is," Hope added. "Yes, he's hot as hell and a professional baseball player, but he's a person just like you. No better."

"Don't think about him on the field or in the media. Remember him racing on the slide with Jeremy or partnering with an old lady at a wedding."

"Okay. I can do that." I took in a deep breath and let it out slowly. "Thank you so much guys. I really don't know what I'd do without the two of you."

"Same goes," they said in unison.

"Shit! I'm down to twenty minutes. Guys, what am I gonna wear?"

"Turn the phone around so we can see what you have again," Hope said.

I did as she told me. They asked me to pull out this item and that, vetoing them all until I was nearly at the end of the line.

"What's that?"

"What?"

Hope pointed, as though I'd have a clue based on that.

"The spot of blue I see tucked between the brown and black blazers."

"This?"

I pulled the sleeveless cobalt wrap dress I'd bought on sale a couple years ago. The tag is still on it because I've never had an occasion to wear it. It always seems too bright.

"Why haven't I seen that before?" Hope asked.

"I don't know."

"It's perfect!" Chloe said.

"Are you sure? You don't think it's too bright?"

"Seriously? That color will look perfect with your hair color and skin tone. Plus it'll make your eyes pop," Hope said. "Put it on."

I held up the dress, still not convinced.

"The clock is ticking," Chloe said.

I walked out of the closet and propped my phone on the dresser then peeled off my T-shirt, careful to not ruin my hair. Removing the dress from its hanger, I slipped it on then fastened the inside closure and wrapped the tie around the outside, securing it with a bow at the side of my waist.

"What do you think?"

"Go to the full-length mirror so I can get the full effect," Hope said.

I walked to my bathroom and stood in front of the mirror, turning my phone so they could see.

"That's the one," Hope said. "Wear your strappy silver sandals, add another coat of mascara, and use that lip stain I put on you the other night."

"Are you sure?"

"Positive."

I shifted my eyes to Chloe.

"What she said."

Seems I'm out numbered.

I was about to end the call, but they said they wanted to see the finished product. It's probably more like they want to make sure I follow their instructions. Which I do to the best of my ability.

Once I finished, Hope told me to pan the camera across my face and thankfully gave me a thumb's up.

"Add your big silver hoop earrings and chunky bracelet and you're good to go."

I tossed my phone on the bed and went into my closet and found my sandals, then grabbed the jewelry she mentioned from the box on top of my dresser.

Chloe and Hope kept yelling out advice on what I should and shouldn't eat as I slipped into my sandals and fastened the jewelry.

I grabbed my phone and held it to my face so they could see as I rolled my eyes at them.

"I don't plan on ordering BBQ ribs, crab legs, or anything other messy food I might embarrass myself with. Geez, I'm not that pathetic. I do eat meals with clients, you know."

"Just making sure," Chloe said.

"Give us one last look in the mirror," Hope added.

I walked into my bathroom and once again stood in front of the full-length mirror. My friends looked at me, then each other, then at me again.

"Our baby bird is ready to leave the nest." Chloe's silly words were said with a sincere smile.

"He's not gonna know what hit him."

"Thanks for your help guys. You're the best."

"Remember to relax and enjoy yourself," Chloe said. "It's just dinner. Like you said, you have dinner with clients all the time."

It was obvious she wanted to say more but didn't want to upset me right before Dale arrived. She's already told me not to mention Jason or talk nonstop about Jeremy.

"I'll talk to you tomorrow."

Hope looked at Chloe. "Oooh, she must think she's gonna be out late if she's not calling us until tomorrow."

Again, I rolled my eyes.

"Goodbye."

I hung up on their chuckling faces and studied myself in the mirror. My hair and makeup actually look decent, which is amazing because I'm not very skilled at doing either. I'm still not sure about the dress, but Hope is the expert. And logically, I know it doesn't really matter. Aside from Sunday, he's only seen me without makeup and in either work or casual clothes. If Dale and I end up hitting it off, it's not like it'll be because of what I'm wearing.

I'd just left my bedroom when the doorbell rang. I continued to the front door and opened it, greeting Dale with a smile. Dressed in khakis and a blue button-down shirt with the sleeves rolled up, he looks good enough to grace the cover of a men's magazine. He smells good, too.

His fresh air and sandalwood scent teases me through the doorway and I want to get closer for a better hit.

Considering how freaked out I was less than a half hour ago, I feel surprisingly calm now that he's here.

"Hi," I said. "Come on in."

Chapter Eight

DALE

I CAN'T STOP STARING at Karen across the candlelit table. She looks absolutely amazing. Her blue dress both hugs and skims her curves and since she first opened her front door, I've fought the urge to run my hands over the silky material.

She looked up from her menu and caught me watching her.

"Do you know what you're having?"

Her small smile drew my gaze to her mouth. She's wearing that pink lipstick again, making her mouth seem even more lush and kissable. Hopefully later I'll get a chance to find out if her lips are as soft as they look.

"I think I'm going with the prosciutto stuffed chicken. How about you?"

"I can't decide between the salmon special and lobster ravioli."

"If you want to order the salmon, we can get a small plate of the lobster ravioli as an appetizer."

"Are you sure?"

"Positive. That is if you don't mind sharing."

She smiled and opened her mouth to say something then stopped herself and just nodded.

"Thanks, you just made my decision easy."

Our waitress, Maria, approached with the drinks we'd ordered after we were seated and a basket of warm bread. We decided on fruit-infused iced tea...peach for her, blackberry for me. And besides the ravioli, I also ordered calamari and bruschetta to start.

Karen's eyes had widened as I placed my order and she smiled as Maria walked away.

"You know, Dan and Jack aren't here to help you eat all that."

"That's a good thing. It means there's more for us."

She shook her head and took a drink of her tea, then looked around the room.

"I like this place. It has such a cozy feel."

Through the years, the guys and I have found the best places to go throughout the country where the food is good and for the most part, we can eat undisturbed. Gianni's is one of my favorite places in all of Florida. The restaurant is welcoming and serves some of the best Italian dishes I've ever eaten.

The women I've dated before have all wanted to see and be seen, but that's not what tonight is about. Which is why this place is perfect. Aside from the larger main room, Gianni's has some smaller spaces perfect for intimate dining. Which is what I'm looking for tonight.

"Yeah, it's pretty great here and the food is amazing." I pulled the napkin off the top of the bread. "You have to try this."

"My mouth has been watering since Maria set it down. It smells amazing." She reached out and took a slice then dipped it in the olive oil and took a big bite. "Mmmm, so good."

Thankfully Karen's not one of those women who doesn't eat. Nothing drives me more crazy than taking a woman out to a nice restaurant and having her order nothing but a small salad with dressing on the side. As I was thinking about that, she took another piece of bread, ripped off a chunk, and placed it in her mouth.

She set what remained on her bread plate and brushed the crumbs off her fingers.

"I better slow down or I'll never eat my meal."

Again she looked like she was about to say something then stopped. I decided to call her out on it this time.

"What?" Her brow raised as she took another drink. "You looked like you had something else to say. It happened earlier, too."

She shook her head as she set her glass down.

"They were just silly things that came to mind."

"I like silly things."

I placed the last bite of bread into my mouth and chewed. She traced her index finger along the rim of her glass as she nibbled on her bottom lip.

Her eyes met mine and she shook her head again, but this time she smiled.

"Both times I was about to make a comment about Jeremy."

"So why'd you stop?"

"Because my friends told me not to talk about him tonight."

"Why?"

Before she could answer, Maria returned with our appetizers. I told her to place them in the center of the table so we could share. Once she left, I repeated my question.

She shrugged. "Because this is a first date and they didn't want me talking about my son all night."

"It's not like I don't know Jeremy exists." I picked up the serving spoon and placed two ravioli on Karen's plate. "What were you going to say about him?"

"Like I said, they were just silly things." With a raised brow, I prompted her to continue. "When you mentioned sharing the ravioli, I was going to say that I've shared most every meal I've eaten for the past ten years. Despite the fact that he's built like a string bean, Jeremy has always been a good eater." She picked up her fork and cut a ravioli in half. "Then I was going to say how I always tell Jeremy not to fill up on the bread whenever we go out to eat."

"Jeremy won't be a string bean for long. He's grown and filled out a lot just in the couple years I've known him."

"I know. He's as tall as me now, and it seems like that happened over night."

"You're pretty tall. Was Jeremy's father tall too?" She'd been about to place a bite of ravioli in her mouth, but froze at my question. "I'm sorry. I didn't mean—"

"No, it's fine." She rested her fork on her plate and let out a short laugh. "Jason is the other subject I was told to avoid and here we are, not even at the main course, and both have been mentioned."

Not able to stop myself, I reached over and placed my hand over hers. She looked over at me with wide eyes but didn't pull away.

"Karen, I want to get to know you better so as far as I'm concerned, no topic is off limits."

She took in a breath and shook her head as she let it out.

"Yes, Jason was tall. About your height."

I acknowledged her words with a nod and reluctantly removed my hand from hers. There's so much I want to ask but I don't just want to bombard her with questions about her late husband. I can't imagine it's easy for her to talk about him no matter how many years have passed since his death. And also, I want her focusing on me tonight, not him. I imagine he's always on her mind somehow but I don't need to put him front and center. Call me selfish, but that's where I want to be.

Trying to lighten things up, I said, "Tell me something about yourself that not many people know."

"Anything?"

"Yep."

She finished a piece of bruschetta seeming to really be thinking. By the time she swallowed, she seemed to have something in mind.

"Well, my only good friends know this but no one else." She hesitated and I nodded, encouraging her to continue. "This is my first real first date." The words tumbled out quickly, then she added. "Ever."

"How's that possible?"

"Jason and I started dating in middle school. For the first couple years, we went places with all of our friends and sometimes we'd hang out together at my house or his. By the time we went somewhere alone, it wasn't really a big deal. So I never had the first date jitters before."

"Were you nervous about tonight?" She nodded. "Me too."

"I find that hard to believe."

"Karen, it took me two years to get you to go out with me. Of course I was nervous."

Her blue eyes met mine, then she gave me a shy smile, hopefully because she saw the truth in my words.

"Okay, your turn. Tell me something not many people know."

"I think I just did. No one knew how nervous I was about tonight."

"You're not getting off that easily."

"Can't blame me for trying," I said around a chuckle. "But you have to promise me that once I tell you this, you'll still look at me as the manly man you see me as now."

"I promise."

"I love chick flicks."

"Chick flicks?"

"Yep. The sillier and sappier the better." I rested my forearm on the table, leaned closer to her, and added in a conspiratorial whisper. "I've even been known to watch the *Hallmark Channel*."

"I can't tell if you're joking or not."

"I wish I was joking. My grandmother used to watch them all the time when I was growing up and I got hooked. Penny and I have marathons on the holidays. We change up what movies we watch every time but always end with *When Harry Met Sally* because that was Gram's favorite."

"That's the sweetest thing I've ever heard."

I sat back, shook my head, and rubbed my forehead.

"See, this is what I was afraid of. You'll just see me as one of the girls now."

Karen had taken a drink and almost spit it out when I spoke that last sentence. She shook her head as she laughed. Her eyes took a quick tour of my chest and arms before meeting mine again.

"I don't think you have to worry about anyone seeing you as one of the girls. Ever."

KAREN

"DID YOU GROW UP HERE?" Dale asked as he navigated the back roads from the restaurant to my house.

"I did. I went to college in Central Florida but was happy to be back here once my four years were up."

"Is your family here?"

"Not full-time. My dad got a promotion right after I graduated college so he, my mom, and younger brother moved to the D.C. area and they all still live up there. They have a condo down here and stay for extended periods of time throughout the year, especially my mom. In fact, she'll be staying for a week once they get back from Orlando."

"What about Jeremy's other grandparents. Do they help you out at all?"

I shook my head. "Jason's mom died when he was in high school and his dad remarried when we were in college. He and his new wife moved to Texas to be closer to her children and grandchildren. It's sad, but Jeremy hardly knows him. My sister-in-law Chloe and I are close and she adores Jeremy. She travels a lot for work but spends a lot of time with both of us whenever she's here."

We drove in silence for a few minutes. I'm not sure what he's thinking. He's commented on how brave I am being a single mom, but I don't see it that way. Jeremy and I are very fortunate. Jason had a generous life insurance policy that paid off the mortgage and put a good-sized nest egg into our savings. As I told him, my job allows me a good deal of flexibility and I make a decent living so we have it better than most.

While the silence was comfortable, I took the opportunity to find out more about him.

"How about you? Where are you from?"

"Until I was thirteen, I bounced back and forth between my parents in Seattle and my grandparents who lived in a little town just outside of Phoenix." He shifted his eyes and met my gaze for just a second before returning his attention to the road. "My parents were addicts, meth mostly, so Penny and I went to live with my grandparents when things got really bad. Then they'd clean themselves up and come get us again. Finally when I was thirteen, my grandparents had enough of a case to get permanent guardianship. My parents overdosed and died the following year."

"Oh Dale, that's horrible." I didn't know what else to say.

"We were lucky to have our grandparents to take us in. I can't imagine they wanted to raise two kids when they were in their late fifties, but they didn't even hesitate. I thank God for them every day. Who knows where Penny and I would have ended up without them?"

"They must be proud of all you've both accomplished. A professional baseball player and an Olympic athlete are pretty impressive things."

"They died five years ago, within two months of each other. So they didn't get to see Penny make the Olympics, but they saw all the rest and yes, they were proud."

"I'm so sorry."

He nodded, acknowledging my words.

How had our conversation gotten so heavy? Definitely not great first-date banter. I mentally shrugged, but at least we're getting to know each other.

"You know, I just told you something most people don't know so I think you owe me another."

It's obvious he's trying to lighten the mood so I went along.

"I'm not sure I agree."

"It's only fair."

I shifted in my seat to face him better. He glanced down when I crossed my right leg over the left. My face heated. I hope he doesn't think I'm trying to be seductive. I wouldn't even know how.

Shaking off that thought, I focused on the topic at hand. Some silly things came to mind that I could tell him but his revelation had been pretty serious so I decided to go with something I consider significant...and potentially embarrassing...but not so somber.

"For the past couple years, I've anticipated going to your games as much, if not more than, Jeremy." Without taking his eyes off the road, he tipped his head slightly in my direction, urging me to continue. "Because I was looking forward to seeing you."

Dale pulled into my driveway and turned off the ignition. I'd been so immersed in the conversation, I hadn't even realized we were here. Without the dash-board lights, the interior darkened but the spotlight on my garage shined on us just enough so I could see him. He reached down and released his seatbelt and turned to face me.

"So I'm not the only one who felt it?" I shook my head. "Then why did it take you two years to say yes to a date?"

"I was afraid." I shook my head. "I'm basically at a tween level when it comes to dating and you're...not."

"What made you say yes this time?"

"Hannah." I chuckled. "I'm sure you've noticed that she's been trying to play matchmaker since last year." He nodded. "She invited me to your birthday dinner and told me that if I was interested in you at all I should give you a chance because you're really a nice guy."

"I really am," he said with a sexy smile.

"And humble, too," I teased.

"When you walked into the restaurant on Sunday, I was speechless. At first I thought I was hallucinating."

"I'm sure you could conjure up something better than me if that was the case."

"I don't think so."

He reached over and wrapped his fingers around the side of my neck with this thumb tracing back and forth across my jaw. The tenderness in his touch had me fighting to keep my breathing under control. It's been a long time since I've been touched so intimately.

"You were the best thing about that night." My heart pounded as the air between us became even more charged. "And I'm so happy you said yes to tonight. I had a really great time."

I felt myself drifting toward him as his thumb continued its hypnotic rhythm. He shifted closer and touched his lips gently to mine for the briefest of seconds. It was a feather light caress, not much more than a mingling of breath, but I felt its effect in every erogenous zone in my body. Pulling back slightly, he searched my gaze, seeming to give me one last chance to back away.

But I didn't. I couldn't.

His oh-so-kissable mouth curled up into a small smile as he tunneled his fingers through my hair and pulled me closer. Tilting my head back and to the side, he opened his mouth over mine. With that, I had expected a full-blown, tongue-tangling kiss, but instead he nibbled at my bottom lip before placing his mouth over mine and applying a wonderful suction.

I dug my fingers into his bicep before slowly dragging my hand up to twist them into his hair. He moaned at the contact and wrapped his arm around my waist, pulling me toward him until my stomach rested against the console and my chest was flush against his. Thankfully his heart is pounding as hard as mine.

And then he *really* kissed me.

Thoroughly.

Completely.

Perfectly.

Oh. My. God. The man can *kiss*.

I eagerly met every thrust, every caress of his tongue.

He wrapped his hand tighter around my waist and pulled me even closer until my hip rested against the console and my whole upper body smashed against his chest. Pulling his mouth from mine for just a second, he shifted his head to come at the kiss from a different angle. Different, but just as good.

It went on and on, long and hot, deep and wet, his tongue stroking mine in a perfect rhythm and I reveled in every second. My entire focus was on Dale and his mouth and what it was doing to me.

I forgot that we're sitting in his truck in my driveway where nosy neighbors can see us, but thankfully he didn't. Some of my sanity returned when I realized Dale had changed the tempo of the kiss. It was more subdued, not burning in intensity like it had been a few short moments before.

He kissed my lips softly one last time before pulling away. My back felt cold as he removed his arm from around my waist. I loosened my grip on his hair and slid back into my own seat. His blue eyes looked darker than usual as they held mine captive.

"Thank you again for coming out with me tonight."

"I had a great time. Thank you for asking me," I said, barely recognizing my husky voice.

Dale looked down at my mouth and I couldn't help but wonder what my lips look like. His are slightly swollen from our kisses so I imagine mine are the same. And the skin around my mouth feels sensitive so it's probably pink from his five o'clock shadow.

He leaned forward and kissed my temple, resting his cheek against my hair for a few breaths before meeting my gaze again.

"Would you like to go out again?"

"I'd like that, but Jeremy is coming home tomorrow so I'm not sure when I'll be free."

"The three of us could go somewhere."

"I'm not sure that's a good idea. We just...and you're..." I gestured helplessly, trying to find the right words.

Dale took my hand in his and kissed my knuckles one at a time.

"I get it. This is all new and you don't want Jeremy to know about it until we're a little further along."

Honestly, I wouldn't be so presumptuous to assume we'd ever be *further along* but I nodded anyway.

"You have a copy of the spring training schedule, right?" I nodded again. "If I don't have a game, consider me free to go out. And if I do have a game, please come to it if you're available. I know Jeremy enjoys attending and it will give me a chance to see you." He looked out the windshield and my window before meeting my gaze again. "I better let you go in the house before one of your neighbors thinks I'm holding you captive in here."

He got out of the truck and jogged around the front then opened my door. I took his proffered hand and stepped down. We walked the few steps to my front porch and I reached into my clutch for my keys.

"Thank you for tonight, Dale. I really had a great time. Dinner was wonderful and so was the company."

"I agree." He gave me a quick kiss then pulled back.

"Check your calendar and let me know when you're available." My stomach flipped at his sweet smile. "The sooner the better."

"I will."

Taking the keys from my hand, he opened the door and stepped back so I could go inside. Handing me my keys, he said, "I'll be looking forward to your call."

That said, he turned and walked back to his truck. I watched him back out of the driveway and drive down the street before I closed and locked the door. Resting my back against it, I reached up and traced my lips with my index finger, remembering every second of Dale's mouth against mine.

From the moment I first met him, I've wondered what it would be like to kiss Dale Montgomery. And now that I know, I'll never be the same.

Chapter Nine

DALE

I RAN along the outfield fence toward right field to complete my last pole. Normally I do three on game days, but today I decided to push myself and run five. Once I reached the foul pole, I did a few stretches then ran five sprints from the line to right-center field and back. I have some excess energy to get rid of today and running is a good way to do it.

Grabbing the bottle of water I left against the fence, I drank it as I walked toward Dan and Jack who were sitting along the first base line doing their usual pre-game stretches. I finished my water then tossed the bottle aside. Standing with my feet shoulder-width apart, I held my arms out and twisted from side to side before bending down to touch my toes. I repeated that three times, going farther and deepening the stretch with each pass.

That done, I sat down on the grass, my legs spread wide. Before I could walk my hands forward to stretch my hip flexors, I noticed Dan and Jack watching me and shifted my eyes between them.

"What?" I stifled my chuckle because I know exactly *what*.

"Seriously?" Jack asked. "I had to hear about your damn date with Karen from both you and my wife for two days and now that it's happened you're sitting here not saying anything?"

I shook my head and stretched from side to side before walking my hands forward as far as I could go. Payback is a bitch and Dan, Jack, and Cal were all busted as they turned into total saps over their women. Now it's my turn. Thankfully I know my friends well and expected this, so I'm prepared.

"We had a good time. The food at *Gianni's* was delicious as usual. Karen actually ate, which was a nice change. And we had some good getting-to-know-you conversation." I walked my hands back, pulled my legs together, and shook them out before stretching again. "It's been a long time since I've had a normal first date, but I think it went well. She agreed to go out with me again, so I'll call it a win."

"Uh oh. You're gonna have to repeat what you just said," Dan said.

"What?"

He nudged his head toward the stands and Jack and I turned to look. Hannah was walking in our direction.

Jack jumped to his feet and kissed his wife as she approached. She smiled up at him and shifted her blue-and-yellow checked glasses back into place then looked at me.

I finished my stretch and stood, relaying my story to Hannah before she had to ask.

"So when are you going out again?" she asked, bouncing on her toes.

"I'm not sure. She's checking her calendar. I also asked her and Jeremy to come to any games they can make so hopefully I'll need some tickets."

"Whatever you need, just let me know."

"Thanks Hannah. For everything."

She nodded, looking very self-satisfied then gave Jack a quick kiss, patted him on the ass, and made her way back toward the stands.

"Isn't she amazing?" Jack asked as he watched her walk away.

I hitched my thumb toward him and looked at Dan.

"Please tell me I don't look that dopey when I'm around Karen."

"Wish I could, buddy." He slapped me on the back and ushered me toward the dugout. "Wish I could."

KAREN

MY MOM LEFT, an exhausted Jeremy went to bed, and I finished putting the leftover pizza away. Time to face the music. Or rather my two best friends. I closed the refrigerator and turned, and there they both were, sitting at the kitchen table, watching me.

"Okay," I said around a sigh as I sank onto the chair across from them. "What do you want to know?"

They did *rock, paper, scissors* to determine who'd go first. Chloe's rock dulled Hope's scissors so she spoke first.

"Tell me about the kiss."

She leaned her arms against the table and angled forward, as if she needed to get closer to hear me.

"How do you know there was a kiss?"

Hope and Chloe shared a look then burst out laughing. Once they quieted, they turned their attention back to me.

"First of all, if you *didn't* kiss that man, I'd have to stop being your friend. And second, I'm pretty sure your lips are still swollen and, if I'm not mistaken, that's beard burn on your chin."

Reaching up, I rubbed my index finger against the abraded skin I'd carefully covered up with concealer this morning.

"Guilty," Hope said in a sing-song voice.

I rolled my eyes and told them what they wanted to know.

"It was amazing."

Before I had to say anything else, they both squealed, sounding like pubescent girls.

"Did anything else happen?" Hope waggled her eyebrows.

"Geez, don't you know me at all?"

"Yeah, I guess that was a stupid question," she said. "So where'd you go?"

"A place called Gianni's. The food was delicious." I chuckled. "Unfortunately, I broke two of our conversation rules before the main course." I went on to explain how both Jeremy and Jason were discussed.

"Did you do anything else?" Hope asked.

"He'd planned on taking me for ice cream afterwards but I was so full we skipped it."

"So he just took you home?" she asked before Chloe could.

I nodded. "We lingered at the restaurant for a while then he took the long way back to my house."

"So when did he kiss you?" Chloe asked.

"At my house. In the truck. In the driveway."

"And how long did it last?" My face heated at Hope's question. "That long, huh?"

"Did you invite him in?" Chloe asked.

"Again, do you know me at all? I wasn't going to have sex with him on the first date and—" I trailed off, realizing I was just going to encourage more questions if I continued.

"That must have been some kiss," Hope said.

Memories of Dale's mouth on mine flashed through my head and I felt my lips curl into a smile. I've always loved kissing and our makeout session had been spectacular. I may have only had one partner but Jason and I had turned kissing into an art form.

My smile faded on that last thought.

"What's wrong?" Chloe asked.

"Nothing." I shook my head. "Both the date and the kiss were great."

"Then why do you look like you're ready to cry?"

"I'm not." She stared at me and when I saw the understanding in her eyes, I fought even harder to hold back the tears.

"Oh honey, you have nothing to feel guilty about." Chloe reached over and squeezed my hand blinking back her own tears. "I know how much you loved...love...Jason. But he's been gone for five years. He'd want you to move on and be happy." She shifted her chair closer. "I knew you were interested in Dale the first time you mentioned his name. I don't expect you to marry the guy, but at least give him a chance."

I wiped the tears that had escaped from my cheeks, still amazed that Chloe keeps encouraging me to go out with Dale.

"I will, I promise."

"When are you going out with him again?" Hope asked. "He did ask you to go out again, right?"

"He did."

"So?" Chloe drew out the word.

"I have to check my calendar and call him."

"So what are you waiting for?" Hope pointed to my phone. "Check it and call the man."

"Now? Tonight?"

"Why not?"

"Shouldn't I wait a couple days?"

Chloe rolled her eyes. "It doesn't sound like Dale is playing it cool with you so you shouldn't do it with him. I know you never miss Jeremy's games, but I'm here for the next two weeks and can take him to practice. And I'm sure your mom will fill in too."

My eyes rounded. "Don't tell my mom about Dale. Please. Obviously I'll tell her once I know if this thing between us is going anywhere. But I don't need her chiming in, too. It's bad enough I have to listen to the two of you."

"You'd be lost without us," Hope said.

"That I would."

Before things could get too sappy, I opened my calendar and scoured my schedule for the rest of the week.

"Jeremy has practice tomorrow and a tournament at home starting Friday night." I switched to the tournament schedule. "The championship game starts Sunday at three if they make it that far."

"So you can go out tomorrow night or Sunday night," Chloe said. "We can just say you have showings."

I zoomed in on the picture of the Waves' schedule.

"Tomorrow is out. Dale has a game."

"What about Sunday?" Hope asked.

"He's off."

"Alrighty then." Chloe stood. "We're gonna head out to give you some privacy so you can make your phone call."

I glanced at the clock. "Now?"

"No time like the present."

Hope grabbed my phone and scrolled with her thumb then dramatically tapped the screen with her index finger before handing it back to me. I looked down and saw Dale's name.

"You dialed his number?" I screeched.

"Bye," my friends said in unison as they slung their purses over their shoulders and ran out the door, slamming it behind them.

It was too late to end the call so I held the phone up to my ear, praying to get his voice mail.

"Karen, hi. I'm so glad you called."

No such luck.

Chapter Ten

DALE

"HI." She sounded unsure. "I hope it's not too late to call."

"Not at all." I muted the TV. "How was your day?"

"Oh, it was good. I closed a sale this afternoon then Jeremy got home around dinnertime."

"Congratulations on the sale."

"Thanks. Congratulations on the win and the home run."

"You watched?"

"It might have been on in my office and I may have seen an inning or two."

I was happy to hear her voice turn less tentative and more flirtatious. Now that I know her dating background, or lack of, I totally understand why she was so reluctant to go out with me and why she's so backwards sometimes.

"I'm glad." She didn't say anything to that, but I didn't really expect her to. I mean, what *could* she say? "Did Jeremy have a good time with your parents?"

"He did. I'm sure he lived on candy and junk food for three days, but after doing the *Harry Potter* ride at *Universal*, he's actually interested in reading the books. So that's a win."

"Do you like to read?"

"I do."

"What kind of books?"

"Romance novels." She raised her voice on *novels* turning her statement into a question.

"Are you sure?"

"I'm sure," she sighed. "But I realize there is a certain stigma attached to them so I don't shout it from the rooftops or anything."

"It's just the two of us on this call and you know I won't tell anyone. After all, you know my movie preference."

"True," she said around a chuckle. "I like them because they always have a happily ever after. I read to relax and escape. It's nice to know that no matter what they go through in the book, the characters will be happy in the end."

After what she's been through, that's totally under-standable. But I don't want her thinking about the bad times so I need to change the subject. Before I could do that, she spoke.

"How about you? Do you like to read?"

"I do. There's a lot of down-time on the road so I read a lot."

"What do you like to read?"

"It varies. I go through spurts where I read a lot of fiction...military thrillers mostly. Then I'll get hooked on non-fiction, like biographies or history of a certain event."

"What's the last book you read?"

"*Notorious RBG*."

"The one about Ruth Bader Ginsburg? Really?"

"Really," I said. "When she died, I kept seeing stories about all the things she

accomplished, so I was curious. The book was written a few years ago, so I might follow it up with something more recent."

"Wow. Now I feel like I need to step up my reading game."

"Don't be too impressed. If this conversation had happened last week, my answer would have been much different. I got into a series by an author I'd never read before and binge read ten books where people kept blowing stuff up."

We talked a little more about books and as much as I was enjoying the conversation, it's almost eleven o'clock and I don't want her to have to rush off the call before we make plans.

"So, did you get a chance to check your calendar?"

"That's actually why I called," she said. "I could be free tomorrow but you have a game. Jeremy has a tournament over the weekend but it's at his home field and we should be done by Sunday evening, if not sooner depending on how his team does."

"So you're free Sunday?"

"I can be. My sister-in-law Chloe said she'd hang out with Jeremy after his game."

"Does she know why?"

"She does. So does my friend Hope."

"I'm glad."

Karen didn't say anything to that, but I swear I could hear her smile across the phone line. Next time I'll have to convince her to FaceTime so I can actually see her reactions.

Then I had a great idea.

"Hey, since we don't have a game, would you mind if the guys and I came and watched Jeremy play?"

"Oh uh." She let out a sharp laugh. "I wouldn't mind at all and I know Jeremy would love it, but I don't think it's a good idea. You'd probably cause a riot."

"I don't think it would be that bad."

"Dale, you'd be at a complex of four baseball fields full of wannabe MLB stars and their parents. The only place you'd be more recognized down here would be at Victory Park standing on first base in your uniform."

Not so much her words but the way she said them made me laugh. As if I was a total dolt for not realizing.

"Okay, you have a point," I said. "But would you still like to go out Sunday night?"

"Yes."

"Great. I promise to take you somewhere I'm not so recognizable."

"Well, you did a good job last night," she said. "I figured we would have been interrupted all through dinner, but I had you all to myself." She sucked in a shocked breath. "I mean——"

"I'm gonna stop you there because I liked that last sentence."

"Yeah?"

"Mmm Hmm. I liked having you all to myself too. Especially at the end."

Her breathing sounded louder in my ear. Hopefully because she'd enjoyed our kisses as much as I did and not because she's about to have a panic attack.

"That was nice."

Thankfully it was the former.

I was up...literally *up*...half the night thinking about my mouth on hers. It's been a long time since I ended a date with just a kiss, no matter how amazing. It's also been a long time since I kissed a woman who didn't either try to take charge or play coy little games. And I really liked it. I really like her.

From the moment I first saw Karen, I felt something special between us. When she kept turning me down when I asked her out, I figured it was a one-sided thing and she just wasn't interested in me. But now that I know she is, I'll do everything I can to move this relationship forward.

"Good."

I was going to say something about repeating it Sunday night but didn't want to make her uncomfortable. Besides the fact I'm the first guy she's gone out with since losing her husband, I'm only the second guy she's gone out with ever. So she's basically a dating newbie and I don't want to scare her in any way.

"I have the perfect place in mind and you can dress casual," I said. "Will six-thirty work again?"

"Yes, but can you pick me up at my office instead of at home? Chloe will probably take Jeremy out to eat after his game but they'll end up at my house. And I don't want him wondering why my car is in the garage."

"Okay."

I agreed to her request, and I definitely understand, but I don't want to have to sneak around. We'll have to figure out where this is going sooner rather than later so we won't have to. My time in St. Pete is limited. Before you know it, the season will start and I'll be either in Myrtle Beach or playing around the country. I need to know where I stand before that happens.

KAREN

. . .

MY DAD PULLED into the parking lot and looped around to the entrance of the complex to drop me off. My parents had come to Jeremy's earlier game, then the three of us went for lunch off site.

"You're sure Chloe is coming?" my mom asked.

"She'll be here in about a half hour."

"We can come in and sit with you until she gets here," she said. "I'd hate for you to be alone."

"No, you guys go home and relax. Dad needs to lie down on the heating pad so his back feels better for your ride home Wednesday."

My father has arthritis in his back from an old injury. Normally it doesn't affect him too much but when he drives too long or doesn't rest it properly, it really bothers him. His famous quote used to be, "Old age doesn't come alone, but it's better than the alternative," but he stopped saying that after Jason died.

"Are you sure, honey?" he asked.

"I'm positive," I said and leaned over the seat to give them each a kiss on the cheek. "I'm normally at these games alone so I'm used to it. But Chloe will be here soon and until then, I have the other parents to talk to if I get lonely."

I stepped out of the car and my dad popped the trunk so I could grab my chair. I slung it over my shoulder and waved goodbye as I walked through the gate of the complex. Jeremy's next game is at the farthest field so I made my way there and found a spot in the shade to set up my chair.

They'd won their game this morning and will be playing in the final championship starting in about an hour. I sat down and spotted the team huddled outside the fence of left field watching the game in progress. The winner of which they'd be playing.

Jeremy pitched this morning so he'll probably be playing shortstop for this whole game, which I'm happy about. I'm getting used to him being on the mound but I still haven't had to watch him pitch a championship game.

With nearly an hour to kill, I swiped open my phone and pulled up the book I'd started reading last night. I'd been so into it then but now I just can't seem to focus on the words and it has nothing to do with the noise of the screaming fans surrounding me. My mind keeps wandering to Dale and our last date, which of course has me wondering what we're doing tonight. He'd told me to dress casual so I'd stuck to skinny jeans, a cute top, and flat sandals.

I'm not gonna lie, I'm also thinking about that kiss. I spent the past few nights tossing and turning, my feelings about it bouncing back and forth. Obviously my variety of experience is limited, but Jason and I had done a lot of kissing, so I know a good kiss when I feel it. And when Dale's lips touched mine, it felt like I'd shoved my finger into an electrical outlet. You can't fake or manufacture that kind of connection.

"Hey."

I jumped at Chloe's voice. I'd been so lost in my thoughts, I hadn't heard her approach or set her chair up next to me or sit down.

"So, do you want to tell me what you were just thinking about or do I have to guess."

I know better than to play dumb or try to lie.

"From the look on your face, I'm guessing you know what I was thinking about. So why even ask?"

"Because it's fun messing with you," she said as she crossed her legs and shifted toward me. "I'm just happy thinking about Dale has your cheeks flush and a smile on your face instead of giving you a panic attack."

"You caught me at a good moment."

"I'm not even gonna comment on that." She sat back in her chair. "So where are you guys going tonight?"

"I'm not sure but he told me to dress casual."

She looked at me, her eyes skimming me from head to toe.

"You look nice."

"Thanks." The wind blew my hair in my face and I dragged my hands through it and twisted it into a bun. "Hey, would you French braid my hair? It's driving me crazy today and that'll look nicer than a regular ponytail."

"Sure." She stood and held out her hand. "Hand me your brush."

Chloe doesn't have a doubt that I have one. She always says I could survive for a week with what I have in my "mom purse." I reached down and dug around for my brush then handed it to her.

I sat up straight as she stood behind me and brushed the knots out of my hair.

"Did Jeremy decide what he wants for dinner?" she asked.

"La Mesa if you're up for it. He said he wants a burrito and chips and queso."

"That sounds good. I could go for a taco." She tugged gently on my hair as she started to braid. "And it's good you know where we'll be so you can stay out of the area."

"Oh God, I didn't even think of that." I started to turn my head to look at her.

"Sit still." She tightened her hold on my hair to keep the braid from unraveling as I shifted to face forward again.

"Sorry."

She finished the braid and secured it with the elastic that had been wrapped around the handle of the brush.

"Thanks."

"You are very welcome." She handed me the brush as she sat and looked me over again. "You look great. Casual but put together. So you should be ready for anything he has planned."

"I hope so."

"Are you still really nervous?"

"Sometimes," I admitted. "I alternate between being excited and being nervous...or something. I don't know. When I'm with him, I feel comfortable and relaxed. It's been that way since I met him. I feel like I've known him forever. But then I remember that he's *Dale Montgomery* and on top of everything else, it freaks me out."

"Kar, he's just a guy. And your friend Hannah said he's a good guy. So stop thinking of him as something more than that," she said. "As far as *everything else*, you'll work that out as you move along. Just take it one day at a time and see what happens."

From her mouth to my brain. Because if I'm being honest, it's not guilt over moving on or the fear of getting involved with someone new that's kept me up the past few nights. It's the fear of falling for Dale...really falling for him...and getting my heart broken. I'm not sure I'm ready for that.

Chapter Eleven

DALE

I FOLLOWED the GPS to the address Karen had texted
me and pulled into the parking lot next to her Subaru. I'd
shifted into park when she walked out of the building. I
quickly turned off the truck and got out.

"Hi."

"Perfect timing," she said. "Jeremy's last game got over
about an hour ago so instead of going home, I decided to
come right here and get a few things done. I just finished
up when you pulled into the lot."

I bent down and kissed her on the cheek.

"I could have met you earlier."

I ushered her around to the passenger side of the truck
and opened the door.

"Oh," she said and stepped on the running board and
climbed into the truck. She sat down, but not before I got a
nice eyeful of her delectable ass in those skinny jeans.
"This actually worked out great. I got some things done

that I would have had to do first thing tomorrow. So now I don't have to come to the office before my showing at eleven."

"Gotcha," I said. "Just remember for next time."

Her eyes widened. I smiled and closed the door then jogged around the front of the truck and slid behind the wheel.

"So, how did Jeremy's tournament go?" I asked as I started the truck, backed out of my spot, and turned left out of the parking lot.

"It was good. They made it to the championship game, but lost four to two," she said. "But Jeremy's team was the youngest in the tournament, so the fact that they got that far was great."

"How'd Jeremy do?"

"Friday night, he hit a single and a double and struck out once. There were two games yesterday and he walked all four times he batted in the first one, and had two singles and flew out to center field in the second. Today he pitched the first game so he didn't hit and he had a triple in the last game. He struck out and popped out to third base the other two times he batted."

"How'd he do on the mound?"

"Pretty good. He pitched all seven innings and only gave up two runs and had one walk. They won five to two."

"That's great. He said he enjoys it."

"He does." She chuckled. "I have a nervous breakdown watching him, but as long as he's having fun."

"You sound like my grandmother when I used to pitch."

"Really?"

I nodded. "She used to sit there with her hands covering her eyes the entire time. She said it was because she was afraid I was going to get hurt but I think she thought I was going to screw up."

"As a parent who's living through it, I'd say it's half and half. I mean, I keep picturing a line drive hitting him in the head but I'm also afraid he's going to get lit up every time he steps on the mound."

"Oh ye of little faith."

"I'm getting better. It's just new. He's never pitched before."

"I really would love to come watch him play some-time." I glanced at her quickly before shifting my eyes back to the road. "Does he have games anywhere that I'd be able to watch away from the crowd or from the parking lot?"

From the corner of my eye, I saw her nibbling at her bottom lip as she thought.

"One of the travel ball teams he plays against holds their tournaments at three separate fields instead of an actual complex like the others. And the fans are spread out a little more since there's more room."

"Any idea when he's playing there?"

"Let me check." She pulled out her phone. "Next weekend and then two weeks after that."

"I'm playing next weekend but I'm not sure about three weeks from now."

She swiped her finger across the screen a couple times. "You don't have a game on Saturday that weekend."

I couldn't hold back my smile at the fact that she has my schedule in her phone.

"Then I'll put it on my calendar."

That'll give me a few weeks to convince her that I'm serious about this thing between us and maybe let Jeremy know we're seeing each other. I realize this is just our second date and that's a big step, but I've never felt this way about anyone before. From the first moment I saw Karen, I knew she was different. For two years, I've waited for her to give me a chance and now that she has, I don't plan on blowing it.

She put her phone back in her purse and looked around.

"Where are we going anyway?"

"To grab some of the best local fare in the area."

I'd just finished my sentence when we came up on the exit. I turned off and followed the winding roads to the roadside shack. It's definitely more casual than our first date but I thought a picnic followed by a walk on the beach would make for a nice, relaxing night.

I pulled into Jimmy D's parking lot. The place doesn't look like much from the outside, but the food is amazing.

"I'll be right back," I said to Karen.

I left the truck running and stepped out, closing the door behind me. I'd called ahead and placed an order so we wouldn't have to wait. I've had two meals with Karen now and she doesn't seem to be a picky eater, but I've ordered a variety of items just to ensure there's something she'll enjoy.

They were just finishing up my order when I approached the window so once I paid, it was ready to go. I grabbed the bag and walked back to the truck and opened the tailgate to stow it in the bed, securing it next to the cooler I'd packed with drinks.

Karen was looking out the window, taking in the area, when I got back in the truck. She looked over at me.

"I've never been out this way before."

"My friend and teammate, John Kasprzyk, lives out here. He's the one who introduced me to Jimmy D's."

I pulled out of the parking lot and drove the few miles to our final destination. Turning off the road, I veered toward the left instead of going right to park in the drive-way. The blacktop ended and things got a little bumpy as the truck ambled over the grassy, sandy terrain. I spotted the wooden deck area and parked just behind it. The sun had already set but the moon was full enough to illuminate our surroundings.

"I thought a picnic on the beach would be nice." I looked at her short sleeves and reached into my back seat, grabbed a sweatshirt, and handed it to her. "Here. There's a heater on the deck, but it might get a little chilly."

She took it from me and hugged it to her chest as I stepped out of the truck. She'd already opened her door by the time I walked around to her side, but I held her hand as she stepped down. Her eyes swept back and forth, taking it all in.

"Do you own this?" she asked, glancing at the house in the near distance.

I opened the tailgate and grabbed the bag, cooler, and blanket then slammed it shut.

"No, that's Kasprzyk's house. He's letting us borrow the deck for the night."

Tossing the blanket over my shoulder, I tucked the cooler under my arm, and held out my hand for her to take. The fact that she did, without hesitation, made me smile.

We walked the short distance to the deck area and I set everything I'd been carrying on the table.

"Have a seat."

I pulled out one of the chairs facing the water and she sat, still holding on to my sweatshirt. Reaching into the large bag, I pulled out the containers of food one by one and set them on the table along with plates, napkins, and plasticware the restaurant had provided.

"Oh wow, that smells delicious."

"Wait until you taste it." I waggled my eyebrows, making her chuckle. Opening the cooler, I asked, "Water or sweet tea?"

"Sweet tea, please."

I grabbed two bottles and set them on the table before setting the cooler on the floor. Walking to the other side of the deck, I switched on the heating lamp and turned it on low before joining Karen at the table.

"I got a variety of food, so it's kind of our own private buffet." I opened each container in turn and named each item. "Help yourself."

"Everything looks delicious." She reached for a fish taco. "I'll start with this."

"Good choice." I followed her lead, but I picked up two tacos, knowing I'd finish the first one in two bites.

We ate in silence for a few minutes, enjoying the food and the sound of the surf.

I was happy to see Karen sampled everything I brought and she liked it all. We'd emptied some of the containers and put a good dent in the others when Karen dropped her fork on her plate, picked up her napkin, and wiped her hands.

"That was all so delicious, but I can't eat another bite." She sat back and finished her sweet tea.

"I'm glad you enjoyed it. Jimmy D's is definitely a hidden gem."

I reached under the table and grabbed the bag the food had come in and filled it with the empty containers. While I did that, Karen replaced the lids on the others.

"It's so pretty here. And quiet."

"The seclusion is one of the things that made Kasprzyk buy the house. He's married with four kids so they wanted somewhere they could enjoy themselves away from the crowds."

"It must be tough, being recognized everywhere you go."

"It goes with the territory." I shrugged. "But honestly, there are ways around it. Like you pointed out when I mentioned going to Jeremy's game, a complex full of baseball fans probably isn't somewhere I'd remain anonymous for long. The guys and I have our favorite spots throughout the country where we can go and not get mobbed. And when I'm by myself wearing regular clothes, only the most dedicated fans recognize me."

The wind kicked up and she shivered.

"Do you want me to turn the heater up?"

"No, I'll just put this on." She picked up the sweatshirt that had been resting on her lap and slipped her arms inside then shifted it over her head. "Thank you for letting me borrow it."

"No problem."

Honestly, I was being practical when I offered her the sweatshirt. I didn't tell her we'd be outside tonight and didn't want her to be chilly. But now, seeing her in a piece of my clothing, especially a Waves sweatshirt with my name and number on it, is making my inner caveman rear his head. I'll have to be sure to give her some gear she can wear to games.

"Would you like another drink?"

She shook her head. "No thanks, I'm good."

"How about a walk on the beach?"

"Sure." She shifted her chair back and hesitated. "I'd better take my sandals off." Reaching down, she slipped them off and placed them under the table. "Ready." She smiled over at me as she stood.

I'd toed off my shoes too. No reason to get them full of sand if she's going barefoot.

Taking her hand, I led her toward the water then slowly strolled along its edge.

"By the way, I don't think I mentioned this yet, but you look really nice tonight. I like your hair like that."

"Thank you." Her voice was quiet, tentative. And I'm sure there's a blush covering her cheeks. "My hair kept whipping at my face so I had Chloe braid it to hold it back."

"Speaking of Chloe, what are she and Jeremy doing tonight?"

"They were going to La Mesa for dinner then probably back to the house to play video games. Chloe is a gamer from way back and she really gives him a run for his money. Which he loves. I can play, but I'm not much competition for him anymore."

"I used to be able to hold my own, but at this point, I'm out of practice."

"I wish Jeremy was out of practice. It's a struggle keeping him from playing when we're home. But at least sports keep him busy so I don't have to nag him about his screen time too much."

"What does he play besides baseball?"

"Basketball. He used to play soccer when he was younger, but once he was old enough for fall ball, he stopped that."

"So you're a real sports mom."

"That's for sure," she said. "Thankfully I like sports...well baseball and basketball anyway. I'm not much of a football fan and I don't mind soccer, but I have no clue about the rules so I never knew what was happening."

"No football, huh?"

"Sorry." She shrugged.

"My grandmother hated when I played football. She and my grandfather fought over whether or not to let me play when I went to live with them. Somehow he won that argument and signed me up."

"Did you play basketball too?"

"Yep."

"So you were a three-sport athlete."

"Guilty."

"Do you like baseball the most or is it just the one you were best at?"

"Both, but I liked playing the other sports in high school because they kept me in shape. What about you? Did you play sports when you were growing up?"

"I did a little bit of everything...softball, basketball, dance, track. I had kind of a jack-of-all-trades, master of none thing going on."

"Nothing wrong with that. As long as you enjoyed it."

"There was nothing I loved doing enough to put my whole heart, soul, and time into. I always envied people who were that passionate about something. My friend Hope knew she wanted to be a cosmetologist back in middle school. I entered college undeclared because I had no clue what I wanted to do with my life."

We'd walked past Kasprzyk's house and were coming to the end of the beach, so I slowed then stopped and turned to face her.

"What major did you end up declaring?"

"Business management, but only because it was practical and there were a lot of things I could do with it."

"That's why I chose communications," I said. "But honestly, my goal with college was to get drafted to play professional baseball."

"Well, that worked out for you."

"Yeah, I've been pretty lucky, getting to do what I do for a living."

Nudging my head toward the deck, I squeezed her hand and started walking in that direction.

"So did your parents stay in town after they brought Jeremy home?"

"Yeah, they're going back Wednesday. They came to a couple of Jeremy's games this weekend which he was happy about."

"Nice."

She told me a little about her parents as we walked back up the beach. They seem pretty involved in her and Jeremy's lives despite the fact they live a thousand miles away. At least she's not totally alone.

"Ready for dessert?" I asked as we stepped onto the deck.

"That depends. What'd you bring?"

"Brownies."

Certain parts of my anatomy perked up at her answering groan.

"Maybe half of one." Her nose scrunched in the most adorable way with her words.

"You can try it, but I think once you've tasted these brownies, you're gonna want the whole thing." I picked the cooler up and unzipped the top revealing the bakery box inside. "Have a seat. I'll bring it over to you."

Karen settled onto the wicker couch toward the back of the deck. I grabbed two napkins from the side of the cooler and placed a brownie on each, grabbed two bottles of sweet tea out of the main compartment, and walked over to join her.

"Oh wow, this is huge."

"These are from a bakery just around the corner from my condo. Cal discovered it a few years ago. That man has the biggest sweet tooth, but I have to admit, he finds some of the best places to get baked goods."

She bit into her brownie and let out a long, low moan as she chewed.

Down boy.

Thankfully we're sitting so she can't see how her sexy moans and groans are affecting me. I shifted to get more comfortable.

"This is amazing." She took another bite, then chuckled. "And you're right, I'm going to finish the whole thing."

"Told ya." I popped the last bite into my mouth and took a long drink of sweet tea. "So is there any chance you can make a game this week? They're all at night."

With her crazy schedule and mine, the days we'll be able to see each other will be few and far between. Add the fact that Jeremy doesn't know we're dating and it's even worse. But if she comes to my games, I'll at least get to see her even if we don't get to spend a whole lot of time together. Unless I can convince her to do something afterwards. I'm sure the guys would join us to make it a group outing.

She finished chewing and wiped some stray crumbs off the side of her mouth with her thumb.

"I'm not sure. Jeremy has practice tomorrow and Wednesday night. He has that tournament this weekend but we won't know if his first game is Friday night or Saturday until mid-week. That leaves Thursday but Chloe is flying to London Saturday and we always do something before her business trips."

"You should bring her to a game. I'd love to meet her."

Her eyes widened and she opened her mouth then closed it. Twisting the cap off her sweet tea, she took a long drink.

"Are you sure about that? You don't think it's kind of soon to meet the friends?"

"You've met my friends so it's only fair."

She finished her brownie and wiped her mouth then crumbled the napkin into her fist, looking unsure of what to say next. I don't want to rush her, but I do want her to understand that I want this relationship to move forward. I'm not just killing time with her while I'm in town. That was how I did things in the past, but I want different things now, and she's the one I want them with.

Taking her hand in mine, I rubbed small circles against her soft skin with my thumb.

"Look, I know this is only our second date, but I want you to know that I'm not just messing around here. There's something special between us. I felt it the first time I saw you. And I understand your reluctance to tell Jeremy we're dating right now, but I'm hoping we can figure out a way to spend time together in the meantime. You guys coming to my games is one way we can see each other and it'll be even better if we can get dinner or something afterwards."

Her clear blue eyes had stayed focused on me while I spoke. Now she blinked and looked down at our joined hands. There's so much more I want to say, but I stayed quiet, letting her absorb my words and collect her thoughts. It seemed like forever, but she finally met my gaze again and spoke.

"I'm not going to lie, this whole thing between us kind of freaks me out. For different reasons at different times. But I can't deny the fact that I enjoy spending time with you and felt that something, too." That last sentence made me smile. "I'll ask Chloe about going to the game Thursday. I'm sure she'll jump at the chance to meet you and probably embarrass me in some way."

"Thank you." I lifted her hand and kissed her knuckles. "And thank you for being so honest."

I shifted closer to her, sliding one arm behind her shoulders. Letting go of her hand, I cupped her jaw. Just like the other night in my truck, the electricity swirled around us. She stayed still for several heartbeats before relaxing into my touch. Closing her eyes, she took in a short breath and let it out on a soft sigh before meeting my gaze again. I looked down at her parted lips and couldn't resist any longer.

Pressing my mouth against hers, I moved slowly, savoring the plump softness of her lips. She let out a soft moan and I firmed my grip on her jaw, holding her in place as I tilted my head to get a better angle. I continued to sip at her mouth before licking at the seam of her lips, asking for entry. She opened up and I touched my tongue to hers, enjoying the lingering taste of chocolate and sweet tea, but as our tongues tangled I got to her true essence. She's delicious.

I angled myself against her, pushing her back against the cushion. She moved one hand up and gripped at my hair as the other wrapped around my waist, pulling me closer. I groaned deep in my chest and opened my mouth, deepening the kiss, kicking it up a notch. It went on and on, and I enjoyed every second, every taste, every touch.

We shifted and inched further down on the couch until she reclined against the arm with me resting between her thighs. I cradled her head in my elbow and shifted my other hand around and up to the middle of her back, holding her tight. Firm, round, and full, her breasts flattened against my chest and I flexed my fingers into her back, fighting the urge to reach around and cop a feel.

Our mouths continued to devour each other and Karen bent her leg and shifted down, putting my throbbing erection right at the apex of her thighs. I pressed against her, easing the ache for a second before making it even worse. She splayed her fingers against my back before digging them into my shirt, grabbing some skin in the process.

Before my last thread of sanity snapped and we hit a point of no return, I slowed the kiss and put some space between our bodies. Reluctantly pulling my mouth from hers, I rested my head against her forehead and fought to slow my breathing.

Pulling back just enough to see her face, I watched as she slowly opened her eyes and took way too much pleasure in her dazed expression. Looking down at her swollen lips, I fought the urge to take her mouth again. Instead, I leaned forward and kissed the tip of her nose, then her forehead before meeting her eyes and shifting back onto my side of the couch.

I held out my hand and pulled her into a sitting position.

"I had a great time tonight, Karen." My voice sounded like I'd swallowed gravel. I cleared my throat. "But I think I should take you home." She looked back at me and dug her teeth into her swollen bottom lip. I reached out and traced my thumb slowly back and forth with the lightest of touches until she released it. "I don't want to mess this up by doing something you're not ready for and I just used every bit of self-control I possess to end that kiss."

Her gaze shifted down to my lap where my khaki shorts were tented with a very visible erection. My groan brought her eyes back to mine and it's pretty obvious that she's mine for the taking if I just make the move. But even if my big brain isn't functioning on all cylinders, I still know she's just caught up in this attraction right now and would regret it if we went any further tonight.

I stood and walked toward the table, adjusting myself on the way so my dick isn't visible from the moon. Next time we go out, I'll be sure to wear compression shorts.

Chapter Twelve

KAREN

"MOM." Jeremy knocked on the bathroom door. "Are you almost ready?"

"Yeah, I'll be out in a minute."

We don't usually do things like this on school nights, so this is a treat for him. He's so busy with his own activities, I figure staying in when he doesn't have anything going on is a good balance. As usual, he asked to get to the stadium early to watch batting practice. And since we're picking Chloe up, we have to give ourselves some extra time since she's a little out of the way.

I looked at myself in the mirror and couldn't stop the smile from spreading across my face. After our date the other night, Dale had told me to keep the sweatshirt I'd borrowed then he sent a box of Waves gear to my office. Of course, every item was branded with his name and number.

He's called me the past three nights after his games,

and even convinced me to FaceTime last night. I'm not thrilled with being on video, but I did enjoy looking at him, especially since he was lying in bed and wasn't wearing a shirt.

I almost bumped into Jeremy as I opened the bathroom door. He was obviously getting ready to knock again. I wish he was this anxious to go to school in the morning. I'm usually the one banging on his bathroom door to get him moving.

He looked at my shirt.

"Is that one of my shirts?"

"No, Hannah gave me some of my own."

Hopefully he won't question why mine all say *Montgomery* on the back. But I doubt he will. I'm sure the thought of me dating has never even crossed his mind, never mind dating one of the Waves.

We walked out of my bedroom and into the kitchen where I grabbed my purse and keys from the island before heading to the garage.

Jeremy slid into the passenger seat.

"I'll move into the back when we pick up Aunt Chloe," he said as he fastened his seatbelt.

"I appreciate you not making me feel like a chauffeur."

"I'm pretty psyched about her coming tonight."

"Yeah, me too."

I'm just hoping she doesn't embarrass me too much around Dale. We're all going out for ice cream after the game to the place he'd planned to take me on our first date. Jack and Hannah are joining us along with Dan and Sabrina and their two kids. Jeremy and Lexi have met a couple times and got along well so hopefully we'll all have a fun night.

"It's awesome that we're going out with Jack and the

guys after the game, too," he said, as if he'd read my thoughts. "I still can't believe that I know them."

I glanced over at him seeing the look of awe on his face before putting my eyes on the road again.

"That's all you, buddy. You met Jack and he liked you enough to introduce you to his friends."

"But like, they're professional baseball players and I get to talk to them and stuff. That's why I never want to bring friends to the games with me. They act all weird around the guys and it's embarrassing. I mean, I remember being nervous the first time I met Jack, because seriously he's *Jack Reagan*, but I don't think I acted like a total idiot."

"No, you didn't. You played it pretty cool."

I blinked back tears as I remembered that night at the CADD beach bash two years ago. Despite the fact that Tampa is our home team, Jason had always been a Waves fan and passed that on to our son. Jack has always been Jeremy's favorite player so when he not only took time to talk to him and sign his shirt, but also raced him on the slide and had Hannah give us tickets to a game, I nearly bawled my eyes out in front of them that night.

"And I'm very proud that you don't brag to your friends about the fact that you get to hang out with Jack and the guys once in a while, not to mention that you have his number saved in your cell."

He shrugged. "I like keeping it to myself. Is that bad?"

"I don't think so."

We pulled into Chloe's driveway and she came out the front door. Jeremy stepped out of the car and gave her a hug before settling into the back. She sat in the passenger seat and after clicking her seatbelt into place, turned and flashed me a big smile.

"Nice shirt."

"Thanks."

I gave her a warning look then backed out of her driveway.

She and Jeremy chatted as I drove to Victory Park. I pulled into the VIP parking lot courtesy of the upgraded passes Hannah included with our tickets. It still amazes me that I've been here more in the past couple years than I was my entire life.

Jeremy jumped out of the car and waited for us before walking toward the entrance. The attendant scanned our tickets and we pushed through the turnstile. The sound of balls being hit echoed through the concourse.

"Can I go watch batting practice and meet you at our seats?" Jeremy asked.

"Sure. See you in a bit."

I watched him run across the concourse, through the opening to the field, and his head disappeared as he started down the steps.

Chloe looked down at her watch. "So we have a couple hours before this game starts?"

"Yep."

"That kid is lucky I love him."

"Yes, he is," I said. "Did you want to get something to eat?"

"Oh no, don't try to distract me with food. I want to go check out your hot baseball player up close."

I rolled my eyes and started walking toward the field. Hannah was standing down the concourse speaking to someone and I waved before continuing to our seats.

"That was Hannah Reagan, Jack's wife and the one who supplies us with what seems like an endless supply of tickets and swag."

"She's adorable. I love her glasses."

"Yeah, that's kind of her thing. She has all kinds of funky frames."

"Wait!" Chloe grabbed my arm and stopped me in my tracks. "Who is she related to?"

"Aaran Diskin is her father."

"That's right." She let go and we started walking again. "Jesus Kar, you're rubbing elbows with professional athletes and Mac Flynn. Who would have thought?"

"I've never met him."

"Still, you're only two degrees of separation away from him. Or is it one degree? I always get that messed up." I stepped ahead of her and started down the stairs. "It doesn't matter. It's still hella cool."

I glanced back at her before heading down our row.

"Hella cool?"

"Hey, I have to use some lingo so I keep my rep as the cool aunt."

Rolling my eyes, I sat down and Chloe took the seat next to me.

Jeremy stood down by the wall watching batting practice. I scanned the stadium looking for Dale and spotted him just off the first base line stretching with Jack and Dan.

"I should come to these games more often," Chloe said with a low whistle. "What a view."

Before I could comment on that, I heard my name and looked up to see Penny Montgomery walking in my direction. Based on the smile on her face, I'm assuming she knows about my dates with Dale. And of course, we met at his birthday party.

"Hi Penny," I said as she sat in the row in front of us.

I introduced her to Chloe being sure to mention that she's a member of the Olympic softball team as well as Dale's sister.

"You guys look like sisters," Penny said.

"We've definitely heard that before," I said, then I

noticed that Lexi had joined Jeremy down by the wall. "Sabrina must be here early, too." I pointed toward the kids.

"No, she'll probably get here just as the game starts so she doesn't have to keep Gavin occupied too long. Lexi came to the stadium with Dan and she hung out with me in the batting cages," she said. "By the way, I stopped by *Courtney's Craft Corner* the other day. What a great place. I'm so glad you told me about it. I got some things and am having her make a few custom items for my friend's bridal shower."

"That's great. It's always my go-to place for gifts, especially when you're buying for someone who has everything."

"Like my brother," she said around a smile. I nodded. "Speaking of…"

I looked at the field and saw Dale walking toward the on-deck circle with a bat tucked under his arm. His eyes were trained on me as he slipped his hand into a batting glove and secured it in place. He dropped his gaze to my shirt and before meeting my eyes again and smiled. I couldn't help but smile back.

"We better move out of the way," Chloe said to Penny. "I'm afraid all these sparks are going to cause a fire."

"Wait until you get them within a couple feet of each other," Penny said.

I decided to ignore them and watched Dale go through his hitting routine. He held the bat in his hands and shifted from side to side before bending and touching it to his toes, giving me a nice view of his ass. After swinging the bat a few times, he leaned it against his upper thigh, drawing my attention to the part of his anatomy I'd been trying to keep from staring at.

That certain part had definitely let itself be known the

other night and I'd almost gasped out loud at the impressive tent in his shorts. I guess his nickname isn't *The Full Monte* for nothing.

He stepped into the batter's box and got into his stance. His muscles bunched and flexed with every swing and I remembered how amazing it had felt to run my hands over them. Once he finished peppering balls all over the field, he signaled for two more pitches and sent them flying into the outfield.

His gaze met mine again as he walked over toward the wall where Dan and Jack were standing talking to Jeremy and Lexi. I watched as he said something to my son then very deliberately took off his batting gloves and handed them to him.

"I think I'm gonna go join my nephew."

"Please behave," I begged.

Chloe stood and smiled down at me.

"Jeremy is down there so I can't be too bad, right?"

No matter who's down there, I'm sure she'll find a way.

DALE

"I'VE LIVED HERE my whole life and somehow you've managed to introduce me to three eating establishments I've never heard of before," Karen said.

Jeremy and Lexi had devoured their sundaes and were now playing catch across the parking lot, safely out of hearing distance.

"One of the groundskeepers at Victory Park told us about this ice cream place years ago and we've been coming here since. It's usually busy during the day, especially on the weekend, but at night it's dead making it a perfect place for us to frequent."

The two girls working the window seemed to panic when she saw us all pull up, but handled the onslaught of orders well.

"These guys find the best places wherever they go," Sabrina said as she fed Gavin vanilla ice cream. He kept sticking his fist in his mouth then rubbing it all over his cheeks. She'd given up trying to clean him up a few spoonfuls ago.

"So how's your wrist?" Dan asked.

I held out my arm showing him the bruise a wild fast ball had given me.

"That sounded awful up in the stands. I can't imagine how bad it was down on the field," Karen's doppelganger, Chloe, said from the other side of the table.

When I saw her walking down toward Jeremy before the game, I couldn't believe my eyes. It would be easy to mistake the two of them for each other from far away, they look that much alike. Of course, I'd never do that. The zing between Karen and me isn't there with Chloe.

"Yeah, it hit right on the bone so it sounded nasty," I said. "It's throbbing a little bit now, but it's nothing ice and *Advil* won't fix."

Wanting to take the attention off me and my ailing wrist, I turned to Jack and Hannah. "Is this the first time you've been here since the proposal?"

"No, we stopped by right after we got down here," he said.

"This is where Jack proposed to me," Hannah said, looking between Karen and Chloe.

When I asked the question, I didn't think about the fact they wouldn't have a clue what I was talking about. I know it's hard hanging out with a tight group like ours, but both

Karen and Chloe are fitting in well. And I love the fact that neither one of them blinked at the fact that Jack, who is basically a multi-millionaire, proposed to his wife at an old ice cream shack.

"So how long are you down here for?" Karen asked Sabrina.

"We fly home Monday night. Then we'll be back the last week of spring training and we'll all go home together," Sabrina said, smiling up at Dan.

"It must be tough, being separated so much," Karen said.

I looked at Sabrina, silently begging her to pick her words wisely. Karen glared at Chloe so I can only assume the thump I heard was a kick to the shin. I get the feeling Chloe's on my side, which kind of surprises me since she's Jason's sister. But hey, I won't look a gift horse in the mouth.

"Most families are separated regularly even when they have normal jobs. Whether they work nine-to-five, nights, or have to travel, it definitely gets in the way of family time," Sabrina said. "Extended road trips are balanced by long home series. And of course, we have the time between October and February together, which is nice. Most families don't get that." She shrugged. "We make it work."

I mouthed a silent "thank you" to Sabrina and she smiled.

All my friends and at least one of Karen's are rooting for us. Hopefully that swings an abundance of good juju in our direction.

Everyone was done with their ice cream, even Gavin, and we just hung out talking for a while. Normally we all would have scattered by now but my friends know how much Karen means to me and they're trying to give us as much time together as possible. They've even asked her when she'll be at another game and if she plans on coming up to Myrtle Beach at some point. Thankfully that last question came from Sabrina. It would have been strange if one of the guys had asked.

"I better get Jeremy home," Karen said. "He has school in the morning and he's been impossible to get up lately so I don't want to be out too late."

I stood with her and looked over at Jeremy, who was still happily playing catch with Lexi.

"Can I get a minute alone?"

"Oh, sure."

Chloe smiled and sat back down as I directed Karen around the back of the building. Pulling her closer, I wrapped my arms around her waist and gave her slow, tongue-tangling, toe-curling kiss. Before things could get too out of hand, I ended it and smiled down at her.

"I've been wanting to do that since I saw you sitting in the stands earlier." I kissed her forehead. "Thank you for coming to the game today. Besides my grandparents and Penny, I've never had anyone special come to watch me play and it meant a lot. Especially since you're wearing my number."

Her light blue eyes stared into mine as if she was searching for the truth of my words. I let her look. I have nothing to hide.

"I had a lot of fun tonight and I know Jeremy did, too. So thank you."

I kissed her again, keeping it PG-rated. I don't need things to get out of control like they did Sunday. Reluctantly, I ended the kiss and stepped back.

"I better let you go so Jeremy can get to sleep."

She nodded then followed me back around the building.

"Jeremy, it's time to go," she yelled over to him.

He didn't look happy as he threw the ball back to Lexi, but he didn't complain.

I followed Karen and Chloe to her car and Dan trailed behind with a sleepy Gavin in his arms.

"We're gonna head out too," he said to Lexi. "Your brother is ready to conk out and he needs a bath before bed."

Lexi looked over at Jeremy. "Are you coming to the game tomorrow night?"

He looked at Karen. "Can we go mom? My first tournament game isn't until noon on Saturday."

She looked over at me and I raised my eyebrows. Does she seriously think I had something to do with this? Nope, it's just dumb luck that Jeremy and Lexi are getting along so well.

Then Chloe chimed in trying to seal the deal. "Since Jeremy doesn't have a game or practice, there's no reason you can't go."

If looks could kill, Chloe would have dropped dead right in front of us, but she just stood there with a cocky smirk on her face.

Karen shook her head and sighed.

"Sure, we can go."

"Yes!" Jeremy and Lexi said at the same time.

"I'll see you tomorrow," Jeremy said to Lexi.

"If you get there early, you can come to the batting cages with Penny and me. She's so awesome," Lexi said.

"I know, I can't believe she's gonna be in the Olympics," Jeremy said then he looked at Karen. "Is that okay, mom?"

She nodded then looked at Dan. "We usually get there just after batting practice starts. Will that work?"

"If you come a few minutes before that we can get Jeremy settled with Penny."

"I'll leave word with the security guard at the VIP parking lot, so just go there," Hannah said as she and Jack approached. "The lower-level entrance, which is the easiest way to get to the cages, is right there so text me when you park and I'll meet you and we'll get him where he needs to go. And instead of you just sitting in the stands for two hours, we can go grab a bite to eat."

Jack put his arm around her shoulders and kissed the top of her head. "That's my girl. The queen of planning." She smiled up at him and settled into his embrace.

Karen's stunned look almost made me laugh but I imagine I don't look much different. My friends know what she means to me and have really closed rank, welcoming her, and doing whatever it takes to make her feel included.

I didn't grow up with a big, extended family but thankfully I managed to piece one together as an adult.

Chapter Thirteen

KAREN

FOR THE SECOND time in as many days, I pulled into the VIP parking lot at Victory Park. The security guard waved me through with a smile after I gave him my name and I settled into a spot.

Jeremy had talked nonstop during the twenty minute drive. He'd had a great time last night and he's excited to hit the batting cages with Penny and Lexi today.

I texted Hannah and she immediately called me and told me which direction to head in. One of the heavy metal doors opened as we approached the side of the stadium and she peeked outside.

"Come on in," she said and held the door open wide.

We stepped over the threshold and she slammed the door shut. As we walked through the beige hallway, she pointed out the trainer's room, gym area, and a couple conference rooms. I heard the ping of an aluminum bat as we approached an open door. Jeremy stepped inside and

Penny stopped mid-pitch and smiled over at him. After reassuring me she was thrilled to have Jeremy join them, Penny told Hannah and me to go enjoy our dinner.

"There's a place right across the street if you don't mind walking. That way we can enjoy a cocktail or two," Hannah said.

"A cocktail sounds amazing right about now."

She led me back out of the stadium and through the parking lot. Thankfully I'd changed out of my work clothes and into jeans, one of the T-shirts Dale had given me, and comfortable sneakers. I'd hate to walk any distance in the heels I had on today. They look amazing but hurt like hell.

"Are you okay with tonight? You kind of got bulldozed into it."

"It's fine. Jeremy loves coming to the games."

She opened her mouth to say something then closed it as we approached the corner.

"That's the place right there."

She pointed to a two-story, glass-fronted building across the street. The light changed and I followed her toward the restaurant.

"It's early yet, so it's nice and quiet. Later there'll be a band downstairs and it'll be packed."

The hostess greeted us and led us to a table against the window, looking over at the stadium. When she asked if we wanted any drinks to start, Hannah ordered a margarita and I did the same.

I opened the menu and since I'd only had time for yogurt for lunch, wanted to order one of everything.

"What's good here?" I asked Hannah.

"The crab cakes, Thai shrimp, and maple-glazed salmon are amazing. They used to be offered as specials but were so popular, they added them to the menu. But honestly, I've never had a bad meal here."

The waitress brought our drinks and set them down along with two glasses of water.

"Are you ready to order or do you need more time?" she asked.

I glanced at Hannah. "I'm ready if you are."

"I know what I want."

We placed our orders...crab cakes for me and Thai shrimp for her...and the waitress promised to return with our salads and some bread.

I picked up my margarita and took a sip. "Mmm, good."

Hannah nodded as she took a drink of hers. "Their mango margarita is good too, but I'm not in the mood for a sweet drink right now. I'm still in sugar shock from my brownie a la mode last night."

"I can't believe the size of their sundaes for the price. How do they make any money?"

"I have no idea. Low overhead, I guess."

"Jack really proposed to you there?"

"He did." A soft smile crossed her face. "He actually introduced me to the place after the CADD beach bash where we met you. When he dropped me off at my hotel afterwards, he kissed me for the first time."

"When I met you that night, I thought you were a couple."

"Well, we *were* after that night." She held up her glass in a mock toast and took another drink.

"But you'd known each other for years beforehand, right?"

Looking up at the ceiling, she tipped her head back and forth. "Yes and no. I mean, we knew each other and worked together, but we didn't hang out socially and didn't really *know* each other." She chuckled. "Like I told you, I had the biggest crush on him for years and I hated myself for it."

"Did he know?"

"God no! Well, not at the time. He does now."

"And what did he think about that?"

"He said he doesn't know why he had his head up his ass for so many years."

"Obviously I don't know Jack very well, but it does sound like something he'd say." I couldn't help but ask, "So what made him get his head out of his ass and notice you?"

She shrugged. "I really don't know. Spending time together, I guess. But one day he just looked at me differently and I'm so glad he did."

"You guys really are adorable together. So are Dan and Sabrina."

"You haven't met Barbara yet, but she and Cal are pretty cute too."

The waitress returned with our salads and a basket of bread. Hannah picked out a slice and slathered it with butter.

She held up her knife. "This butter is amazing. I have no idea what they add to it, but it's delicious." She took a big bite, chewed and swallowed as I followed her lead and added a generous amount of butter to my own bread. "But you asked about the proposal, which is a funny story. Jack had this whole big party planned. He invited my father and his wife and the rest of the gang." She gestured with her bread. "Private room, fancy food, music, flowers. You name it, he had it there and he planned on proposing in between dinner and dessert, in front of everyone."

"So what happened?"

After popping the last of her bread into her mouth, she shook her head as she swallowed.

"I'm not really sure. I had no idea all that was planned obviously. All I knew is that we were meeting everyone for dinner. On our way there, he veered off, and took me to the ice cream place. We shared a banana split then he got down on one knee and asked me to marry him. So by the time we got to the venue where he was supposed to pop the question, we were already engaged."

She picked up her fork and dug into her salad. I know there's a reason for this dinner beyond her not wanting me to sit at the stadium for two hours, but I'm not sure what it is. But I'm enjoying my drink and her company so I just ate my salad, figuring she'd get to the point eventually.

When the waitress delivered our entrees, we both decided to have another margarita. I also asked for a pitcher of water so she doesn't have to keep refilling mine. The older I get, the more I focus on staying hydrated whenever I drink. There was a time I could drink all night and wake up the next day without so much as a headache. Now if I have one cocktail too many it takes me two days to recover.

"I know you're sitting there wondering what this dinner is about."

I placed a big piece of crab into my mouth and smiled over at her.

"I figured you'd let me know eventually."

"Like I said earlier, before I got involved with Jack, I didn't hang out with him or his friends, so I know how overwhelming it can be spending time with them at first. And trust me when I tell you that they've been on pretty good behavior around you. There's normally a lot more teasing and smartass comments. Honestly, it's like spending time with teenage boys sometimes. But they're going to continue to invite you to things and include you and

Jeremy in whatever is going on because they know Dale wants you there."

The waitress returned with our fresh margaritas and the pitcher of water. After checking that everything was prepared to our liking, she left us alone.

"If you'd told me five years ago that I'd be married to Jack Reagan, I would have laughed in your face. Despite my ridiculous crush, I never even thought it was in the realm of possibility. I mean, he's *Jack Reagan*. Why would he ever notice me?" She smiled. "But then he did." She popped a shrimp into her mouth, chewed, and swallowed before speaking again. "Remember I told you why I set up that PR blitz for Jack two years ago?"

"Because of the book, right?"

"Yes, the book." She rolled her eyes. "Jack lived his life a certain way and I definitely didn't fit into that mold, nor did I want to. So I crushed on him from a distance. Then we were thrown together and this thing just grew between us until we couldn't ignore it anymore. I understand my circumstances weren't the same as yours. I don't have your history and I wasn't a single mother, but we do have some things in common. We're pretty low-key women who caught the eye of some extraordinary men, and that can be scary as hell. But it can also be worth it. Remember that whenever you have doubts or when a gang of people are overwhelming you with invitations and smothering you with attention."

I smiled at that last sentence. They've always been friendly with Jeremy and me, but since Dale's party, we've been welcomed at a whole different level. It's both flattering and overwhelming, especially since I'm still not sure where this thing between Dale and me is going, or even where I want it to go.

We finished our meals and the waitress refilled our

water glasses before clearing our plates and the empty pitcher.

"Would you like two more margaritas?" she asked.

"No thank you. Water is good for me."

Hannah turned down a third drink as well.

"Technically I'm on the clock, so another one wouldn't be a good idea," she said around a chuckle.

I grabbed the check when the waitress brought it over.

"I've got it," I said.

"No, I invited you, so hand it over."

"Dinner may have been your idea but I appreciate you asking me and sharing everything you did."

And that's the truth. Chloe and Hope can offer advice but they don't have first-hand experience like Hannah. I realize that I have my own issues and insecurities, but getting involved with Dale comes with its own real list of complications.

I won the battle for the check and once it was paid, we left and headed back toward the stadium. Hannah led me through a side door and walked with me to the main concourse.

"I have to run up to my office to make a few phone calls but I should be down by the time the game starts." Before I walked away, she added, "I know you have a lot going on in your head with this, so if you ever want to talk, please give me a call." She smiled. "He's worth it. I promise."

DALE

. . .

I SWEAR I play better when Karen's here. I'm seeing the ball better when I bat and my reflexes are sharper in the field.

Standing in the on-deck circle, I keep looking up at her in the stands as I go through my usual pre-bat ritual. I've been doing the same thing for so long it's second-nature at this point, so staring at Karen isn't taking away from my game.

And thankfully I'm good at multi-tasking so I know exactly what's going on with Kasprzyk at the plate. He'd taken two strikes followed by three balls then fouled one off. I shifted my eyes toward the field as the umpire settled behind the catcher and the pitcher went into his windup. The ball was low and outside for ball four. Kasprzyk jogged down to first base, handing his bat to the bat boy along the way.

That gives us a big opportunity. We're losing three to two and since it's the bottom of the eighth, we're running out of chances to catch up. There's only one out, so I have to do something here to move Kasprzyk around the bases.

I banged the handle of my bat against the dirt to dislodge the donut then walked toward the plate and stepped into the box to face the pitcher. A fastball came flying at my head and I ducked out of the way then got right back into the box. He released the ball and again, it came at me high and inside again.

The pitching coach called time and jogged out to settle his pitcher down. He just took the mound this inning and he's missed his spots on most of his pitches.

Stepping out of the box, I leaned the bat against my hip and tightened my batting gloves. Looking up into the stands, I zeroed in on Karen who was having an animated conversation with Penny. They're probably talking about how Jeremy did with her in the cages today. But regardless of the topic, I'm just happy to see them getting along. Penny and I are really close and I'm hoping Karen and I will be, too.

Her head had been turned as she listened to whatever Penny was saying but she looked in my direction as if I'd willed her attention my way. I smiled and that roller coaster feeling flowed through me again when she smiled back. I don't know what it is about her that makes me feel all warm and fuzzy inside, but I really like it.

The umpire stepped into position and I got into the box and took my stance. The pitcher looked over his shoulder at Kasprzyk then stepped his foot off the rubber.

Seriously?

With the way he's been pitching, he needs to concentrate on putting the ball over the plate instead of dicking around with the guy he put on first base.

I stepped back into the box and glared at the pitcher. He glared back but didn't look very intimidating.

Throwing from the stretch, he reached back then released the ball. Since he's having trouble finding the zone, I wouldn't normally swing at anything until he throws a strike, but as soon as the ball left his hand, I knew the pitch coming at me was my idea of perfect when I'm hitting from the left side of the plate. Thigh high and between the center of the plate and the inside corner.

A satisfying crack sounded as the bat vibrated in my grip when it made contact with the ball. Once the line drive sailed over the first baseman's head, no one else had a chance of catching it. Kasprzyk had had a big lead and was already rounding second as the ball bounced just inside the foul line in right field. The first base coach rotated his arm in big circles waving me toward second. I glanced over my shoulder just before I rounded the bag and saw the ball bounce into the corner so I kept going.

The third base coach held up his hands letting me know I could go in standing.

Clapping my hands together, I looked over at the dugout watching my teammates celebrate the tying run before glancing up at Karen, who was on her feet cheering. I tipped my helmet in her direction then slapped it back on my head.

The bat boy ran over and I removed my elbow and ankle guards and handed them to him. I watched the pitcher circle the mound. During the regular season, he would have been yanked by now, but I'm guessing they're letting him in to see how he'll do to get out of this mess. The guy has been a reliever for Boston for three years now and he's either unhittable or all over the place. There's no in between.

Jimmy Chavez stepped up to the plate and I took a decent-sized lead. The first pitch was a fastball right down the middle for a called strike. Chavez hit a long fly ball to left field on the next pitch but it curved foul. Too bad the fielder didn't catch up to it so I could tag up and put us ahead.

But what happened next was just as good.

After looking over to check on me, the pitcher threw a changeup into the dirt and it caught the edge of the plate and went sailing over the catcher's head. I took off down the line as Chavez stepped out of the box and waved me home. The ball went flying over my head as I dove head first and slid, swiping my hand across the plate. Using my forward momentum, I jumped up and bumped Chavez's waiting fist before jogging to the dugout.

The pitcher was taken out after that, replaced with their closer, who got the next two outs with five pitches. After a quick ninth inning, with three up and three down for both teams, we ended up winning the game four to three.

I took my time getting my stuff together in the dugout, knowing Lexi would come down onto the field once the crowd thinned out. I'm hoping Jeremy joins her. This is the last time I'll see Karen for a few days so I'll take any contact I can get. It's kind of pathetic, really. But I have no shame when it comes to her.

My patience paid off. Lexi ran over and hugged Dan and Jeremy followed behind her.

"That was awesome," he said. "The hit and the slide."

"Thanks, Bud." I held up my hand for a high five and he didn't leave me hanging. "Speaking of slides...how's your pop-up slide coming along?"

He'd mentioned last year that he'd gone to a camp and learned how to slide properly. But it's definitely a learning process and he said he was working on it.

"It's getting better." He scrunched his nose the same way Karen does. "Sometimes I still don't make it all the way to standing and end up on my knees."

"You'll get there. It just takes a lot of practice."

Jeremy scratched his head and looked back toward home plate then back at me.

"When did you start switch hitting?"

"Uh, I think I started fooling around with it when I was about your age. Not in games or anything, but in the yard with my grandfather and off the tee. You interested in hitting from the other side of the plate?"

"Yeah, kinda."

The thing is, I know it's not the kind of thing coaches work on. They're more interested in having their players perfect hitting from their natural side instead of splitting their efforts. Switch hitting is more something that's worked on with a parent, or in my case a grandparent.

I'd love to work with Jeremy but I'm not sure how his mother would feel about that. Karen and I are still figuring things out and I don't want to overstep my boundaries. But there is something I can do.

"I have a tee and net you can have to practice on. That's really the best way to get started working on your swing from the other side."

His eyes lit up. "That'd be cool. Thanks Monte."

"Any idea when you'll be at another game?"

"I'm not sure. I have a tournament this weekend and practice every day this week."

I already knew that of course, and besides helping Jeremy out it might be a way for me to see Karen during the week. A win-win as far as I'm concerned.

Chapter Fourteen

DALE

DAN FOLLOWED me onto the balcony as I turned on the grill. We had an afternoon game and didn't feel like going out for dinner so we decided to grab a couple steaks and chill at my place. Jack and Hannah are doing a date night so it's just us two tonight.

We sat at the small table with our beers while the grill heated.

"I hope we get all that shitty play out of our systems down here," Dan said.

We'd played Philadelphia and looked like *The Bad News Bears*. No one that played today could point a finger at anyone else because we all sucked one way or another. I'd gone one for four. Dan had misjudged and ended up missing two pretty routine fly balls. Jack hadn't done any better than me at the plate. And the rest of the team had the same kind of issues. That combined with the fact that none of our pitchers could put the ball over the plate had us losing fifteen to three. Not our finest moment for sure. But like Dan said, hopefully we'll get all our bad play out of the way before the regular season starts.

I got up and tossed the steaks on the grill, then set the timer on my phone so I know when to flip them. Sitting back down, I drained the rest of my beer in one long chug then set the bottle down on the table with a little too much force. The noise it made had me checking to make sure the glass didn't crack.

"Everything okay?"

I dragged my thumb along the remaining condensation on my empty bottle and nodded.

"I haven't seen Karen since last Friday at the game. We've talked on the phone a couple times, but that's it." I shrugged. "I miss her."

"You didn't see her when you brought the tee over for Jeremy?"

"No, she had a meeting with a client that ran over, so she couldn't make it home. By the time she texted me, I was halfway to her house, so I just let myself into the yard and set it up so he'd have it." I looked over at him. "How do you handle not seeing Sabrina all the time?"

"Well, things are different for us now because we're married. And they were different when we were in the stage you're at because I was out with my leg injury and Sabrina was staying at the house with me for therapy. So we saw each other all the time. You're in a totally different situation because you're working around your schedule, hers, and Jeremy's. Add the fact that Jeremy doesn't know you're dating and you have a tiny window to see each other in person and do the getting-to-know-you thing."

The timer dinged and I got up to flip the steaks. After

closing the lid, I flopped back into my chair and set the timer again.

"You know, this really sucks. All my other relationships were much easier." Dan looked at me with raised brows. "What?"

"Monte, you didn't really have any other relationships. Yes, there were women you spent time with, but they weren't real relationships and you know that."

He's not wrong and I *do* know that but it's still not an easy thing to hear.

"Will you talk to her later?"

"I told her to call me when she gets home from Jeremy's game, or to at least text."

"The only thing I can recommend is to be honest with her. You know how things were with Sabrina and me when I basically bribed her then boss to get her to rehabilitate my knee. She hated me for what I did to her back in college. But I got her at the house and was determined to convince her to give me a second chance. She barely wanted to speak to me so it wasn't easy. Anytime I had an opening I let her know what I was feeling and tried to show her that I changed. It wasn't easy putting it all out there but I knew I had to do it because I wouldn't get another chance. And I think that's what you have to do, too. I know you've been trying but all I can say is you have to try harder. Literally spell things out for her if you're that sure she's the person for you."

The timer went off again and I stood to shut off the grill. Thankfully I'd had the good sense to set it or our steaks would have turned to shoe leather because I wasn't paying attention. I placed one steak on each of the plates I'd brought out earlier and we went inside.

Sitting at the kitchen table, Dan and I filled the rest of

our plates with the salad he brought and dug in. I thought about what he said and realized he was right. Yes, Karen and I have only been on two official dates, but I know I want to move this thing along. I've been trying not to freak her out by coming on too strong but maybe I need to share more of what I'm thinking.

"I can practically see your thoughts," he said around a laugh. "You're gonna have to be more subtle than what I see you contemplating. It's definitely a balance. Let her know how you're feeling and what you want without being a total caveman."

"You know something, this really sucks."

"I know, but trust me, it's worth it."

Yeah, as long as I end up getting the girl like Dan, Jack, and Cal did.

KAREN

I GLANCED AT THE CLOCK. Only a half hour to go. Of course, then I have to run home to change and pick up Jeremy to take him to his games. This weekend's tournament is at a complex forty-five minutes away so there's not much time to spare. Hopefully I don't hit traffic along the way or we'll be late.

Settling onto a bar stool at the kitchen island, I looked over the sign-in sheet, happy with the results of this open house so far. It had a lot of traffic initially, with a few of the attendees interested in coming back next week to look at the house again.

With no one here now, I let my thoughts wander to my

conversation with Dale last night. I texted him after I got home and he asked if we could FaceTime. He'd been in a strange mood and after we talked for a few minutes, I found out why. He's interested in moving things forward with our relationship and even mentioned telling Jeremy we're dating.

I'm not sure how I feel about that at this point. I mean, we've only been on two dates. Before I could ponder the situation any more, a couple entered with two children around Jeremy's age and I turned my attention to them.

After introducing myself and giving them my usual spiel, I urged them to check out the house and let me know if they had any questions. I'm hoping they don't take too long exploring because I want to be out of here on time.

Thankfully it didn't take them too long to look around and come back into the kitchen.

The woman, Cara, told me she loved the house and asked when they could come back and bring her father, who is a carpenter, to check it out. Her husband, Mark, said he was going to take the kids out back to explore the yard.

I had her add her name and contact information to the sign-in sheet then handed her my card. "My information is on there. I'll talk to the owners to find out their schedule and let you know what time slots are available this week."

"I know I shouldn't sound too eager, but we love this house," she said. "It's the first one we've looked at that works for all of us and is in move-in condition."

"I'm not using a typical sales tactic when I say that there were a few other people who came through today that are interested in the house. But we'll get you back so your father can check things out as soon as possible so you can make an offer if he gives it his approval."

Mark and the kids came back into the house and the girl, Sophia, ran over to Cara.

"Mom, Mark said there's probably room for a pool!"

I'd wrongly assumed the children were both Mark's but it turns out he and Cara had just gotten married the previous year. My surprise must have shown on my face because she went on to explain that they both had lost their spouses...her to a brain aneurysm and him to breast cancer. The two met at a grief support group.

"I was afraid to get involved again after losing my late husband but I'm so glad I took the chance." Cara looked at the clock. "I'm sorry we came last minute then talked your ear off about our newly-blended family."

I realized it was eleven o'clock and I really need to get moving within the next five minutes if I want to wear comfy clothes to the game.

"No problem." I packed the leftover fliers and sign-in sheet into my computer bag and slung it over my shoulder. "I'll check with the owners and get back to you by tomorrow with a time."

Thankfully I can do that kind of stuff while watching Jeremy play. Part of my success as a realtor is that I get back to people as quickly as possible. After walking them to the door, I did a quick check of the house to make sure all the lights were off before heading out myself.

Jeremy was sitting on the couch watching TV in his uniform when I got home.

"I'm going to change and I'll be right out," I said as I headed to my bedroom and quickly changed into a pair of jeans, a T-shirt, and sneakers. I grabbed a sweatshirt and was walking back to the living room in record time. Jeremy had his head in the refrigerator when I returned and he emerged holding a brown bag and a bottle of water.

"I packed you a sandwich, chips, and some grapes," he said.

"Oh honey, thank you." I took the bag from him and kissed his forehead. "I appreciate that."

He followed me out to the car and tossed his bag in the back before settling into the passenger seat.

"Are you pitching today?" I asked as we hit the road. I like to mentally prepare myself.

"No, maybe tomorrow," he said. "How did your open house go?"

"It went well. There are a few people interested in coming to look at it again."

"Cool."

I thought about Cara and Mark and their newly-blended family. And also what she said about being afraid. It was in the back of my mind as I drove the rest of the way to the complex while Jeremy and I talked, jumping from topic to topic.

"Do you think we can go to the Waves' game Wednesday night? I don't have practice or anything." Before I could answer he added, "I know we don't usually go out when I have a day off from activities, but I took some video of me hitting lefty off the tee and I want to show it to Monte and see if he has any pointers."

I'm still amazed Dale came over even after I got held up and couldn't meet him to set up the net and tee in the backyard. Jeremy has been out there practicing with it every day, trying to perfect his swing.

But as I thought back to our conversation last night, it kind of makes sense. He basically told me that he wants to move forward with this relationship and that would definitely include Jeremy.

"I think we can make an exception and go to the game," I said.

"Thanks Mom. I can't wait to hear what Monte says about the video."

I made a mental note to text Chloe and Hope as soon as I get to the field to set up an emergency FaceTime session with them for later tonight. My thoughts about what Dale said last night are so jumbled. Hopefully my friends can help me sort them all out before I see him again.

Chapter Fifteen

DALE

I TOWEL DRIED my hair then pulled on a T-shirt. Dan and Jack did the same at their lockers next to me. Thankfully our weekend games have gone better than the one on Friday. It definitely helps the mood in the locker room.

My phone buzzed on the shelf and I grabbed it to check the text message.

> Karen: I was hoping to talk to you about a couple things. Are you available for lunch tomorrow?

"What's wrong?" Jack asked.

I turned the phone to face him and Dan. They both read the text and looked up at me with raised brows.

"We haven't spoken since Friday night when I basically spilled my guts to her over FaceTime. I'm thinking this isn't good."

"You don't know that," Dan said.

"Yeah, don't jump to any conclusions."

I took in a breath and let it out slowly.

"Well, whatever it is, I can't avoid it."

> Dale: Sure. What time?

> Karen: Twelve-thirty? I'll meet you at Rudy's Place?

> Dale: Sounds good. I'll see you then.

> Karen: See you.

No emojis, no xoxo, no "looking forward to it." I'm not sure what to expect.

"I'm gonna pass on dinner. I don't think I'll be very good company tonight."

Dan and Jack just looked at me but didn't say anything as we walked out of the locker room. Hannah stood in the hallway talking on the phone. She smiled at Jack and wrapped up her call as we joined her. He kissed her then wrapped his arm around her shoulders, pulling her close and nudging his chin in my direction.

"Show Hannah and get her take on it," he said.

I pulled up the texts and handed Hannah my phone.

"This is it?" she asked.

"That's it until lunch tomorrow."

She looked up at me. "Don't get all freaked out. This isn't necessarily a bad thing." I raised my brow. "It's not. You said you missed seeing her this week. She probably feels the same."

I reached over and pointed to the *I was hoping to talk to you about a couple things* line.

"Again, it could be anything," she said.

Taking my phone from her, I stuck it in my back pocket as we started walking toward the exit.

"Where are we going?" Hannah asked, looking at each of us in turn.

"I'm just gonna grab a pizza and go veg on the couch," I said. "I'm tired."

Hannah stared at me, "Dale Montgomery, do not go home and pout."

"I promise I won't pout," I said around a chuckle. She didn't look convinced. "Seriously, it's fine. I really just want to go relax, unwind, and watch some TV."

And think about how I'm going to keep Karen Walsh in my life beyond tomorrow.

KAREN

I WALKED into Rudy's with a sense of déjà vu. Last time I was here, I was attending Dale's birthday dinner and felt just as nervous. I really didn't want to do this over the phone or FaceTime. It's definitely a conversation that needs to happen in person.

As I approached the hostess, I spotted Dale at a table over by the window. He had his

hands clasped behind his head, his eyes focused on the ceiling and looked more stressed than I've ever seen him. He must have spotted me out of the corner of his eye because he shifted his gaze to me then stood as I got closer to him. He awkwardly kissed my cheek then held my chair and pushed it in as I sat.

"Thank you."

The waitress came over before he could respond and

took our drink orders. I'd love nothing more than a few shots of tequila to get through this conversation but ordered lemonade like a responsible adult.

I didn't want to get into anything too heavy before the waitress came back with our drinks and to take our orders, so I opted for small talk.

"Great game yesterday."

His smile didn't reach his eyes. "Yeah, thankfully Friday's game was a one off and we got it together again."

"Thank you again for the tee and net. Jeremy has used it every day since you set it up."

The waitress brought our drinks and asked if we're ready to order. I hadn't even looked at the menu, but wanted to get our orders out of the way so she didn't have to come back immediately. I really want to get this conversation at least started before I lose my nerve.

I ordered a tuna poke bowl and Dale got a crabby burger.

"What exactly is a crabby burger?" I asked once she left.

"A burger with crab meat piled on top. It's also served with crab fries."

"Sounds yummy." His eyes didn't leave my face as I took a long drink of lemonade and swallowed. I set my glass aside, placed my hands in my lap, and twisted my fingers together. "I appreciate you meeting me for lunch. Jeremy has practice every day this week except for Wednesday and after our conversation Friday night, I wanted to speak to you in person."

He drank half of his sweet tea in one long gulp, looking like he wished it was whiskey instead.

"I'm sorry if I came on too strong Friday." He dragged his fingers through his hair, leaving it looking sexy and rumpled. "Spring training will be over before you know it and I wanted to be honest with you about how I'm feeling, what I'm hoping for here."

"And I do appreciate your honesty. Really. It just gave me a lot to think about." He nodded, but stayed silent. "Dale I—" I gestured helplessly.

I've thought about this conversation all day yesterday and can't think of a single word to say right now. It really shouldn't be this difficult. I reached for my lemonade and took another sip.

"Dale, I think you were right. We can't fully explore this attraction between us if we only see each other alone once every couple weeks." He blinked slowly and his hands gripped the edges of the table until his knuckles turned white. "And unless Jeremy knows about us, we can't jump in one hundred percent and give it a fair shot."

"So what are you saying?"

"I'm saying that I'd like to tell Jeremy we're dating and really see where this can go. If that's still what you want."

Dale stayed still for a few seconds just looking at me before a smile spread across his face.

"Yeah?"

"Yeah."

He stood and took the two steps that put him in front of me then placed his hands on either side of my face, bent down, and kissed me. Resting his forehead against mine, he breathed out a sigh and said, "I thought you wanted to meet me to end things."

"Why did you think that?"

He pulled back to look me in the eye.

"Because we've only had two dates and I dumped a shit-ton of crap on you during our conversation Friday night. I was worried I'd scared you away."

I shook my head then shrugged. "I mean, this whole

thing scares me but ignoring it or pushing you away won't make it go away."

The waitress approached with our meals and Dale stood as she placed them on the table. After assuring her we didn't need anything else, she left, and he took his seat looking much more relaxed than he had since I got here.

"So when did you want to tell Jeremy?"

"I thought I'd tell him tonight or tomorrow. He doesn't have practice Wednesday and already asked if we could go to your game. Like I said, he's been working on the tee every night and apparently took some videos he wants to show you to see if you have any pointers."

"Would you want to go for pizza or something after the game? It should be over by eight so if we keep it simple, you guys could be home by ten."

"Sure, that sounds good."

He picked up his burger and took a big bite. Now that we've faced the elephant in the room, I feel more relaxed and it seems like he does too. And that's obviously kicked our appetites into full gear and we both dug into our lunch with gusto.

"What do you think he's gonna say?" he asked, then bit into a fry.

"I'm not sure. I discussed this with Chloe and Hope and asked how they think he'll react and they seem to think he'll be thrilled. He knows and likes you so I'm leaning in that direction too but there's still the unknown factor of how he'll feel about me being with anyone who isn't his father. So I'm hoping for the best and preparing for the worst."

"Do you want me to be there when you tell him?"

"No, I don't think so, but I appreciate you offering. I think I'd rather tell him without you there so I can get his honest reaction. I don't want him holding his true feelings in just because you're there. I mean, I'm not sure that he would, but I don't want it to even be a possibility."

"I understand." He finished the last bite of his burger and wiped his hands on his napkin. "But will you do me a favor?"

"Sure."

"Please tell me how he reacts. Don't sugar coat it."

I nodded. "I can do that."

Chapter Sixteen

DALE

"DON'T EVEN START," I said to Jack as he caught me looking up at the stands as we stretched.

He just laughed.

"You busted my ass about Hannah so you have to let me have some fun."

Dan just ran to get a drink but I'm sure he'll join in the fun once he gets over here.

"So you're all going for pizza after the game?" Jack asked.

"Yep. She said he wasn't upset about us dating, so that's a positive thing. I don't imagine I'd have a chance if he was against it."

Dan walked over and joined in the conversation.

"Yeah, as much as I had my sights set on getting Sabrina back, if Lexi didn't like her, it never would have worked out." He folded over to touch his toes. "Thankfully they loved each other from day one. And you're lucky with that, too." He rolled back up. "Jeremy already knows and likes you."

"Yeah he likes me as me, not as his mother's boyfriend."

"It'll be fine, I'm sure," Jack said. "Jeremy's a great kid."

"Yeah, he is."

For the past couple years I've thought about what it would be like to get involved with Karen. I've never dated anyone with children, or if I did, I wasn't involved enough to know. I know they're a package deal and I think I understand what that entails.

I finished with my stretches and headed back to the dugout. Just before I walked down the steps, I spotted Jeremy and Karen settling into their seats. I'm not reading too much into the fact that he's not coming down by the wall because they're arriving later than usual.

I waved and they both waved back so that's a good sign. Karen and I FaceTimed after their conversation Monday night and she said Jeremy seemed okay about us dating, but I'm still a little nervous. Like I said to Jack, Jeremy knowing and liking me as a ballplayer is totally different than him liking me as the guy who's dating his mother. But all I can do is take her word for it and be as good to the two of them as possible and hope for the best.

KAREN

I TOLD Dale we'd meet him at Antonio's after the game. Since he had to shower and change, we beat him to the restaurant and ordered a pitcher of sweet tea and a large pie, half plain, half pepperoni and an order of boneless chicken wings.

"Practice is at the high school field tomorrow, right?"

Jeremy nodded. "At six o'clock."

"Okay, we can make that work. But I'm going to need you to come to another showing at that same house we were at today. It's closer to the field than home."

Coming to the office or showings and open houses with me is old hat for him. He's been doing it since he was little, even before Jason died. Thankfully he was always well-behaved, even as a toddler, so I felt comfortable taking him anywhere. I don't bring him too often now that I let him stay home by himself for short periods of time. Today he came with me so I didn't have to backtrack to get him at home before heading to the stadium. Tomorrow is the same. I'll probably have plenty of time to get him to practice after the showing but I don't want to take the chance the couple will linger and I'll be running late.

"Monte is here."

Jeremy must have seen his truck pull up because as I looked toward the door, Dale was standing just outside. I watched as he opened the door and stepped aside so an older woman could enter ahead of him.

He looked around and smiled when he saw us. More than one woman glanced in his direction as he walked across the restaurant to our table. That could be either because they recognize him or just because he's sexy as hell. Since no one approached him or stopped him to talk, I'm assuming it's the latter.

"I hope I didn't keep you waiting too long," he said as he pulled out a chair and sat between Jeremy and me.

"No, we haven't been here too long," I said. "But we

did order so we don't have to wait to eat. Despite the fact that he ate at the stadium, this guy is starving," I said hitching my thumb in Jeremy's direction. "And you probably are too."

I'd just finished that sentence when the waiter came out carrying our pizza and wing bites.

"Oh wow." His eyes rounded. "Monte." He set the food on the table then held out his hand. "It's a pleasure, sir."

Dale shook his hand and read the waiter's name tag.

"Nice to meet you, Darren."

Then he introduced Jeremy and me, but of course, Darren could care less about us. Dale talked baseball with the young waiter for a few minutes before politely ending the conversation.

"This looks great," he said.

Darren took the hint and told us to let him know if we needed anything then left. He practically ran into the kitchen, I'm assuming to alert the entire staff that *Dale Montgomery* is in the house. Thankfully it's not too crowded, so if people do start coming over to the table, it shouldn't be too bad.

"Sorry about that," Dale said.

"Goes with the territory," I said.

He nodded and looked at the pizza. "This looks awesome. And pepperoni is my favorite."

"Mine too," Jeremy said as he helped himself to a slice. "And here they put a lot of pepperoni on, not like at Anthony's. They only give you a couple pieces per slice."

"A pizza connoisseur." Dale smiled at Jeremy. "Now I know who to call when I want a good pizza."

Jeremy smiled at that, but didn't stop eating long enough to comment. He's always been a good eater, but the past couple years, that's been taken to a whole different level. I've heard teenage boys have big appetites and now I'm seeing it firsthand.

The conversation flowed while we put a decent-sized dent in the food. Jeremy asked Dale some questions about today's game. I was happy to see their banter was as relaxed as usual. Jeremy had been surprised when I told him about Dale and me but he didn't seem upset.

I'm going to take things at face value and believe him when he says he's okay with it. I'm sure it will be an adjustment for all of us but we'll deal with things as they come up.

"So your mom said you have some videos for me to look at," Dale said as he picked up a napkin and wiped his hands.

Jeremy shoved a wing bite into his mouth and nodded then picked up his phone. His fingers swiped at the screen as he chewed then swallowed.

"This is the first day I used the tee." He leaned toward Dale and held the phone so they both could see. "I spent a lot of time putting the tee back together at first because I kept hitting it instead of the ball. But I took this video on the last few swings." They stared at the phone for a few seconds. "Then if you just swipe, the other videos will play."

He handed the phone to Dale and they leaned even closer together. Dale made a few comments as they watched. I know what they're looking at because Jeremy showed me the videos every day after he recorded them. I'm no expert, but it seems like his left-side swing is getting better.

Dale swiped the screen a few times, I'm assuming to watch certain videos a second or even third time.

"Look at this," he said as he pointed at the screen. "From this video to this one, you started dropping your elbow. That's why you're popping it up more than hitting it straight ahead."

Jeremy asked him to replay the videos and scratched his head as he watched.

"I didn't even notice that."

"It's pretty subtle but it's enough that you're not getting a flat swing," Dale said. "If just being conscious of it isn't enough to help fix it, raise the tee as high as it will go. That'll force you to keep your elbow up. Once you get the feel, lower it in small increments."

"Thanks Monte. I'll work on that this week."

"You're welcome," Dale said then took a long drink of sweet tea. "If we ever have the same day off, maybe I can throw to you so you can try to hit off live pitching." He glanced at me. "If it's okay with your mom."

"That'd be awesome!" Jeremy turned pleading eyes my way. "Wouldn't it, Mom?"

"Sure."

Of course, I know how difficult it is to blend our schedules so hopefully he won't be too disappointed if it doesn't happen anytime soon.

"I'm off Saturday," Dale said. "Do you have any games that day?"

Dale knows Jeremy has games Saturday and had already planned on coming, but I like how he's asking my son about his schedule instead of me.

"Yeah, my first game is at eleven."

"Would you mind if I came to watch you play?"

Jeremy's eyes widened. "Seriously?" Dale nodded. "Dude, that'd be so cool. Mom?"

"It's fine with me."

"What time do you have to be at the field?"

"Ten, but it takes a while to get there." Jeremy looked at me.

"It's about an hour away," I said.

"How about if I pick you up at eight and we get some breakfast before we hit the road?"

Jeremy liked that idea. We...or rather they...were discussing potential breakfast spots when our waiter, Darren, approached. He'd checked on us once while we ate and refilled our pitcher, but other than that kept his distance, which I appreciated.

He left the check and took the two leftover slices and handful of chicken wings to wrap for us to take home. Dale insisted on paying the bill and pulled out a few bills that would not only cover the total, but would also give Darren a generous tip.

Jeremy took the take-out container when Darren brought it out and the three of us walked out of the restaurant together. He commented on how *awesome* Dale's truck is then said goodbye to "Monte" before continuing to my car, asking me to unlock it. I heard the door open and close then looked up at Dale and chuckled.

"Well, I'm no expert, but I think that went well," he said.

"I have to agree."

He stepped closer and cupped my jaw with his hand. His denim eyes turned serious as they stared into mine.

"You're going to have to guide me here. I want to get to know both of you but don't want to make you uncomfortable or overstep my bounds in any way. So please tell me if I'm doing either."

His thumb stroking my cheek was having a hypnotic effect so I just nodded my response.

Closing the space between us, he leaned down and gave me a quick kiss before pulling back.

"Call or text to let me know you got home safely please."

I promised that I would and practically floated over to my car excited about the fact that we get to see each other in three short days.

Chapter Seventeen

DALE

I JUST GOT out of the shower when I heard my front door
open and close. Wrapping a towel around my waist, I
walked out of the bedroom. Jack and I just finished a run
on the beach a little while ago and he went to his place
while I got cleaned up to grab some brownies Hannah had
packed for me to bring to Jeremy's game.

"Tell Hannah I said thank you again."

He nodded and set the container on the kitchen table.

I went back into my room to get dressed but left the
door open.

"I told you Jeremy would be okay with you and Karen
dating," he said loudly enough for me to hear him.

I slipped into a pair of boxer briefs then pulled khakis
from the next drawer and put them on.

"He really is a great kid." I grabbed a plain black T-
shirt out of another drawer and walked back out into the
living room. Jeremy told me his team colors are black and

light blue so it should help me blend in with the other parents. "But you had no way of knowing that. You just got lucky. *We* got lucky." Pulling the shirt over my head, I added, "For now anyway. Hopefully it stays that way."

Jack shrugged. "As long as you're good to them, I don't see why it wouldn't."

"I guess."

"So what's the plan today?"

"Karen said the fans are usually more spread out at the field we're going to so I'm hoping no one recognizes me." He looked at me with raised brows. "I know, Karen seems to think I'm dreaming but I still have high hopes. Or at least if they do recognize me, I hope they respect the fact that I'm there to enjoy the game and not hang out with them and talk baseball strategy." I sat on the couch and put on a pair of deck shoes. "Since none of you guys will be there and I'm not in Waves gear, I think it'll be easier to blend in. I'm trying to keep things as normal as possible."

"Like you're normal," he snorted.

I stood and punched him on the arm.

"I know Jeremy would love for you to come see one of his games sometime. After all, you're his favorite player."

"And don't you forget it," he said around a cocky smile. "I'd love to go see him play sometime but today is for you guys."

Up until he noticed Hannah as something more than a kickass PR person, Jack exuded an I-don't-give-a-fuck attitude, but he's always been deeper than that. Case in point, how he met Jeremy at that CADD event and befriended him. Which I thank every deity for because it brought Karen into my life. Even if it did take two years to get her firmly in place...or at least semi-firmly.

I grabbed my keys and the container of brownies and

followed Jack out the door. He headed back to his condo and I got in the elevator to head down to the garage.

Jeremy came running out of the house with his bag slung over his shoulder and a cooler in his hand as soon as I pulled into the driveway.

"Hey bud," I said as I got out and opened the back door for him.

He slid inside and dropped his bags onto the seat beside him.

"Mom will be right out," he said as he clicked his seatbelt into place.

He'd just said that when Karen stepped out onto the porch carrying her purse, a cooler, and two chairs. Two items were slung over each shoulder and she struggled to get out of the way of the door so she could close it behind her.

I jogged over to her side.

"Let me help you with that."

Wrapping my hand around the strap of the chairs, I pulled them off her arm, taking the opportunity to steal a kiss.

"Thank you."

I walked down the steps, giving her room to close the door and screen door.

"For taking the chairs off your hands or the kiss?"

"Both." Karen smiled up at me as we walked the short distance to the truck.

I opened the passenger door and kissed her again before she stepped up and settled into the seat. After closing the door behind her, I walked around the back of the truck, opened the tailgate, and secured the chairs and cooler before slamming it shut.

"Ready?" I asked as I got behind the wheel then looked back to Jeremy. "Have everything you need?"

"Yep."

"Then let's go eat. I'm starving."

"Me too," Jeremy said.

I backed out of the driveway and turned left onto the street. We'd decided to stop at a diner a few blocks from Karen's house so Jeremy isn't eating a big breakfast and playing immediately.

"This truck is awesome, Monte."

"Thanks."

"Do you have any other cars?" he asked.

"I have a Mercedes, but I don't drive it that often."

Not anymore anyway. That was my see-and-be-seen-in car and the women I spent time with in the past would have expected me to pick them up in it rather than a truck, no matter how fancy.

"I also have an old pick-up truck and a 1955 Ford Thunderbird convertible that were my grandfather's. Penny thinks at least one of them should be hers but I told her that he'd already given them to me before she was born." I smiled at him through the rearview mirror. "That drives her crazy."

"You're awful," Karen said around a chuckle.

"Where do you keep them?" Jeremy asked.

"The Mercedes is at my house in South Carolina and the other two are at the ranch in Aspen."

That led to questions about my houses. Are they big? Who takes care of them when I'm not there? Which one do I like best?

I just pulled into the parking lot of the diner when he asked that last one. After turning off the truck, I unbuckled my seatbelt and shifted to face them.

"It used to be my ranch but now my favorite is my condo in Clearwater because it's closer to the two of you."

KAREN

"YOU LOOK as excited here as Jeremy does at your games."

Dale shifted toward me and lifted the brim of his hat so I could see his dark blue eyes.

"That's because this, watching Jeremy, is amazing. Thank you for letting me come today. I'm having a great time." He looked dramatically from side to side before giving me a quick kiss. "Of course, that probably has just as much to do with my present company as it does the game."

"Well, I'm enjoying myself more than I usually do."

We're in the sixth inning of Jeremy's first game and so far, so good. Dale has drawn some attention, but I'm not sure if that's because he's sitting with me or he's been recognized. Either way, no one has approached us as we sit just outside the fence along the third base line.

I looked up at Jeremy's team logo on the hat Dale is wearing.

"It's strange to see you in a hat with a logo other than the Waves."

"It helps me blend in though, right? I'm just glad Jeremy thought to bring it for me to borrow."

I'm not sure Dale could ever truly blend in anywhere. He's just too charismatic and sexy so he'll always stand out. But Jeremy stepped up to bat before I could comment on that. Which is probably just as well.

Dale sat forward in his seat as he watched Jeremy step into the batter's box. He practically vibrated as the pitcher went into his windup. That pitch was called a ball and he relaxed a few seconds until the next one was thrown. And so it went, him tensing up every time Jeremy stepped into the box and relaxing between pitches.

Jeremy had a full count on him and fouled off two pitches to stay alive. Dale was literally sitting on the edge of his seat when Jeremy swung and hit a line drive into left-center field. He jumped to his feet and yelled as we watched Jeremy round first base and slide in safe at second for a double.

Dale let out an ear-piercing whistle and yelled, "Way to go, Jeremy!" before settling back into his seat.

His honest reaction both amused me and tugged at my heart. It's obvious when they spend time together that Dale really cares for Jeremy and he's not just nice to him to score points with me. Then again, they sort of had a relationship before the two of us did.

"That was an awesome hit," he said.

"I probably should have warned you that Jeremy is the king of the full count. On average, it happens two out of three at bats."

Which was the case today.

"He's really good," Dale said. "He has a good swing, he's fast, and he always knows what he's supposed to be doing. The shortstop is supposed to lead the infield and he definitely does that."

"When his junior high coach suggested he try out for this team I was hesitant. Besides the cost, it's a huge time commitment and our schedules were already pretty full. But he was so excited about the opportunity, I couldn't tell him no. Then he not only made the team, but scored a starting position and the coach has him pitching. He really loves it and his game has really improved in the past year."

Jeremy stole third base on a wild pitch, but the batter hit a fly ball to center field for the third out. The next inning and a half went pretty quickly, with three up and three down for both teams.

Dale and I stood and packed our chairs then headed to the truck. After a quick team meeting with the coach, Jeremy joined us. Normally the team hangs out for short breaks between games, but since we're moving to a whole other location, they've all scattered.

We'd researched local restaurants using our cell phones during the game and decided on a place called La Taberna. It has great reviews as a local favorite and Jeremy loves Mexican food.

It was just a short drive from the field so we were seated with drinks in front of us a few minutes later. Jeremy had scarfed down two brownies on the way and was now digging into the salsa and chips the waitress put in the middle of the table.

He and Dale were discussing the game, and Jeremy glowed as my...*boyfriend?*...gushed about what an amazing job he did today. They dissected every play and hit. Then Dale offered some pointers, but he did it in such a positive way, and Jeremy lapped up every word.

I couldn't help but feel a little melancholy at the fact that Jason should be having this conversation with Jeremy not Dale, but shook it off. Jason is gone. Wishing won't bring him back. I know, I tried. And I also know that not moving forward won't bring him back either.

I'm still not sure how this thing between Dale and me is going to work, especially once the season starts, but I'm trying to enjoy the moment and not obsess about it. For now, I just have to appreciate how wonderful he treats me and how great he is to Jeremy.

The waitress brought our entrees and refilled our drinks and we all dug in.

"Did Aunt Chloe tell you she's coming home Thursday?" Jeremy asked after he'd nearly cleared his plate.

"She texted me earlier."

"Did she tell you she wants me to sleep over Saturday after my game?"

"She did. I told her it was up to you."

"I definitely want to."

"Sounds like a plan then."

Chloe had texted me during the game and thankfully Dale's full attention had been on the game because she'd included a very inappropriate gif. She's more anxious for me to have a full night alone with Dale than I am. And that's saying a lot. After five years of celibacy, since my first kiss from the sexy first baseman, sex is all I can think about.

"What time is your tournament Saturday?" Dale asked Jeremy.

"It's not a tournament this weekend, just games. I'm playing at eleven Saturday then three on Sunday."

"I have a game at noon, but then John Kasprzyk is having some people over after that for a barbecue. I was going to ask if you'd like to come with me. And now that Chloe is in town, maybe she'd like to join us."

Jeremy looked at me with pleading eyes. He'll take any opportunity to hang out with his idols. And I'm sure Chloe would be up for it.

"We'll talk to Aunt Chloe and see what she thinks. Then we can figure out the plan for the night."

Dale glanced at me out of the corner of his eye as he finished the last of his water in one long gulp. If I'd had any doubt that he's thinking the same thing as I am, that cleared it up. With Jeremy staying at Chloe's, I'll have the entire night free.

Chapter Eighteen

KAREN

"YOU KNOW, I've always thought Jeremy was good, but he looks totally amazing today," Chloe said.

"He definitely has more confidence since getting a thumb's up from Dale. Plus he got some pointers from Dale so I'm sure that's helped."

"Speaking of Dale, have you discussed tonight in any specific detail?" She wagged her eyebrows.

"Not like you're suggesting." I laughed. "Do *you* discuss details beforehand?"

"No, but I'm not you."

"That's a fair point."

Jeremy had a ball hit to him and he made the play for the third out. Then he was up first to bat the next inning so we gave the game our full attention.

I cringed as he got hit by a pitch just above his elbow. Even though it must hurt like hell, he just ran to first base and took his lead. The pitcher had been doing well up until now but after hitting Jeremy, he walked the next batter then gave up a hit to the outfield that allowed Jeremy to score.

The game stopped as the coach changed pitchers and with Jeremy back in the dugout, Chloe picked up the conversation right where we'd left it.

"So did you? Discuss things?"

"Sort of. It's kind of floating out there that we're going to spend the night together, but we haven't dissected things. That would be unromantic, not to mention embarrassing."

"So we're going to that party, Jeremy and I will hang out for a little bit, then we'll leave you two alone. What are you doing then?"

"The plan is for us to go back to his place when we leave the party."

"Are you nervous?"

"Not right now but if I think about it too much I will be." I thought about that for a few minutes then added, "I mean, once we're together I'll be fine, and once things get started, I'll be really fine. But for the past few days I've studiously avoided thinking about it because I didn't want to psych myself out."

She leaned down and reached into her purse then sat back and handed me a box.

"Chloe! Seriously?"

I shoved the box into my purse when her answering laugh drew the attention of some of the parents.

"They're Waves blue. When I saw them, I couldn't resist."

"Why would anyone want to use a colored condom?"

She shrugged. "Just to change things up."

"But they look ridiculous enough wearing a condom, never mind a colored one."

"Well at least you have some on you in case he doesn't."

Jeremy's team took the field again after the longest at-bat ever. They'd scored five runs, putting them ahead seven to two. I turned my full attention to the game, more to take my focus off blue condoms and the fact that I'll probably be breaking my sex fast tonight.

DALE

"I'LL SEE you tomorrow at the game," Karen said to Jeremy as he got into the passenger seat of Chloe's car. "Text if you need me to bring anything for you."

"I will," he said. "See you tomorrow, Monte."

"I'm looking forward to it." I leaned down to look at Chloe. "See you tomorrow."

"Yep," she said with a big smile.

We stood in Kasprzyk's driveway and watched them drive away.

I swear Chloe Walsh is my own personal angel. She not only asked Jeremy to stay with her tonight, she also drove her own car today leaving Karen with me when they left. As much as I love spending time with Jeremy, I'm looking forward to having his mother all to myself tonight.

"They seemed to have a good time."

"I think they did. I know I am. Thanks for bringing us along."

I pulled her to my side and kissed the top of her head.

"Thanks for coming."

Natalie Kasprzyk and Hannah were consolidating what

food was left over on the platters as we walked through the gate to the backyard.

"I'm gonna help them clean up," she said then stood on tiptoe to give me a quick kiss. Before I got over the shock that it's the first time she initiated a kiss, she was walking across the patio. I would have offered to help too, but I figured I'd give Karen time alone with the women.

Jack, Dan, and Kasprzyk were sprawled on lounge chairs across the patio and I walked over to join them. After spending part of the day at the stadium and the rest of it either in the pool or running around on the beach, the kids were all tired and went inside to watch a movie. Natalie's parents had also gone in to relax. And even though it's not even ten o'clock, everyone else had left.

"Remember when these parties used to go until dawn?" I asked as I sat on the edge of a lawn chair. I don't plan on getting too comfortable. As soon as Karen is done, I want to get out of here.

"We're older and wiser now," Dan said.

"Older anyway," Kasprzyk said.

"Thanks for including Karen and her family today," I said to Kasprzyk.

"The more, the merrier," he said.

"What time will you guys be getting to the game tomorrow?" Jack asked.

"I'm not sure. I'll text and let you know."

He and Hannah are coming to Jeremy's game. I've no doubt with the two of us there, we'll be recognized. But at least Hannah and Chloe will be there to keep Karen company while we do our thing.

"Wait until you see him play. He's really good," I said to Jack.

"You sound like a proud papa."

I shrugged. "He's a great kid and I'm enjoying getting to know him and his mother."

"Did Hannah write that quote for you? It sounded like something right from the PR department," Jack said.

"She's taught me well. I thought that one up all by myself."

They laughed at that then Dan said, "But seriously, things must be going well. Karen seems much more relaxed. She doesn't have that deer-in-the-headlights look anymore."

"Things are good."

Before anyone could comment on that, I spotted the ladies making their way toward us. Karen laughed at something Natalie said and it warmed my heart to see her so comfortable with my friends.

I stood as they got closer.

"Do you want to hit the road or hang out a little while longer?" I asked.

"Um, we can go," she said to me then turned toward Natalie and John. "I had a lot of fun and the food was amazing. Thank you again for inviting Chloe, Jeremy, and me."

"You're welcome," Natalie said. "Hopefully I'll see you again soon."

After everyone said their goodbyes, I led Karen toward my truck and held her hand as she stepped inside and settled into the passenger seat. I don't want to assume anything so as I got behind the wheel, I asked her if she still wanted to go back to my condo.

When she looked me in the eye and said, "Yes please" I had to fight the urge to push the gas pedal to the floor and break every speed limit going home.

Chapter Nineteen

DALE

I TURNED into the entrance of the garage and keyed in my code. The gate seemed to take forever to open and when it finally did, I stepped on the gas too hard and spun the tires before pulling inside.

It's been a long time since I've been even slightly nervous about the prospect of having sex, but I realized during the drive that's exactly what I'm feeling. And if I'm nervous, I figure Karen must be freaking out.

Only as I park the truck, she seems calm.

I held her hand as we walked toward the elevator and didn't let it go as we stepped inside. As the doors closed, the same electricity that zinged between us the first time we were in here together darted and dashed between us now. Only this time, I don't have to keep my distance. Her sweet vanilla scent commanded my senses as I pulled her to me and covered her mouth with mine.

Whenever I've kissed her before, I've slowly pressed our

mouths together, taking time to enjoy the softness of her lips. But not this time.

I thrust my tongue inside, and my knees nearly buckled. Leaning back against the side of the elevator, I held her close, unwilling to let her mouth go for one split second. She let out a little moan and I curled my hand around the back of her head, wrapping my fingers into her long hair to keep her close. Her tongue kept pace with mine, exploring and feeling, kissing me back and echoing my intensity.

The elevator stopped, jerking to a halt as the loud ding sounded, pulling me back to my senses. I ended the kiss and stared into her eyes feeling like I've taken a fastball to the heart.

Before the door could close, I shoved my arm out holding it open so she could exit the elevator. I followed her down the hall to my condo and punched in the code to unlock the door.

I took a deep breath as we stepped over the threshold and slowly let it out as I closed the door behind me. As surprised as I am about my reaction to her, to this, I'm happy I'm feeling something more. Because this thing between Karen and me is definitely more than anything I've experienced before and should be treated special.

"Would you like something to drink? I have wine and beer. Or water and sweet tea if you'd rather something non-alcoholic."

She looked at me and smiled.

"Wine sounds wonderful."

"Make yourself comfortable and I'll bring it over."

I watched her sit, then went to the kitchen and pulled two wine glasses out of the cupboard and retrieved the bottle of Riesling from the refrigerator.

From her perch on the corner of the couch, she looked

around my condo. Her eyes widened when they landed on *The Office* glasses she'd given me for my birthday lined on the edge of the kitchen island.

Picking up the two glasses in one hand, I grabbed the bottle with the other and walked the short distance to her side. I held out my hand and she took one of the glasses then I set the bottle on the coffee table and sat next to her.

I raised my glass.

"Here's to possibilities."

She clinked her glass to mine then took a quick sip of wine, then a longer drink.

Nudging her head toward the kitchen, she said, "You have the glasses I gave you on display."

"I love them. They're one of the best birthday presents I've ever received. And you can't see it but the mug is in the dish drainer. I drink my coffee from it every morning."

She bit her lip and smiled then took another drink. Her knuckles turned white as she wrapped her hands around the wine glass.

I put my glass down next to the bottle then placed my hands over hers. I leaned forward and kissed her forehead before pulling back to meet her gaze.

"Karen, you don't have to do anything here that you don't want to do. We can take this as slow as you need. We're starting a marathon here, not a sprint."

I cringed at the corny comparison, but she must have liked it because I felt some of the tension leave her hands as she released her grip on the wine glass. With my hands still over hers, she moved her arms to place her glass next to mine then entwined her fingers with mine and smiled up at me.

"Kiss me, Dale."

The air left my lungs at her sweet request and I fought the urge to pounce on her. Instead, with our hands still joined, I touched my lips to hers, taking it slow just like I'd promised we could.

Gently, leisurely, I moved my mouth against hers, deepening the kiss in deliberate increments until I couldn't wait another second to taste her again. I licked at the seam of her lips and she opened to me, her tongue meeting mine, matching me stroke for stroke.

Her fingers dug into my hair and she held me tight. I shifted closer, needing to feel her. She sank against the arm of the couch and I followed, my chest pressing against hers. Keeping one hand against my scalp, she dragged the other around my back and moved slowly from side to side, rubbing her erect nipples against my chest.

Shifting, I pulled her further down onto the couch and settled between her widespread thighs. She bent her leg and rested her foot against the back of my knee and I dragged my hand up the long length of her leg, over her hip, across her waist, and up to cup her breast. She didn't stiffen or move to stop me. Instead, she arched her back and moaned as I rubbed my thumb back and forth against her nipple through her soft cotton shirt and the bra underneath. It pebbled even further and I pinched it between my thumb and index finger and gently tugged.

She thrust her hips up against my rock hard cock and pulsed twice and I swear I almost came in my shorts. I pressed my hips against hers to hold her in place and dragged my mouth from hers.

I need to get myself under control or this will be over before it really gets started. I also need to make sure she really wants to move forward with this and isn't just getting caught up in the moment.

I pulled back, feeling a surge of satisfaction when she whimpered and dug her fingers into my shirt as if trying to hold me in place. Kneeling back, I wrapped my hands around her wrists and waited until she opened her eyes to pull her up into a sitting position.

I slipped my hands down to hold hers and raised them to my lips and placed a kiss on the back of each before resting them between us.

"Karen, we're getting to the point of no return here. Are you sure?"

She nodded and if I wasn't already on them, her words would have brought me to my knees.

"I've been standing still for years and now it's time to move forward. And I want to do that with you."

KAREN

DALE WENT TOTALLY STILL for several heartbeats, his dark blue eyes studying mine, as if he was processing my words. Then they must have registered correctly in his brain because he blinked and stood as a sexy smile lit up his face. I hadn't been expecting him to pick me up so I shrieked and wrapped my arms around his neck when he reached down and pulled me into his arms.

I floated through the air snug and secure in his strong embrace as his mouth devoured mine. Then he stopped and shifted me until I was flush against his body and let me slide down against him until my feet hit the floor. His erection poked into my belly feeling just as impressive as it had last time I'd encountered it.

We just stood there staring at each other, breathing hard, long enough for my eyes to adjust to the dark room. Dale's hands moved down my body and around to squeeze my ass before reversing direction and dragging my shirt up over my head. I heard it drop to the floor as his big hands circled my waist and he pulled me closer and devoured my mouth again.

His kiss had my head spinning as he changed tempo and pressure, kissing me long and hard then angling my head to go deeper, fusing our mouths together to create a tight suction as our tongues tangled and explored. I twisted one hand into his hair and dug the other into his bicep as I enjoyed his every taste and texture then groaned in protest when he pulled back. But I was rewarded when he slid his open mouth down my neck to lick at the pulse hammering at its base before making his way up the other side to nibble at a particularly sensitive spot on the side of my neck.

"You are so sweet," he whispered against my ear just before he dipped his tongue inside then sucked at my lobe.

My entire body broke out in goosebumps which he must have felt because he looked down, his heavy-lidded gaze staring at my breasts. His bicep flexed as he reached up to cup me though my bra. My nipple poked through the lace begging for attention, which he seemed more than happy to give.

I felt his warm breath on me a split second before his mouth covered my nipple. His tongue flicked at it through the lace as his thumb mirrored the action on my other breast. I moved both hands to his broad shoulders and held on because honestly if I didn't, I'd probably melt into a puddle of want.

What he was doing felt so good, too good, and as he moved back and forth alternately licking and sucking and flicking my overly-sensitive nipples, my hips pulsed forward of their own accord.

Dale pulled back and looked down at his handiwork and his mouth curled into a satisfied smile. I followed his gaze and saw my nipples thrusting forward through my pink lacy bra which now sported twin wet spots.

With that sexy smile still in place, Dale's eyes met mine and he slowly lowered to his knees. His hot mouth skimmed down my stomach and nibbled at my navel. I dug my fingers into his hair and held on, unable to do anything else. My pants and moans filled the room as I eagerly awaited his next touch.

My befuddled brain didn't quite register when he popped the button of my shorts open until he pulled the zipper down and spread his hands wide over my exposed belly. He kissed his way from my belly button to my panties then dragged his open mouth along the waistband.

Dale's hands shifted to my ass then I felt my shorts slide down my legs. He sat back and held my hand while I stepped out of them then took the opportunity to look his fill. Thankfully, I'd worn my sexy underwear. He stared at me for what seemed like forever before meeting my gaze.

"You're so beautiful," he said. "Perfect." He stroked his hand across my abdomen then, leaning forward, he dragged his tongue against the juncture of my thighs making me shiver. "Sweet."

He stood and wrapped his hand around my waist, then walked me backward until the back of my legs hit the bed. Following me down onto the mattress, he pushed me until I was sprawled in the center with him between my thighs.

After kissing me senseless yet again, Dale pulled back and traced his index finger along the edge of my bra before dipping it inside and pulling one cup down then the other. My breasts were on full display for him and I should have felt at least a little embarrassed, but I didn't.

I held out my arm to stop him when he started to lean down and kiss me again. His eyes widened and he moved to pull back, but I dug my fingers into his shirt to hold him in place and smiled.

"Take off your shirt."

He did as I asked and I itched to touch his smooth skin and well-developed muscles. So I did. He sucked in a sharp breath as my fingers traced down his six pack to the cut of his hips and over to the other side and up again. I moved them down to unbutton his shorts but he grabbed my hands and stopped me then entwined our fingers and shifted down on top of me, our joined hands on either side of my head.

"It's best if I keep my shorts on for now." He gave me a lingering kiss then pulled back and smiled. "I don't want this to be over before it gets started."

Then he took my mouth again almost frantically, with much less finesse, but still so good. His hands let go of mine and he wrapped his arms around my waist shifting me further down as he settled between my thighs, the ridge of his erection pressing against me *right there* and I rocked against him. He rested more of his weight on me, holding me still.

Somewhere in the back of my mind it registered that he'd unhooked my bra, but it wasn't until I felt my breasts fully pressed against his naked chest that I realized it was gone. Dale dragged his mouth from mine and shifted down to pull my nipple into his warm mouth. I let out a long, low moan as he licked and sucked one nipple then the other. Back and forth he went, and every touch of his mouth sent zings of sensation down to my clit but when I tried to push up against him seeking relief, his hips held me in place.

I slid my hands up his back then dragged my nails down and cupped his ass, pulling him forward to help ease my ache. Only it just made it worse.

Dale pulled back and drew in a big breath.

"Christ Karen. You're driving me fucking crazy."

Dale sat back on his knees and hooked his thumbs in the waistband of my panties and slowly dragged them down my legs. He stared at me for several heartbeats, heating me with his gaze, before leaning down and kissing my knee. Slowly, deliberately, he inched his way up my leg, alternately kissing and nibbling my skin.

When he reached the juncture of my thighs and kissed right over the center of my core, I nearly jumped off the bed. He placed a restraining hand on my belly and his eyes met mine over the expanse of my body as he opened his mouth and licked between my folds over and over again, flicking his tongue against the nub of nerves at each pass.

My chest rose and fell as I fought to steady my breathing while he continued his sensuous torture, licking and nipping and sucking until I didn't think I could take anymore.

I closed my eyes as though blocking out the sight of what he was doing would help dull the sensation, giving me a modicum of control. But it only intensified the feeling so I opened them again and dug my fingers into his scalp holding him in place, surrendering to wherever he wanted to take me.

Every touch of his mouth felt so damn good, I was barely holding on to my senses. So when Dale slipped one finger inside me, then another, and stroked as he sucked hard on my clit, I shattered.

When I came back to reality, he was beside me, naked, condom in hand. I blinked twice before looking down and focusing on his enormous erection.

"Oh wow." I reached out to touch it, but again he grabbed my hand and stopped me.

"Next time, okay?" Resting his forehead against mine,

he kissed the corner of my mouth and flashed a pained smile. "I'm hanging on by a thread here."

I pulled my hand back and he ripped open the foil packet and watched, fascinated, as he rolled the condom down his impressive length. That done, he met my gaze and settled back between my thighs. He reached down and lined himself up at my entrance and pushed forward, sinking into me in one, long thrust. I gasped at the same time he groaned. He stayed still for a minute and my inner muscles relaxed as I adjusted to his size. He's really big and it's been a long time.

"Damn." The way he said the word, it sounded more like a prayer than a curse. "You feel so good. So tight." He pulled back and slowly thrust forward and stilled again. His brow wrinkled as his gaze met mine. "I'm really sorry, but this isn't gonna last very long. But I swear I'll make it up to you next time."

That's the second time he's mentioned doing this again. Not that I'm complaining.

Again, he pulled back and pushed forward, but this time he kept repeating that motion, pumping in and out, slow and steady. My inner muscles gripped at him every time he pulled out and clenched against him with every thrust forward.

He settled into a perfect rhythm and I moved my hips to counter his movement, adding to the sensation. I pulled my legs further back as he picked up the pace and gripped his ass. With each forward motion, he nudged against my clit and I shifted my hands to his shoulders and wrapped my right leg around his waist, wanting more. He sank further against me and hit *that* spot.

I let out a long, low groan as I felt my inner muscles spasm against him again and again. My orgasm went on and on and I fought to suck in air.

Dale moved his hands down to grip my hips and slammed into me twice more before he let out a low growl and collapsed on my chest.

I wrapped my arms around him and held him close. His weight felt so good against me and when he tried to pull away, I tightened my arms. He rested his head against my shoulder and still joined, we held each other as our breathing slowed back to normal. After kissing my chest and chin, he looked up at me.

"I'll be right back."

I felt cold as he pulled away so I shifted under the blankets. My eyes half closed, I watched him walk back to the bed and crawl under the covers. He pulled me into the circle of his arms and I rested my head against his chest, exhausted.

As I drifted off to sleep, I focused on how amazing this had been instead of allowing the guilt nudging at the corners of my mind into my thoughts.

Chapter Twenty

DALE

I JUST FLIPPED the last pancake onto the stack when I heard Karen come out of the bedroom. Looking over my shoulder, I smiled when I saw her standing by the table wearing my T-shirt from yesterday.

"Good morning," I said. "Have a seat. Would you like some coffee?"

"That'd be great. Thanks."

It might make me a sick bastard but my chest swelled a little bit at her sex-rumpled appearance and tired eyes. Not to mention the fact that she's moving slower than usual.

She pulled out a chair and lowered onto it, then picked up the glass of orange juice I'd set out earlier and took a long drink. As she swallowed, she held up the glass and smiled.

"I get Pam, huh?"

Of course, I had to serve the juice in *The Office* glasses

she'd given me. I handed her a mug of coffee and set the plate of pancakes in the middle of the table then sat down.

"Well, if you'd taken this seat, you would have been Jim."

She added a teaspoon of sugar and a splash of cream to her coffee then looked at the breakfast I'd prepared.

"But regardless, I always have Dwight." I held up my coffee mug. Her shy smile made me add, "I do love these. They really were the perfect present for me."

"I'm glad you like them." She picked a strawberry out of the bowl and popped it in her mouth. "The pancakes look delicious. The smell of them cooking is what woke me up."

"Help yourself."

I was happy to see her take three pancakes and place them on her plate. Then she smothered them with butter and syrup, cut off a piece, and placed it in her mouth. Closing her eyes, she let out a long groan as she chewed. The sound had my dick standing at attention. After all, he recognized that sound. He'd heard it quite a lot last night and it usually meant good things for him.

"These are amazing," she said as she swallowed. "I didn't know you could cook."

I filled my own plate and cleared my throat as I willed my raging erection to settle down. After our amazing first time, we'd both fallen asleep then woke in the middle of the night and as promised, I did things a little better the second time around. So she's probably not only tired, but sore as well.

"I'm no gourmet, but I can make most basic breakfast foods and few other things that keep me from ordering out all the time." I fixed my pancakes to my liking then cut them into bite-sized pieces. "Before Penny and I moved in with our grandparents for good, we were left alone a lot so it was either learn how to cook, or live on cereal, ramen, and boxed mac and cheese."

"Speaking of Penny, Jeremy told me she'll be leaving in a couple weeks."

I nodded and swallowed. "Yeah, she'll have to report to training camp soon. But it was nice seeing her so much the past couple months. It's been a long time since we've been in the same zip code for so long."

"She's really great, and I *love* her hair. It's gorgeous."

"Everyone seems to love it but her." I popped another forkful into my mouth and chewed, thinking about that. "Actually, I think she's come to terms with it now. But she went through a rebellious phase and dyed it all different colors when she was a teenager. She was blonde for a little while then black when she went through her Goth stage Jack mentioned the other day. I thought she looked ridiculous and told her so, but my grandmother said she wasn't gonna argue about hair."

Karen took a sip of coffee then cradled the mug in her hands, rubbing her thumb back and forth across the smooth surface. I was happy to see she'd cleared her plate.

"I can understand that. I hated my hair when I was a kid and used to tell my mother that I was going to dye it black when I grew up."

"Why? Your hair is beautiful."

And I learned last night she is in fact a natural blonde.

"When I was a kid, it was white blonde. I swear it was fluorescent. And people commented on it all the time calling me a little towhead. Of course, when I was little, I thought they meant toe head, like a toe on your foot, not tow as in flax."

I laughed at that.

"That is seriously the most adorable thing I've ever heard."

She scrunched her nose, trying to look annoyed, but her smile won out.

"Want more pancakes?"

"No." She sat back and patted her stomach. "I'm full. Although I'll probably have more strawberries. They're really good."

I'm really hungry this morning so I took the last two pancakes.

"Did Penny tell you that she was named for her hair?"

"No."

I nodded and chewed the mouthful of pancakes then swallowed.

"My parents planned on naming her Lillian. Why? I have no idea." I shrugged. "Anyway, once she was born with that copper hair, my mom said it was the same color as a shiny penny and decided to name her that."

"That's kind of cool."

"It's better than how they came up with my name." She raised her brow as she bit into a strawberry. "There was some grunge band they followed whose lead singer was named Dale. But if anyone asks I say I was named after either Dale Murphy or Dale Earnhardt, depending on the audience." I shrugged. "I haven't been asked too often though. Most people call me Monte so I think they forget that's not my first name."

Her eyes rounded. "Would you rather I call you Monte?"

I shook my head and smiled. "No, I kind of like you calling me Dale."

Especially when she says it in a breathy voice like she did last night. But I decided to keep that to myself, for now anyway.

"What about you? Does your name have an embarrassing origin?"

"No, my parents just liked it I guess. And I never minded my name until it became a universal synonym for all entitled women with irritating demands." She chuckled. "I never in all my life thought I'd be a meme."

"I didn't even think about that," I said around a short laugh then reached over and squeezed her hand. "But you're none of those things. In fact, you're the sweetest woman I've ever met." I shifted closer and held her gaze. "And I had an amazing time last night."

I didn't take my eyes off hers, but still saw the blush that stained her cheeks.

"I had a great time, too."

When she bit her lip, I couldn't resist her anymore. I leaned closer and kissed her. Her lips are still a little swollen from my kisses last night and they feel plumper and softer.

"I love your mouth," I said then shifted out of my chair to kneel before her. "And I love kissing you. I swear I could do it forever."

I sealed my mouth over hers and thrust my tongue inside. The kiss was so wet and wild and earthy, you'd never know we'd had our fill of each other mere hours before. Then again, I'm not sure I'll ever get my fill of her.

Wrapping my hands around her waist, I pulled her forward so she slipped off the chair and onto my lap and took her mouth again. Her thighs rested on either side of mine and my cock settled between her warm folds, her lacy panties and my basketball shorts not adding much of a barrier.

I moved my hands down to squeeze her ass and pull her closer. She held onto my shoulders and as our tongues tangled and explored and her hips rocked against mine. I swallowed her low groan just before she pulled back, her breathing harsh.

"Dale."

I recognized that breathy tone. Looking into her glazed eyes, I tightened my grip on her ass and pressed her down against me as the movement of her hips became more frantic.

"Come for me," I whispered. "I want to watch you."

She lost her rhythm and let out an adorable distressed groan before picking it up again.

I didn't take my eyes off her face, not wanting to miss a single nuance as she rode me. She dug her fingers into my shoulders and let out a long, low moan as her eyes widened then fluttered shut.

Tightening my grip, I held her in place when she sagged as her orgasm ended. She rested her cheek against my chest and I felt her warm breath against my neck. When her breathing slowed, she pressed a kiss against my chest and pulled back.

I shifted my hand up to cup her jaw.

"That was beautiful." I placed a gentle kiss on her lips. "Thank you."

The corners of her mouth curled up then she let out a short snort of laughter.

"I think I should be the one saying thank you." She shifted off my still-hard cock. "As a matter of fact, you made me a promise you didn't keep last night."

Since she already had my dick in her grip, I knew exactly what she was talking about, but I asked anyway.

"What promise is that?"

I followed her gaze down to watch her hand tighten on my shaft as she used her thumb to rub the drop of precum that had escaped into the head.

My breath shuddered in my chest and I leaned back and rested my hands on the floor behind me and sat back.

Which Karen took full advantage of. She shifted to her knees and leaned over me.

Licking her lips, she met my gaze.

"You said I'd get a chance to touch you, but I never did." She lowered her head and placed her tongue along the base of my shaft and dragged it up to circle around the tip. "Not that I'm complaining. Last night was amazing, but now I want to play."

She'd addressed those two sentences to my dick and the warm puff of her breath nearly put me over the edge. Once she actually puts her mouth on me again, I'll be a goner. I swear I don't usually have the control of a teenage boy scoring for the first time but with her it's just different. I'm totally at her mercy.

"Aaahhhh, that feels so good."

She pushed at my chest until my back rested against the floor. Grabbing the waistband of my shorts, she tugged them down to the middle of my thighs. My dick bobbed toward my stomach and she leaned forward and flicked her tongue against the tip before opening her mouth wide and sliding her lips down my shaft then back up again.

Wrapping her hand around the base, she slowly moved down until her mouth met her fist then she squeezed and did it again. She bobbed up and down on my cock, her warm mouth pulling me closer and closer to the edge. I wrapped my fingers in her hair and held on, reciting baseball stats to keep from coming as I watched her head move up and down in a hypnotic rhythm.

She tightened her grip around my shaft as her mouth moved back up my length. Her tongue swirled around the tip over and over and my balls tightened. I grabbed at her shoulder.

"Karen." She didn't stop so I said her name louder.

With her lips still wrapped around my dick, she looked

up at me with those cornflower blue eyes and I forgot what I was going to say. Then my balls tightened even more and I felt the telltale tingle at the base of my spine.

"I'm gonna come." I dug my fingers into her skull. "Karen, I'm gonna come if you don't stop."

Apparently she didn't care because she pulled her hand from my shaft and reached down to alternately cradle and tug my balls. She lowered her head, taking as much of me into her mouth as she could and sucked, and kept sucking until I lost it.

Chapter Twenty-One

KAREN

"STOP STARING at the hot guy in your backyard." Chloe stood directly behind me on her tiptoes, looking over my shoulder. "Not that I blame you for enjoying the view."

I finished drying my hands on the towel and draped it over the edge of the sink.

"He's really good with Jeremy."

"Judging by the glow on your face, he's really good with you, too." She bobbed her eyebrows.

I can't argue with that. And it's not just the sex.

After I basically attacked him on the floor next to the kitchen table, we showered...separately thank God, or I probably wouldn't be able to walk...and got dressed.

Since Jeremy's game wasn't until three o'clock, we had some time to kill, so Dale took me for ice cream. And I realized he was correct when he said the place is usually crowded during the day. He handled the fans who approached like the pro that he is and I enjoyed watching him in action as I ate my sundae.

As we'd expected, with both Jack and Dale at the game, they were easily recognized. They talked and shook hands and took pictures, and whatever else their fans requested until the game started. Then they excused themselves to sit with Hannah, Chloe, and me and give it their full attention.

The game was a nail-biter, and I nearly had a stroke when Jeremy took the mound with the score tied three to three in the top of the sixth inning. Dale held my hand as I watched my son pitch two perfect innings. Then one of his teammates hit a walk-off home run in the bottom of the seventh giving them the victory.

It had been an amazing night followed by a great day and I really enjoyed spending time with Dale and getting to know him better. After the game, we got takeout and came back to my house to eat and while Chloe and I cleaned up, Dale and Jeremy went outside to play catch.

"So, how was it?" Chloe asked as she settled onto the chair in the living room. "Inquiring minds want to know."

I sat on the couch across from her.

"Chloe, I've never given you details of my sex life before," I said around a chuckle. "Why would I start now?"

She scrunched her nose.

"That's because *before* you were having sex with my brother and I didn't even want to think about that much less hear about it. But *Dale Montgomery* is a whole other story. Besides, I don't want details, just a general summary." She held up her index finger. "One, did you enjoy yourself?" Then she added another finger. "And two, are you okay? Mentally, emotionally."

I smiled, memories of the previous night flashing through my head.

"Yes, I enjoyed myself." I grabbed the throw pillow next to me and squeezed it against my stomach. "As for if I'm okay, I'll say yes. There was a moment of guilt after, well after the first time, but I fell asleep before it could take root."

Her eyes widened and a cat-that-swallowed-the-canary smile spread across her face.

"The *first time?*" I threw the pillow across the room and it hit her right in the center of the chest. She just laughed and hugged it to her. "He really likes you."

"I really like him, too. More than I thought I would."

"Well, the air practically crackles when you're with each other."

"I know, I can feel it. But aside from the physical attraction, I just enjoy his company. He's very nice and thoughtful, not to mention funny and easy to talk to. Our phone conversations have been amazing."

""But?" I frowned at her. "I've known you too long for you to tell me there's not a 'but' in there somewhere."

I reached over and grabbed another throw pillow and hugged it to my chest.

"I just don't know what's going to happen when the season starts. We have enough trouble getting together now." I traced the pattern of the pillow with my index finger. "I mean, you broke up with your guy because he's in Chicago so you don't have a future. You have a lot more experience with relationships than I do and if you can't make it work, how am I going to?"

"First of all, Elliott and I didn't have the connection you and Dale have. Honestly, if we had been in the same city we probably wouldn't have lasted as long as we did. But you guys really have something and I'm sure you'll figure out the logistics as you go along."

She'd just said that when I heard the back door open.

"Thanks Monte. I'll show my coach that pitch at practice tomorrow."

"The circle change is a great pitch and yours looks really good. For now if you use that and hit your spots, you'll be golden."

I looked over and saw him hand Jeremy a glove as they walked into the living room. Dale sat next to me on the couch and rested his arm behind me.

We've been slowly showing affection in front of Jeremy and he doesn't seem to mind. In fact, he's been amazingly cool about our relationship, thankfully.

"Mom, I'm really tired. I'm gonna go take a shower."

"Okay, don't forget to put your uniform in the laundry room before you go to bed."

"I will. Thanks again for coming today, Monte. And you too, Aunt Chloe."

He gave Chloe a hug and kiss then went off to shower.

"I didn't think you guys were ever going to come inside."

"We were having fun, but it got too dark to see the ball."

"Isn't playing catch like working on your day off?" Chloe asked.

"Nah, that was fun. And Jeremy is fun to show stuff to because he really pays attention."

"He loves the game," I said.

"That's pretty obvious," he said. "Speaking of, Jeremy said you can come to the game Friday night."

"If that's okay?"

"Do you even have to ask that?" He wrapped his arm around my shoulder and pulled me close for a quick kiss. "Maybe we can grab something to eat afterwards?"

"Sure."

"What about you, Aunt Chloe? Are you still in town on Friday?" he asked.

"I am, but I actually have a date." She tapped her index finger against her chin. "Although, it would probably score me a lot of points if I took him to a game and introduced him to you."

Dale bobbed his eyebrows. "Are you looking to score points with him?"

"You know, I'm not sure yet. The phone conversations have been good, but let me get through the first date before I bring him to meet the family and the team."

Chloe dates a lot and that's the way she likes it. Or at least it's the way she always has liked it. Where Jason and I got together young and then got married and had Jeremy young as well, she never wanted that. Getting married has never been part of her life plan and she's never wanted children of her own.

Dale asked her questions about the guy, sounding like a protective older brother. Then when she mentioned when she'll be leaving on her next business trip, he asked her about work too.

I shifted in my seat and rested against his side. Without missing a beat in the conversation, Dale moved his arm from the back of the couch to rest on my shoulder.

While he and Chloe talked, I thought about today and the other days we've spent together and couldn't help but smile at how nicely he fits into my life.

Chapter Twenty-Two

"YOU MUST HAVE DONE something to piss off all the pitchers," Jack said, checking out the bruise just above my elbow. Even though my elbow pad took most of the impact of the wild pitch, it's still swollen and purple.

"Seriously, you've been dinged more this spring training than all of last season," Dan added.

"Maybe they're just intimidated by my prowess at the plate."

They looked at each other and burst out laughing. I flipped them off then picked up my mug of beer and took a long drink.

Rudy's Place is pretty crowded for a Monday night but the hostess sat us at a table in a little alcove so we're not out in the open. But instead of paying attention to the guys or checking out the room, my eyes keep straying to the hallway leading to the deck. As much as I'd protested about Hannah arranging a birthday dinner for me, I'm so happy she did, mostly because she'd used her super persuasion powers to get Karen to attend.

And life has been pretty incredible since then.

I'm not sure what changed for Karen, but since that night, she's been different. Before I felt like she was fighting to keep me at arm's length, but now she seems to have jumped into this relationship with both feet. Especially since the last time we were here and Karen told me she wanted to tell Jeremy about us.

I realized the guys weren't talking anymore and looked across the table and found them both staring at me.

"What are you two idiots smiling about?"

"The dumb, lovestruck look on your face," Jack said.

"But I have to admit that it's better than the pathetic, lovelorn look you had for the past two years," Dan added.

I just chuckled and shook my head. Let them have their fun. Turnabout is definitely fair play and I enjoyed busting their asses when they turned into lovesick fools. I'm just happy they have something to tease me about.

"Seriously though, it looks like things are going well."

While Jack phrased that as a sentence, it was definitely a question

"Yeah, things are going well. Karen is amazing and Jeremy is so great. He's been really cool about us dating." Then I figured I'd bring up the elephant in the room. These guys would understand the impending issue better than anyone. "I just don't know what's going to happen after next week."

They shook their heads, looking almost solemn.

"Have you talked to her about it?" Dan asked.

"Not yet. I didn't want to give her a reason to end things before they got started. I thought we'd figure it out when the time came but now that it's here, I'm not exactly sure how to handle it."

"You really need to talk to her and find out what she's thinking."

The fact that Jack just uttered that sentence shows how much he's changed. Before Hannah he never would have even thought something like that, never mind said it out loud.

"I know. It just sucks that I'm going to have to use some of the time we have left together here discussing it."

"When are you seeing her again?" Dan asked.

"We usually FaceTime every night but I won't see her in person until Friday at the game." I rubbed the back of my neck. "I'll have to see if we can get together before then. It's not a conversation I want to have over the phone, even if I can see her face."

"You've seen guys juggle baseball and family your whole career. I'm sure you'll figure it out," Dan said.

He's right, but I also know that figuring it out is the easy part, following through and making it work is what's difficult.

KAREN

"DO YOU NEED HELP?" I asked Sabrina as she made her way down the aisle with a sleeping Gavin in her arms.

"No, I'm good. Thanks." She sat in the seat next to me. "He conked out about five minutes ago."

"He's so adorable."

He's a mini Dan McMullen and right now, his chubby cheeks are rosy with sleep. Sabrina looked down at her son and smiled.

"That he is." She shifted him down to rest in her lap and he snuggled into place. "So how are you doing?"

"I'm doing well. So is Jeremy."

"And?"

I laughed when she dragged out the word. Honestly, I'm not sure whose friends are more invested in my relationship with Dale, his or mine.

"Things are going well there, too."

I'm just not sure what's going to happen after this week. Dale and I got together Wednesday night after his game and talked about how we're going to handle the season starting. He made it very clear that he's dedicated to our relationship but I still have lingering doubts. Once he's traveling around the country and I'm out of his sight, will I also be out of his mind?

"Do you and Jeremy have plans to come up to Myrtle Beach?"

"Dale and I have discussed it, but nothing is set in stone. We won't be able to go until Jeremy is out of school. Then I have to figure out when he doesn't have games and I can get away from work. There's a home stretch at the end of May that I think might work."

"If you can, plan some extra time. Jeremy and Lexi get along well so I'm sure they'd enjoy hanging out. And we can just relax by the pool."

"I'll see what I can do."

Thankfully I'm at the point in my career where I'm not expected to be in the office all the time. As long as I don't have a showing or a closing, there's a lot I'd be able to do from South Carolina if necessary.

I looked down at the field and spotted Dan and Dale walking toward the dugout. Dale looked up and smiled. I waved, feeling my face heat.

"This is all still very surreal to me. How on Earth am I dating Dale Montgomery?"

Like Hannah, Sabrina has been in my shoes. And, even though I haven't spent as much time with her as I have with Hannah, I still feel comfortable talking to her.

"I know. When Dan and I got together, he was injured so we were in our own little bubble. So it was a bit of a shock when I had to deal with all this." She adjusted her hold on Gavin and shifted slightly to face me. "At home he's just Dan, but to the rest of the world, he's a sports idol. It's definitely surreal." Chuckling, she added, "Cal's wife Barbara always says she forgets he's 'kind of a big deal' until they go out and he's recognized."

"I can understand that since both you and Barbara knew your guys before they were *kind of big deals*. But don't forget, Jack is Jeremy's idol and my late husband was a big Waves fan so I've been watching these guys play since they started with the team. It's strange to see them socially now."

"I get it, but as you've probably figured out by now, they're just regular guys. And I'm amazed at how they've found places to go all over the country where they can remain relatively anonymous."

"That is pretty impressive. When Dale and I went on our first date, I'd expected to be interrupted all night, but we weren't. Not once."

As we watched the game, I thought about my conversation with Dale the other day. He was pretty adamant about the fact that he wants to see each other as often as possible during the season. While I'm thrilled he doesn't just consider what we're doing here a spring training fling, I had to make him understand that I can't just pick up and fly off to see him. He was okay with that and asked that I not give up on him even when things get tough.

"What does Jeremy think about you and Dale dating?"

"He's okay with it."

"You sound surprised by that."

"Part of me is and part of me isn't. I mean, Dale is the first guy I've dated since Jason died so I thought Jeremy might be upset that I'm moving on from his father. But he said he wants me to be happy and that I laugh a lot when I'm with Dale."

She was about to say something when Jeremy and Lexi appeared at the end of the aisle, each carrying a drink in one hand and a food container in the other. They sat in the two seats in front of us so Sabrina and I shifted our attention to them.

We were invited to their condo after the game for a late dinner. Jeremy brought a change of clothes and he and Lexi plan to go swimming. He doesn't have a tournament or practice this weekend so we won't have to leave early. We'll also be able to attend the final spring training games tomorrow and Sunday.

As if she read my mind, Sabrina asked, "You guys will be hanging out with us this weekend, right?"

I nodded. "You're leaving Monday, right?"

"Yeah, we're flying home in the afternoon." She bobbed her eyebrows and flashed a big smile. "But I understand Dale is staying until Wednesday morning."

Glancing down at Jeremy to remind her he's sitting right there, I said, "He chartered a flight that leaves at 5 a.m. so we can hang out after Jeremy's practice Tuesday night."

What I didn't mention is that I'm taking the day off so Dale and I can spend it together. I also arranged for Jeremy to go home from school with one of his teammates and his mom will take them to practice. So Dale and I have an entire uninterrupted day together to do whatever we want.

Chapter Twenty-Three

DALE

THE FRONT DOOR opened as I stepped onto the front porch. Karen stood behind the screen door, looking adorable in a pair of cotton shorts and one of my Waves T-shirts. Her hair was piled on top of her head in a lopsided bun.

"Good morning. These are for you."

I handed her the spring bouquet I'd picked up at the florist last night. I'd put it in the refrigerator as I was told to do and was thrilled when it still looked perfect this morning.

"Thank you Dale, they're beautiful." She tipped them toward her nose and inhaled. "Mmm, they smell good too. Let me go put them in water."

I followed her to the kitchen and watched as she stood on her tiptoes and pulled a vase out of a top cupboard. Grabbing a pair of shears out of her knife block, she expertly clipped the end off the stems and arranged the flowers in the vase.

"We didn't really discuss what we're doing today so I wasn't sure what to wear." She placed the vase in the middle of the dining room table and stood back to admire her handiwork. Seemingly satisfied, she turned and faced me. "I know I look a mess, but I'm showered. I just need to get dressed and brush my hair."

I heard what she was saying but was too distracted watching her to answer. She somehow looks adorable and sexy as hell at the same time and I can't take my eyes off her.

"What?" she asked as I continued to stare.

Closing the distance between us with three short steps, I placed my hands on her waist and pulled her close.

"You look beautiful."

She simultaneously scrunched her nose and patted her hair. I reached up and took her

hand in mine then lifted it to my mouth to kiss the center of her palm before placing it flat over my chest.

"I'm sure it makes me some kind of misogynistic asshole, but I love it when you wear my shirts. But besides that, you always look beautiful."

Biting her lip, she looked straight at my chest before meeting my gaze again.

"Thank you."

I gave her a quick kiss, making sure to keep it short so things didn't get out of control.

"As for today, we can do whatever you want. It really doesn't matter to me as long as

we're together."

"Have you eaten?"

"No."

"Why don't we run to the diner for a quick breakfast

then come back here and…" Her eyes shifted from me toward her bedroom. "Hang out."

"Hanging out sounds great." I kissed her forehead.

"I'm gonna go change." She shifted out of my embrace. "I'll be right back."

I walked into the living room to sit on the couch to wait but got sidetracked by the pictures on the mantle. I'd noticed the family photos when I was here before but didn't want to gawk at them. Now that I'm alone, I can check them out.

They're a mix of posed professional shots and candids of Jeremy at various ages. Over on the end table, there's a family portrait of the three of them. I can't say who Jeremy looks like because Karen and Jason can pass for brother and sister. No wonder she and Chloe look so much alike.

Karen and I haven't talked about Jason too much. I mean, part of me feels like I should know about him but another part thinks it might be creepy for us to spend our time together discussing her late husband.

"That's the last family portrait that was taken before Jason died."

I turned and found Karen standing across the room, wearing an orange sundress. She'd taken her hair down and it flowed over her shoulders.

"Sorry, I didn't mean to snoop. I started looking at the pictures of Jeremy and just kept going."

"No, it's fine. I mean, they are on display." She let out a nervous chuckle and shifted her gaze from me to the pictures. "I guess we've never really talked about Jason." Looking me in the eye again, she said, "This is all new to me. I'm not really sure exactly what's appropriate, how much to share."

"Karen, this is all new to me, too." I crossed the room,

needing to be closer to her. "And I don't think anything is right, wrong, or appropriate. I want to know whatever you want to share. But please don't feel like you can't talk about Jason. He was a huge part of your life and he's Jeremy's father."

I was totally surprised when she wrapped her arms around my waist and hugged me tight.

"Thank you. You really are too good to be true."

Resting her chin on my chest, she looked up and gave me the sweetest smile. And at that moment, something happened to me. A warmth flowed through me and my chest tightened, then it felt like my heart skidded to a halt and started really beating for the first time.

KAREN

I SET the bag of food on the coffee table.

"I'm gonna take a quick shower," Jeremy said and ran off toward his room.

I went into the kitchen to get drinks, plates, and utensils then returned to the living room. Sitting on the floor between the couch and coffee table, I set out the Chinese food containers then picked up the remote and turned on the game.

It's opening night for the Waves and I breathed a sigh of relief this morning when Dale texted and let me know he'd made it to Myrtle Beach. He waited until last minute to leave and I was so worried something was going to happen and he wouldn't make it back in time. But despite that, I was so happy he'd stayed in town to spend the day with me.

Jeremy ran into the living room and sat next to me, looking squeaky clean. He quickly filled his plate and dug into the food.

"I'm so hungry," he said in-between bites.

"I guess so."

Of course, it had been three hours since he ate and nowadays that's like a lifetime to his teenage appetite. He picked up the remote and turned up the volume while I filled my plate.

"Cool. Cal is in the booth tonight."

I looked at the TV and saw Cal Chase's face on the screen next to the regular Waves announcer, Jay Glasser. Jeremy and I met him at a couple of the first games we had attended but he got hurt and then retired so I don't know him very well.

The national anthem ended and the camera focused on the starting pitcher, Chris Russell. I'd sat next to his girlfriend Ivy at a few games but never met him, although Jeremy has.

I've been watching Waves games for years but after meeting the players and having spent time with them, it's different. I feel more connected and invested, especially to one player in particular.

Jeremy cheered as the first batter struck out.

"Rusty looks awesome this year," he said as he added more sweet and sour chicken to his plate. "Remember he struggled the first half of last season, but he figured it out by the end. And now—Yes!" He cheered and banged his fist on the table as with just one more pitch thrown, the Waves had their second out as the batter hit the ball right at Jack Reagan. He didn't even have to move to catch it. "Anyway, now he looks better than ever."

The next batter stepped up to the plate. Rusty threw the first pitch in for a strike but then just barely missed the zone the next three times. Cal and Jay discussed how close the pitches were and whether or not they should have been strikes while the camera stayed on Rusty as he stood at the back of the mound rubbing the ball between his hands.

Finally, he stepped back on the rubber and went into his windup and fired a fastball right down the middle. The batter swung and popped it up. The camera panned to Dale as he tracked the ball toward the stands. I watched, fascinated, as he navigated the foul territory and stopped next to the wall and caught the ball for the third out. He smiled then turned and tossed it to a little boy in the second row.

"It was so great of Monte to stay and hang out with us yesterday," Jeremy said.

"Yeah, it was."

"You really like him, don't you?"

I looked over and saw my son's eyes looking serious as they studied me.

"I really do."

"Good. Because he really likes you and I really like him too."

The commercial break ended and Jeremy turned his attention back to the game. Of course, my attention was still on what he'd said and brought my thoughts back to yesterday. The three of us did have a great time together but it was before that, when it was just the two of us, that was really special.

We went to breakfast and ended up sharing stories, me about Jason and him about his parents and grandparents. You'd think that our libidos would have been killed after that topic, but when we came back to the house, we'd gone at it like teenagers. *Three* times. The last time had been in the shower and I was amazed at how effortlessly he'd held me against the wall.

After we got cleaned up, we went to pick Jeremy up at practice and we all went out to dinner, then came back to the house to watch a movie. He stayed later than I'd expected considering his flight was leaving at five o'clock, but I appreciated the extra time with him.

I really will miss him. We've gotten really close in six short weeks and yesterday something shifted bringing it to a whole other level.

After Jason died, I never thought I'd fall in love again, but now I'm pretty sure that's not true.

Chapter Twenty-Four

DALE

I GOT OFF THE PLANE, exhausted but excited to see Karen. Through the years I've watched various teammates rush from one location to another just to spend an extra few hours with wives, girlfriends, or family, but never thought I'd be one of them.

Yet here I am rushing to meet my girlfriend at the gate.

My girlfriend.

That's another thing I thought I'd never do. I've spent time with a lot of women, but never felt enough of a connection with even one of them to introduce them by anything other than their name. But I refer to Karen as my girlfriend, to anyone who will listen.

Speaking of…

There she is standing at the end of the gate waiting for me. She smiled and waved when she spotted me and I had to fight the urge to push the couple in front of me out of the way so I could rush toward her.

Finally they shuffled out of my way and I jogged toward Karen, pulled her into my arms, and kissed her.

"I've missed you so much," I said when we pulled apart. Slinging my arm around her shoulders, I led her toward the exit.

"Don't you have any bags?"

I kissed the top of her head. "Nope. I have clothes at the condo."

"Is that where we're heading?"

"I have five hours before I have to be at the stadium. What would you like to do?"

She flashed a wicked smile and I threw my head back and laughed as we walked through the automatic doors toward the parking lot.

"Then to the condo it is."

The fifteen-minute drive seemed to take forever but she finally turned into the parking garage of my complex. She remembered the code and keyed it in, then drove through the garage and pulled into my spot.

I jumped out of the car, jogged around to her side, grabbed her hand, and pulled her toward the elevator. We stepped inside and I pushed her against the wall and lowered my mouth to hers. She twisted her hands into my hair and kissed me back, echoing my desperation.

The elevator came to a stop and I dragged my mouth from hers then led her down the hall to my condo.

As we stepped inside, she launched herself at me. Cupping her ass, I picked her up and walked to the bedroom with her clinging to me, our mouths devouring each other. I held her close to me and lowered her onto the bed before resting on top of her. Groaning against her mouth, I pulled back, panting.

"Two weeks is too long," I said, kissing my way down

her neck. "It's great getting to see you on FaceTime, but I miss touching you."

I ran my hands down her body then back up again, cherishing every dip and curve before settling on her breast.

"I missed you so much," she said, repeating what I'd said to her at the airport.

I pressed my lips to hers and took small tastes, nibbling and licking before opening my mouth fully and taking hers in a tongue-tangling kiss. Karen gave as good as she got, meeting my tongue stroke for stroke. Her legs wrapped around my waist and she shifted forward, whimpering as she ground herself against my erection.

The woman drives me insane.

Shifting back, I dragged my shirt over my head and tossed it behind me. Karen reached up and ran her hands up and down my chest before settling on the button of my shorts. After popping it through the buttonhole, she carefully lowered the zipper then cupped me through my briefs.

"Why don't we get you undressed before you start doing that?"

She smiled then held her arms up so I could pull off her shirt. I removed her shorts and panties in one sweep. Stepping back off the bed, I dropped my shorts and briefs and crawled back onto the bed.

I lowered my mouth to hers again then rested my hands on either side of her head. I couldn't get enough of her lips, her tongue, and the hot sweetness of her mouth. But I wanted more. Grazing my hand down her stomach, I moved lower still and slipped a finger into her slick heat and groaned deep in my chest. She's so wet. I added a second finger and groaned again as she tightened around me.

Dragging my mouth from hers, I shifted back and looked down at her. She looked so beautiful lying in my bed wearing just a pale blue bra, writhing as I fucked her with my fingers.

"You feel so amazing. I can't wait to be inside you."

"So what are you waiting for?"

She whimpered as I slowly removed my fingers and shifted off the bed. I opened the nightstand drawer and pulled out a condom then climbed back into bed. Handing the foil packet to her, I rested back against the pillows.

Karen smiled as though I just handed her a winning lottery ticket and ripped it open. Moving onto her knees next to me, she wrapped her hand around the head and slowly rolled the condom down my shaft. By the time she had me fully sheathed, I was panting.

I wrapped my hands around her waist.

"Come here."

She shifted her leg to straddle me. I reached around and unhooked her bra as she thrust forward, pulling me into her wet heat. We both moaned as she slid down my length until I filled her completely.

I leaned forward to lick and suck her nipple into a tight peak before moving to give the other one the same treatment. Karen moved against me and my self-control eroded with each long, slow stroke. She grabbed onto my shoulder and picked up the pace, grinding herself against me with each forward thrust.

Resting back against the pillows, I moved my hands down to cup her ass, pulling her closer as she rode me faster and faster. She panted my name and fell forward, dragging her nipples against my chest as she moved up and down and back and forth.

Her movements became more and more frantic and she dug her fingers into my chest, holding me close. She let out a long, low groan and her head dropped to my shoulder as I felt the first ripples of her orgasm. I thrust my hips up to move in time with hers, then kept up the rhythm when she couldn't until I followed her over the edge.

KAREN

FOUR DAYS FLEW by and while Dale spent every possible second with us, it wasn't enough.

"I miss you already," I said as we cuddled in my bed.

He'd come over for breakfast and drove Jeremy to school then came back and gave me three mind-blowing orgasms. It's a perfect start to a day that will end with him catching a late flight to the west coast for a ten-day stint.

"I know." He kissed my forehead. "Did you figure out if you can come up to Myrtle Beach next month?"

"So far, it looks good. Right now, Jeremy doesn't have anything going on. He's out of school and has a break in baseball."

"Have you mentioned it to him?"

"Yes, and he's excited."

"I'll be home for eight days, but you know you can stay at the house as long as you want, right?"

I traced my index finger up and down his six pack abs.

"I appreciate that."

He pulled me closer. "I kind of like the idea of the two of you there."

"Tell me about it."

"My house?" I nodded. "I just bought it a couple years ago. It's right on the beach, not too far from Cal's place. It has four bedrooms, each with its own bathroom. Three of them are upstairs and the fourth is downstairs. That's the one Penny uses when she stays with me. There's also a rec room and living area down there. Upstairs, it has a big deck off the living room that looks out over the ocean. There's a pool and hot tub, too."

"It sounds amazing."

He shifted me onto the pillow and rolled to his side to face me.

"I understand that you and Jeremy have your own lives here, but I'm serious about you staying in Myrtle Beach as long as possible. Consider it a vacation." He tucked my hair behind my ear and stroked his finger down my cheek. "I know my life is crazy and this schedule isn't easy. It means a lot that you're willing to put up with all this just to be with me."

"You're definitely worth it."

He stared into my eyes for what seemed like forever then he spoke.

"This thing between us, it's pretty special, isn't it?"

I swallowed the lump in my throat and nodded. "It is."

He took in a short breath and let it out on a sigh.

"I've never done this before so I need you to tell me if I screw up somehow."

"So far you're doing great."

"Yeah?" An adorable smile spread across his face.

"Yeah." I kissed the tip of his nose then his lips before pulling back to look at him again. "Honestly, you're pretty perfect."

"As much as I appreciate that, I know it's not totally true."

"How about you're perfect for me?"

"That I agree with one hundred percent."

He placed his mouth over mine and shifted until he covered my body with his. And for the second time this morning, we made slow, sweet love.

I dozed off as he spooned me from behind and I thought I heard him whisper "I love you" but figured I must be dreaming.

Chapter Twenty-Five

DALE

I DRANK in the sight of Karen through my computer screen, wishing I was lying next to her instead of three thousand miles away.

"Sorry it's so late."

"You can't control how long a game goes."

"I could have if I hit the ball in the ninth instead of stranding the go-ahead run on second base."

She laughed and shook her head, then snuggled farther into the pillow.

"You got a hit every other time you batted and had two RBIs."

I love the fact that she watches my games. It's better when she's actually in the stands, but beggars can't be choosers.

"But at least we pulled it off in the end. Even if it did take thirteen innings." She chuckled then tried, unsuccessfully, to hold in a yawn. "I'm sorry. I'll let you get to sleep."

"No, it's fine. I'm okay for a little while longer."

"Well before you totally fade, I wanted to ask you something."

"What's that?"

"You know I talked to Jeremy earlier and he told me about his game." She nodded. "I was wondering if you'd be willing to video his games so I can actually see what he's doing."

Her eyes widened. "Really?"

"Yeah, I realize you probably can't tape the entire thing but even if you got when he bats and pitches."

"Sure, I can do that."

"Great. He was trying to describe something to me today and I gave him the best advice I could but if I could actually see what he's doing I could be more helpful."

"Okay, we'll just have to figure out how I can transfer them to you."

"Now that that's taken care of, how was your day?"

Karen told me about her day then I ended the call before she fell asleep. It's one-thirty on the East Coast and she's had a long day, plus she has to get up early and do it all again tomorrow.

Closing my computer, I rolled over and stared at the ceiling.

It's been five days since I chickened out and whispered *I love you* to Karen while she was asleep. I hadn't meant to do it that way, it just came out. But since then, there hasn't been a good moment to repeat it.

We'd woken up late that day and had just enough time to get dressed and pick Jeremy up from school. After dinner, we hung out for a while, then they dropped me off at the airport. And it's not something I want her to hear for the first time over FaceTime.

I won't see her in person again for a few weeks when

KAREN

"SO WHEN ARE you going to see your guy in person again?" Chloe asked.

"Not until the end of the month when we go up to Myrtle Beach."

The Waves are in Colorado finishing their time out west before heading home for four games. Then they're away again for a week, first to Boston then New York. After that, they have an eight-day home stretch before heading to Chicago then Texas.

I don't know how Dale handles this schedule. I'm exhausted just following it, never mind living it.

"How are you holding up?"

"I miss being with him, but we FaceTime every day, which is better than nothing." I tucked my feet up onto the couch. "I'll admit, all the years I watched baseball, I never thought about how stressful the schedule is for the players and their families."

"It's probably easier if they live wherever their team is based. Then at least they're together when they play at home."

"True."

"What are your plans if this thing between you guys keeps moving forward? Would you move up there with him?"

"I can't even think that far ahead. Besides, he doesn't live in Myrtle Beach all year. He's in Aspen during the off season. Jeremy and I couldn't do that. We need some stability. I have my job and he has school and sports." I shook my head. "I'm getting ahead of myself here. We're a long way away from worrying about who's going to live where."

"Have you seen the way that man looks at you?" She raised her brow. "Or the way you look at him?"

"Regardless, we've only been together for a short time. I'm not going to waste my time figuring it all out when it might not even happen."

She was about to say something else when Jeremy came back into the room. We got home from his game just in time for him to shower and catch the Waves game. He helped himself to two slices of pizza and settled in on the couch next to Chloe. Picking up the remote, he turned up the volume.

This game flew by. At the top of the eighth inning, there was still no score.

"What a pitcher's duel," Jeremy said. "But now they'll probably put their relief pitchers in. It'll be interesting to see if they do as well."

I looked over at my son with wide eyes. He sounded like a professional announcer. Of course, he watches enough games and really pays attention to pick things up. Plus I have to remember that he's a teenager now, not a little boy.

Blinking away tears at the bittersweet thought of Jeremy growing up, I stood.

"I'll put this in the refrigerator if you're done."

He looked at the pizza, seemingly deep in thought. "I'll have one more."

I dropped a slice on his plate then closed the box and carried it to the kitchen. After finding a spot for it in the refrigerator, I washed my hands and looked out the window as I dried them.

Chloe came up behind me and squeezed my shoulder.

"I know, it's weird when he opens his mouth and an adult speaks."

She opened the refrigerator and filled her glass with sweet tea. I just nodded, trying to

swallow the lump in my throat.

"What's wrong?" she asked. "All of a sudden you look like you're ready to cry."

I looked into the living room to make sure Jeremy wasn't paying attention to us. He was happily eating his pizza with his eyes glued to the TV so I figured I'd share my thoughts with Chloe. She's been with me through the good and the bad. And even though the bad times are few and far between at this point, every once in a while something triggers them. Often it's something silly, like my son sounding like a grownup. The last time it was watching Jeremy and Dale play catch.

Wiping away the tear that had escaped, I said, "Jason should be here for all this."

She wrapped her arms around me and kissed the top of my head.

"Yes, he should, but a cruel twist of fate and a dickhead drunk driver took him away."

I pulled back and looked her in the eye, voicing my biggest fear.

"I'm afraid I'm forgetting him. That Jeremy is forgetting him. And that's not right."

"Kar, you're not. He's always here with both of you. Just because you're moving on and not spending every waking moment thinking about Jason doesn't mean you've forgotten him." She looked up at the ceiling and shook her head before meeting my gaze again. "I didn't mean to freak you out with all the talk of moving forward with Dale. I just thought that if we discussed it, you wouldn't run scared when he brings it up."

I was about to say that she doesn't know he will bring it up when Jeremy yelled, "Mom, Monte is up to bat."

Chloe hugged me again and kissed me on the cheek.

"Come on, let's go watch your hot baseball player hit. Because we're lucky enough to be alive and that man has a fine ass."

I chuckled and followed her back into the living room, some of my melancholy lifted. She's right on both counts. We are lucky to be alive and Dale definitely has a fine ass.

Chapter Twenty-Six

DALE

I PACED BACK and forth at the gate, watching the boards, making sure their flight was still landing on time. It seemed like this day would never come but finally Karen and Jeremy are arriving and will be here for the next two weeks. I'll only be here for eight of those days, but I'm thrilled she took me up on my invitation to stay longer. I want her to be comfortable in my home and the only way that will happen is if she spends time here.

Since I've been at the gate, a few people approached to either shake my hand, ask for an autograph, or take a selfie with me. But for the past few minutes I've just been impatiently waiting. Finally I heard the announcement that their plane landed.

Even though Karen had initially protested, I'd purchased their tickets, rationalizing with her that they were coming to see me so it made sense for me to pay. And

I put them in first class so they should be some of the first people walking through the gate.

I'm tall enough to see and be seen over the small crowd so I stood toward the back. An older couple emerged followed by an airport employee pushing an elderly man in a wheelchair. Then I saw them. My heart skipped a beat then pounded as I watched first Jeremy then Karen emerge through the tunnel and walk toward me. Jeremy reached my side first and I wrapped my arm around his shoulders, giving him a hug.

"This is awesome. Thanks for inviting us, Monte."

"I'm so happy you're here," I said before pulling Karen into my arms and giving her a quick kiss. It wasn't nearly enough but would have to do for now. Taking her bag, I asked, "Do you have any checked bags?"

"Nope, just our carry-ons."

"That's pretty impressive for two weeks."

I held her hand as we walked through the airport toward the parking lot.

"We each have enough for at least a week. I'd rather wash clothes than lug a bunch with me." She smiled up at me. "Plus I think you have stores here if we need anything, right?"

"Last time I checked." I chuckled and pulled her close to kiss the top of her head.

We piled into the truck and headed toward my house. Traffic was heavy so the ride took a little longer than usual, but it doesn't matter now that Karen and Jeremy are with me.

"The weather is supposed to be nice this week. I know both Sabrina and Barbara are planning get-togethers. And you know my game schedule, but I'm yours whenever I don't have to be at the field."

"Do we get to go to all the games?"

I stopped at a red light and glanced back at Jeremy through the rearview mirror.

"Absolutely if you want to. Hannah has seats saved for both of you."

As much as I love it when she's at my games, I'm not sure Karen wants to spend half of her vacation sitting at the stadium. But we can work that out.

We turned off the main road and it was only a few more blocks to my house. The garage door opened as I approached and Karen looked over at me. I pointed to the small sensor mounted on the dashboard toward the windshield.

"That triggers the door to open when I approach."

"Because pushing a button on a remote is such hard work." She rolled her eyes and chuckled.

I pulled into the garage and turned off the truck.

Shifting in my seat to look at her, I said, "I actually got that because Penny broke the remote for the door opener and she had issues with the app. So it seemed like a good solution." Giving her a quick kiss, I added, "But now that I have it, I'm kind of spoiled. I'd probably run right through the garage door if it didn't automatically open for me."

I stepped down and closed the door behind me. Karen was at my side before I could go help her out. Jeremy had already hopped out of the truck and was looking around the three-car garage. The middle stall where Penny parks when she's here is empty but my Mercedes is in the other one.

"That car is awesome!"

"Unfortunately it only has two seats so we won't be able to take it when the three of us go out, but you and your mom can have fun in it after I hit the road."

Karen made a choking noise and looked up at me.

"I can't drive *that*."

"Why not?"

"Because it probably cost more than my house."

I chuckled and wrapped my arm around her waist.

"Well it's either that or the truck. Take your pick." I kissed her cheek. "If it tips the scales at all, the Mercedes is a convertible."

"That's even more awesome," Jeremy said.

Keeping my arm around Karen's waist, I led her to the door and through to the lower level. Jeremy took one last look around then followed.

Other than the bedroom and bathroom, the downstairs is one large room.

"Penny calls this the man cave, which is pretty funny since she spends more time down here than I do."

At least she used to. Now she stays with Kenny.

Jeremy was happy to see the Playstation and even though he'd probably rather stream whatever he's watching, I pointed out the DVDs too.

I led them upstairs and Karen gasped as we stepped into the living room.

"Dale, that view is amazing."

The open-concept is continued up here and the living room and dining room flow into each other, with the kitchen separated by a breakfast bar. The view from the floor to ceiling windows is visible from anywhere in the room. I opened the sliding glass door and the sound of the ocean filled the space.

I followed them out onto the deck. Karen leaned against the railing and looked out at the horizon.

"You'll probably be more interested in this," I said to Jeremy and he followed me to the other side of the deck.

He looked down at the pool area then back at me with a big smile on his face.

"Can I use that?"

"Absolutely. I put it there for you so you can practice while you're here if you want."

I'd put up a pitching net and target. I also borrowed a portable mound from Cal. He had an extra at the training facility he and Dan opened that he was willing to share.

"There's a tee and two buckets of balls in the garage."

"Thanks Monte."

Karen looked like she was blinking back tears when she joined us to see what we were talking about. I smiled at her and held out my hand.

"Come on, I'll show you your rooms."

Jeremy was thrilled with his, which is right near the stairs leading to the lower level. Of course, I put Karen in the room directly next to mine. I'm keeping things all proper setting her up in her own room, but with Jeremy either on the other side of the house or downstairs, hopefully we'll be able to sneak in some sexy time.

After putting Karen's bag in her room, we went onto the deck while Jeremy got familiar with the entertainment system downstairs. We're going out for dinner a little later, but for now we're just relaxing.

I sat on the rattan sofa then pulled her onto my lap. Wrapping my arms around her, I shifted her closer and brushed my lips against hers once, twice before pressing my open mouth against hers and kissing her the way I'd wanted to when I first saw her at the airport. Deeply. Desperately.

She twisted her fingers into my scalp, holding me in place. Not that I was going anywhere. It seems like forever since we've been together and I'd love nothing more than to bury myself inside her, but this isn't the time or the place.

I slowly ended the kiss and shifted her onto the cushion next to me.

"I missed you so much."

I tucked her hair behind her ear then dragged my index finger down her cheek. She shivered at that simple touch.

"I missed you too." She rested her head on my shoulder and took in a deep breath. "Dale, this house is gorgeous. It's so homey and comfortable. I love it."

"I'm glad." I kissed the top of her head. "Because I hope you and Jeremy will be spending a lot of time here."

KAREN

EIGHT AMAZING DAYS have flown by and Dale will be leaving for Chicago in the morning. Besides Saturday when we arrived, he's had games every day, but we've still managed to do a lot together. Jeremy has been in heaven hanging out at First Allegiant Bank Park. Lexi has shown him around the whole stadium and just attending all the games is a treat for him.

Today's game was in the afternoon and afterward we went to Cal and Barbara's for dinner. I just met Barbara this week, but she's as welcoming as Sabrina and Hannah and we became fast friends.

Now I'm relaxing on the deck while both Dale and Jeremy went to shower. They'd gotten all sandy playing beach volleyball.

"Mind if I join you?"

I looked up and found Dale looking deliciously sexy wearing just a pair of basketball shorts low on his hips. Patting the couch, I smiled.

"Please."

He settled in next to me and wrapped his arm around my shoulders, pulling me to his side. I settled my cheek on his chest enjoying his fresh-from-the-shower scent. It's amazing how even surrounded by the ocean, he smells like fresh mountain air.

"I peeked in on Jeremy on my way out here and he's already asleep. Like, dead to the world asleep with the remote still in his hand."

"He's always been like that. He goes and goes then just crashes."

Dale shifted and pulled me closer then kissed the top of my head. We sat like that for a long while, just listening to the sound of the waves. His thumb traced a lazy pattern on my arm and I snuggled in and just enjoyed being with him.

I have no idea how long we stayed like that before he spoke.

"This has been such a spectacular week."

Pulling back just enough to look him in the eye, I said, "Yes it has. Thank you so much for inviting us."

"Hopefully you won't need to be invited going forward." He kissed the tip of my nose. "*Hopefully* you'll feel comfortable enough to come here whenever you can." After placing his mouth on mine and giving me a slow, lingering kiss, he pulled back. "I like you in my space. And even though I'll be away next week, I'll be happy knowing you're still here."

"It's going to be different without you."

His playful smile nearly melted my panties off.

"You'll be so busy, you won't even notice I'm gone."

"With what Sabrina, Hannah, and Barbara have planned I'll definitely be busy. But I will also most definitely notice you're gone. I'm going to miss you so much."

My voice cracked on the last word and I cleared my

throat. I want to enjoy our last night together, not sit here pouting because he has to go.

Dale shifted to face me and took my hand in his, looking down to watch as his thumb traced back and forth over my knuckles. After taking in a breath and slowly letting it out, his eyes met mine and in them I saw everything I could have if I just let myself take it.

This man. This life. This...love?

He must have read the understanding in my gaze because the corners of his mouth curled up into an adorable smile.

"I love you." He let out a relieved breath. "I've wanted to say that for weeks now, but it was never the right time. I'm not sure now is either, but I couldn't keep the words inside anymore. I love you."

I stared at him with wide eyes, unable to move or speak. This feels like a dream.

"Karen? Baby?" I blinked, bringing him into focus. "I know I've always been a few steps ahead of you in this relationship so I understand—"

I lunged at him, stopping his words as I took his mouth in a fierce, possessive kiss. His surprise only lasted a second then he was kissing me back with just as much passion.

Shifting my leg, I rose up and moved over to straddle his lap. His hands cupped my ass and pulled me down onto his erection as our mouths continued to consume each other. I pulsed my hips against him and groaned deep in my throat when he hit just the right spot sending zinging sensations throughout my entire body. My nipples tightened and tingled as they rubbed against his bare chest.

I pulled my mouth off his and sucked in a deep breath, needing to tell him before this goes any further.

"I love you," I gasped. "I love you, too."

"Thank fuck."

His words had barely registered when he stood, gripping my ass to take me with him. I wrapped my arms around his neck and held on as he carried me across the deck and through the sliding glass door.

"Your room is closer," he muttered and walked through the living room to the bedroom I've been using, kicking the door closed behind him.

After setting me down next to the bed, he had me naked in two seconds flat. He cupped one breast then the other, squeezing and molding them in his big hands before swiping his thumbs over my nipples again and again. I dropped my head back and let out a long, low groan when he placed his mouth over me and sucked, hard.

When he pulled me farther into his mouth and feasted, I thought I was going to come right then and there. My hips moved against his and when that wasn't enough, I slid my leg up and wrapped it around his thigh to pull him closer.

Dale released my nipple then moved back and forth, licking and teasing one nipple then the other.

"Mmmm," he moaned, the vibration heightening the sensation. He pulled back, looking down to admire his handiwork. "Beautiful."

Placing his hands on my waist, he pushed me back until I was lying on the bed.

"Prop yourself up on your elbows," he said, his voice gravelly.

When I did as he said, he knelt in front of me then rested my legs against his shoulders, opening me to his gaze. He looked his fill before meeting my eyes over the expanse of my body.

"Watch."

I did as he commanded and he leaned forward, placing an open-mouthed kiss right at my core before licking me from bottom to top, circling my clit, before doing it again and again. Our eyes stayed locked on each other as he took me higher and higher, my inner muscles tightening. I thrust my hips up and he placed a restraining hand on my belly, holding me in place as he continued to tease and taste until an orgasm slammed through me.

My arms collapsed and I fell back onto the bed. As soon as I caught my breath, I felt Dale slip a finger inside me and slowly pump in and out. He added a second finger then a third, plunging deep before curling them to stroke me.

"You feel so good. So tight. So wet." He kissed my inner thighs between each sentence. The feel of his lips on my skin and his fingers inside me combined with his sex-deep voice tantalized my senses, pushing me toward the edge again.

"Dale." I drew his name out on a long groan that echoed through the room. He leaned forward and teased my clit with the tip of his tongue then opened his mouth over me and sucked and I couldn't hold back anymore. "Oh God."

He stayed with me, stroking and soothing, through the aftershocks until I got my breathing under control. I lay limp and exhausted, but despite that and after two mind-blowing orgasms, I still want him inside me. My inner muscles clenched and released as he removed his fingers and stood. I shifted my legs farther apart and held out my arms, offering an invitation. Which he immediately took me up on.

His thick erection rested against my inner thigh as he settled on top of me.

"Shit." He rested his head against my shoulder. "The condoms are in my room. I'll be right back."

I wrapped my arms around his shoulders, holding him in place.

"Don't go."

"But—"

"I'm on the pill."

"Are you sure?"

I nodded.

He closed his eyes and I felt a shudder rack through his body. After taking in a deep breath, his dark blue gaze met mine.

"I love you. So much."

Then he plunged inside me with one, long thrust. I wrapped my legs around his waist, pulling him in even deeper. He's such a snug fit and without a condom, he feels even more amazing than usual.

"Are you okay?"

"God yes."

He moved, slowly at first, then faster and faster still. My inner walls gripped and released him as he settled into a rhythm, in and out, in and out, in and out.

"You feel so fucking good," he said through gritted teeth. "Too good," he added on a

groan.

He lowered his head and licked my nipple before pulling it into his mouth and sucking on it in rhythm with his hips. My fingers and toes started to tingle and the sensation moved up my arms and legs and exploded through my core. I felt my inner muscles clamp down on him before clenching and releasing over and over again.

"Karen," Dale groaned and with one last hard thrust collapsed on top of me.

Chapter Twenty-Seven

KAREN

MY MOTHER and I ordered lunch and the waitress was barely out of ear shot when she pounced.

"So, Dale Montgomery?" She took a sip of sweet tea. "It must be serious since you went up to visit him in Myrtle Beach."

Actually I'm surprised it's taken her this long to bring up the subject. Jeremy is playing golf with my dad and my mom and I spent the morning shopping.

"It's getting there," I said.

I love my parents and don't know what I would have done without them after Jason died, but I've been reluctant to discuss Dale with them. And since they haven't been in town at the same time, it really hasn't been an issue. It's not like I'm hiding him from them but as an adult, I didn't feel the need to announce it when we started dating.

"Are you sure he's someone you should be getting involved with?"

"Mom, you don't even know him. Why are you saying it like that?"

"Well, he's a professional baseball player. They do have a certain reputation."

I can't chastise her for saying that. I thought the same thing before I started dating Dale. It's one of the reasons I was reluctant to go out with him in the beginning.

"He's a really great guy and Jeremy loves him." I smiled thinking about our time together in Myrtle Beach. "And he loves Jeremy."

She stared at me, obviously reading the happiness and love on my face but still not looking convinced.

"So when do we get to meet him?"

"Actually, if you're going to stick around, he'll be back in town at the end of next month when the Waves play Tampa."

Dale has asked about meeting my parents a few times, so he'll be happy when I tell him I have plans in place.

It's obvious I've surprised my mother because she's quiet. She probably expected me to make up some lame excuse why they couldn't meet and had a whole argument prepared.

"We can go to his game and then to dinner."

"His game?" She wrinkled her nose.

"I know you're not a baseball fan, but dad and Jeremy are, and so am I. But if you don't want to go to the game, we can just pick you up afterwards."

"No, I'll go. That way I can see him in his natural element."

I'm not really sure what that means and don't want to ask and ruin our day together. I love my mom, but she can be judgmental and opinionated. And it's obvious her opinion is that Dale is all wrong for me.

I'll admit that's what I thought two years ago when he

first asked me out, but he's managed to change my opinion. Hopefully he'll work his magic on my mom, too.

The waitress brought out entrees and we ate in silence for a while before she spoke.

"You were so devastated when Jason died. I just want to make sure you're not jumping into this relationship to escape your grief."

I carefully placed my fork on my plate and pushed it away. Taking a drink, I simultaneously tried to collect my thoughts and control my temper. Of all the things she could say, that's probably the worst. She's making it sound like I'm some fickle female who hops from one man to another to avoid facing her feelings.

"Mom, I loved Jason and you probably know better than most how devastated I was when he died. I'm not sure how I would have survived if I didn't have Jeremy to focus on. But Jason is gone and I'm still here. Dale asked me out more than once over the two years I've known him and I turned him down for a variety of reasons, mostly because I didn't feel ready. But something just clicked this year and when he asked me out again, I decided to give him a chance."

I didn't dare mention that Chloe and Hope kind of nudged me in Dale's direction. She's not a big fan of either of them for reasons I'll never understand. For the most part she loved Jason but she never liked his sister, saying she didn't trust her. Ditto for Hope.

"And I'm really happy. So when you meet him, please set all your judgements and preconceived notions aside and give him a chance."

DALE

. . .

"GREAT GAME TONIGHT."

Karen smiled at me through my computer.

"Thanks." I smiled back.

I don't think I'm being cocky when I admit that I've been playing great lately. There's probably some logical explanation for it, but I'm chalking it up to the fact that I'm so happy.

"But I don't want to talk about my game or Jeremy's right now. I want to discuss that text you sent me about meeting your parents."

"You brought it up and now so did my mom. Since they'll be in town when you play Tampa, I figured I'd do my best to make it happen."

I settled onto my side and propped my computer on the pillow next to me.

"Meeting the parents is a pretty big step," I said.

Her eyes widened. "Oh."

"I'm just teasing. Seriously, I'm thrilled. What do you have planned?"

"I figured we'd go to your game then out to dinner if that works. Wednesday's game is at four so I thought that'd be the best day."

"Did you talk to Hannah about tickets?"

"No, I wanted to talk to you first." That adorable crease formed between her eyes with her frown. "And I just figured I'd buy tickets."

I shook my head. "Talk to Hannah."

Since the game isn't at our home field I'll have to buy the tickets, but that's not a big deal. Plus I'll get better seats than she will.

"Okay I'll call her tomorrow," she said. "Any ideas for dinner?"

"Do you think your parents would like Gianni's?"

"Definitely. The food was so good there."

"It's always been one of my favorite restaurants, but since I had an amazing first date

there with an even more amazing woman, it's bumped up to the top of my list."

"You are such a sweet-talker."

Her tone was light but her pink cheeks told me she liked what I'd said.

"I just speak the truth."

"Then you're incredibly sweet and I'm very lucky."

"I'm the lucky one," I said. "And I'll make reservations for eight o'clock. If the game goes into extra innings we may have to bump it back, but they're very accommodating there."

"Sounds good."

"Since we're talking about reservations, there's something else I wanted to discuss with you."

"What's that?"

"I'm playing in New York in a couple weeks. It's a three-day series, Friday through Sunday. I already checked Jeremy's schedule and he doesn't have a tournament so I was thinking maybe the two of you could fly up for the weekend and I'd get to see you, plus you could visit with your friend Hope. I haven't met her yet and I'm looking forward to it. You can invite Aunt Chloe and bring the perfect storm to New York."

"Oh wow, that's...wow, I wasn't expecting that."

"What do you think?"

She nibbled at her bottom lip for what seemed like forever before her face broke out into a big smile.

"I think it'll be fun. And I will invite Chloe...who loves that you call her *Aunt* Chloe by the way."

"Is there something special I should be calling Hope? I wouldn't want her to feel left out."

"Nope, she's just Hope," she said. "And I'll text her letting her know we'll be invading her town."

"I'll make sure to get a suite so you and Jeremy can stay with me."

We discussed more details before hanging up and she seemed really excited about the trip. I'm so happy she agreed. It puts us in the same city for a few days, plus I get to meet her good friend, Hope.

Even though this whole relationship thing is new to me, Dan and Jack are right. Karen and I are figuring it out as we go along and so far, we're making it work.

Chapter Twenty-Eight

KAREN

I'VE BEEN to regular season games in Tampa and Myrtle Beach, but those didn't prepare

me for New York. It was so loud and the fans cheered and booed with equal intensity. Jeremy was fascinated with the legendary stadium and thrilled when Dale called him down onto the field before the game.

This is his first time in the city and I'm afraid he's getting a skewed view. Dale had once again booked us a first-class flight...Chloe too...then he had a limo pick us up at the airport and drop us off at our five-star hotel. The three-bedroom suite he booked is gorgeous. I don't even want to know what he's paying per night.

We've also had door-to-door car service wherever we want to go and sat in the cushy seats right along the third-base line at the game. Definitely not the trip Jeremy would have had if I'd planned it.

Unfortunately the Waves lost by one run, but I suppose they can't win them all.

After the game, we left the stadium and met my friends for dinner at a restaurant not far from Hope's apartment. She and Dale were formally introduced and he bantered back and forth with both her and Chloe throughout the meal.

"I've been living in the city for years now and have never been to any of the sporting events," Hope said. "Tomorrow will be a whole new experience."

"The stadium is so awesome, Hope. If I lived here, I'd go to every game," Jeremy said then let out a big yawn.

Dale looked from Jeremy to me and said, "If you guys are done eating, would you mind if we headed back to the hotel. I'm bushed."

"I'm kind of tired, too," I said. "It's been a long day."

And while Dale might have said that so we can leave without making Jeremy feel like a child, I actually am tired. It *has* been a long day.

Dale paid the check and we said our goodbyes. Chloe and Hope were moving on to the bar next door, probably to compare notes on Dale. I'll get a full report at some point but right now, I just want to go relax.

Jeremy went right to his room when we got back to the hotel and Dale and I settled onto the couch.

"This day has been surreal," I said. "You're spoiling us."

He rested against the arm of the couch and pulled me farther into his embrace.

"That's my evil plan." He kissed my temple. "To spoil you until you can't live without me."

I wrapped my arm around his waist, snuggled my cheek against his chest, and closed my eyes. His fresh air and sandalwood scent filled my senses and I felt like I was floating on a cloud of happiness.

"I already can't live without you."

DALE

"I DON'T THINK I've ever cheered so much at a game. I may not have a voice tomorrow," Chloe said.

"I believe it," I said. "Fifty thousand people in the stadium and yours was the only voice I could hear."

Everyone at the table laughed at that. We're eating at a little place Hope recommended. Jack and Dan came along and so did Hope's boyfriend, Hanley. Our friends are meshing well and Jeremy is holding his own at a table full of rowdy adults.

It was really nice having my own personal cheering section, especially at an away game. And it was great bringing Jeremy onto the field and even introducing him to some of my friends on the other team. Even though he's a die-hard Waves fan, he respects and appreciates the tradition and history of New York.

Hanley is a born and bred New Yorker but he's been cool about the Waves' victory and the skewed discussion of the game. Honestly, it could have gone either way. All of the pitchers were on fire and the game was tied at one through the eleventh inning. We got lucky when Jack hit a long shot over the right field fence putting us ahead and then we managed to hold them in the bottom of the inning. It was a sweet victory after last night's loss.

"I'll be right back," Hope said. "That DJ is a friend and I want to go say hello."

She walked to the corner of the room and hugged the stocky man who had been setting up equipment.

"Just like at home," I said to Chloe, then explained to the guys. "No matter where we go, we run into someone she knows. And it's been that way as long as I've known her. She even ran into a friend at the stadium today."

Hope returned and leaned over and whispered something in Chloe's ear. She nodded and then smiled when she caught me watching. Karen was talking to Jack so she missed the exchange, but I'm wondering what it's all about. Instead of asking, I figure I'll let it all play out.

Hope's DJ friend introduced himself then said he was starting things off "old school" and put on a song from the early nineties. The music was loud enough to be heard, but not so obnoxious to inhibit conversation.

The waiter came over and cleared our empty dishes then rolled over the dessert cart. Karen and Hope groaned, saying they couldn't eat another bite, but the rest of us took something. And Hope stole bits of Hanley's strawberry-topped flan while Karen sampled my Baileys cheesecake.

"Hey, I have a great idea," Chloe said. "Why doesn't Jeremy hang out with Hope and me tonight and you can meet us for lunch tomorrow and drop your bags off at the apartment so we don't have to lug them to the game."

Jeremy looked from Chloe to Karen and smiled. This must be what they were discussing. And I have to say, I approve. I love Jeremy and having him around is never a hardship, but Karen and I haven't been together in weeks. I had high hopes last night but after uttering the sweetest words, she conked out. I'd carried her to her room and tucked her in so she'd get a good night's sleep.

Since they're flying home tomorrow after the game, tonight is my last chance to get her naked until I'm in

Tampa in a couple weeks. We can make it work once Jeremy goes to bed, but this way, we won't have to wait.

"He doesn't have any clothes with him."

"He's going to sleep and you'll be over with his bag tomorrow," Chloe said.

Karen looked at Jeremy, who was smiling at her with pleading eyes.

"Okay. If you want to."

"Yes!" Jeremy said. "Thanks Mom."

Once that was settled, Hope looked over at her DJ friend and nodded. Once the song that was playing ended, he picked up the microphone.

"We have a celebration happening tonight," he said. "I've been told we have a perfect storm happening here in our fine city and to mark the occasion, I was asked to play a special song." He looked over at our table, "Hope, Chloe, and Karen, come on up and show us what you've got."

Chloe and Hope jumped up but Karen sat rooted to her seat.

"What did you do?" she asked her friends.

Chloe grabbed her hand and pulled her up. She looked back at me as she was dragged toward the DJ and handed a microphone.

"Karen always says the way we interact reminds her of her friends and I definitely see it," Jack said.

"They're a lot of fun," Dan said. "I'm glad you talked us into coming with you guys tonight. I wouldn't have wanted to miss this."

The ladies were handed microphones as the beginning notes of *Put Your Records On* by Corinne Bailey Rae started to play. Karen looked like she wanted to strangle her friends at first, but by the end of the song, she was laughing as the three of them sang in perfect harmony.

"This is their favorite song," Jeremy said. "They have a

dance too but there's not enough room here for them to do it."

Good to know. Maybe I'll be able to convince Karen to give me a private show sometime.

I kept my gaze glued to her as she belted out the words, a big smile on her face. She definitely seems happier these days. When we first met, she had an undertone of melancholy. I didn't know her whole story at the time, but even then, it was obvious she'd experienced some kind of tragedy.

But now that veil of sadness seems to be gone, for the most part anyway. Logically I know that's just because time is dulling the pain of her loss, but I like to think I have at least something to do with the fact that she smiles more these days.

We paid the check and left the restaurant shortly after their performance. Hanley walked with Chloe, Hope, and Jeremy to Hope's apartment since it's on the way to his. Dan, Jack, Karen, and I called the car service to pick us up and take us back to the hotel.

Our floor was first so we said our goodbyes and got off the elevator. No one was in the hallway so as soon as the doors closed behind us, I leaned down and tossed her over my shoulder.

"Dale!" she screeched.

We both laughed as I practically ran to our room. I fumbled with the keycard then opened the door and slammed it shut behind us before setting her back on her feet.

Karen's smile faded as I looked deeply into her blue eyes and backed her against the door. Pinning her against it with my body, I rubbed my erection into her hip and pressed my open mouth against her neck, licking and sucking my way down one side and up the other before whispering in her ear.

"I've missed you. It's been too fucking long since I've touched you."

She moaned low in her throat and wrapped her arms around my neck. My mouth met hers and there was nothing soft or sweet about the kiss. As soon as our lips touched, it was hot and wild and sexy as hell.

I grabbed her ass and she wrapped her legs around my waist. She writhed as I thrust against her again and again, putting me too close to the edge. Based on her breathy moans, she's right there, too.

Before I embarrass myself by exploding in my pants, I eased my grip and set her back on the floor, holding her waist while she gained her balance. I unbuttoned her shorts, slid the zipper open, and shoved them down her thighs. Her panties quickly followed. I looked down and admired what I'd uncovered.

I dragged my finger through the glistening wetness on her trimmed blonde curls.

"Mmm, so wet for me. I love it." I lowered my head and she curled her fingers into my hair and met me stroke for stroke as I took her mouth in a tongue-tangling kiss before pulling back. "I love you. So much."

I pulled her T-shirt over her head, tossed it to the floor, then reached around to open her bra and added it to the pile. Lowering my head, I licked one nipple then the other, moving back and forth before settling in on one side. When I drew her into my mouth and sucked hard, she arched and reached her hands under my shirt then scratched her nails down my bare back. One of her hands continued down to squeeze my ass before continuing around to cup the front of my tented shorts.

Since I was distracted with her breasts, I didn't notice when her dexterous fingers opened my shorts until she reached in to wrap her fingers around my cock. I let out a strangled groan as she pumped up and down then drew slow circles around the head with her thumb nearly making me blow.

I backed away and tore off my clothes before reaching out to cup her bottom in my hands again and lift her against the door. Covering her mouth with mine, I buried myself inside her completely with one thrust, groaning at the sense of homecoming that washed over me.

She wrapped her arms around my neck and held tight as I rocked against her, pressing as high and hard as I could. With each stroke she tightened around me until I didn't think I could take it anymore.

Without losing my rhythm, I dragged my mouth from hers and looked into her hooded eyes.

"I can't hold on much longer."

I pumped harder and faster, barely holding back my release. She closed her eyes and dropped her head back against the door as she let out a long groan. I lowered my head and licked at the pulse beating wildly at the base of the throat and felt the first gentle quivers at the tip of my dick. Squeezing her ass, I angled her forward slightly, increasing the pressure on her clit.

That did it. She tightened her legs around my waist and dug her fingers into my shoulders as her inner muscles milked me dry.

I pressed her against the door, holding her tight as I fought to catch my breath. Once my legs felt stable again, I shifted her up, walked her to my bedroom, and placed her gently on the bed.

Leaning down, I kissed her forehead. "I'll be right back."

I went into the bathroom and cleaned myself off then wet a washcloth with warm water and returned to Karen to do the same for her. This is something new for me, too. I've never *never* had sex without a condom before that night in Myrtle Beach.

Through the years, there have been women I've spent a lot of time with who told me they were on birth control, but I never trusted them enough to not use my own. Besides the potential for disease, I was always afraid of pregnancy. While a baby wouldn't have been the worst thing to happen, being tied to some of those women for the rest of my life would be.

Shoving away the thoughts of my shallow past, I concentrated on what I was doing. Karen watched with sleepy eyes as I completed the task. Climbing into bed next to her, I tossed the washcloth toward the bathroom where it landed on the tile floor with a splat.

Pulling her into my arms, I rolled onto my side, taking her with me, until I was spooning her from behind.

"I love you."

"Mmm, I love you, too."

Closing my eyes, I fell into a deep sleep with her sweet vanilla scent surrounding me.

Chapter Twenty-Nine

DALE

IT'S BEEN a long first half of the season, or maybe it just feels that way. Juggling a relationship with my crazy schedule takes more mental energy than I would have thought, but it's definitely worth it. And thankfully Karen has been great about working with me even though, as a single working mom, she has a full schedule of her own.

Standing with my feet shoulder-width apart, I slowly twisted from side to side to loosen my back. I looked up into the stands but didn't see Karen or Jeremy. Bending forward, I placed my palms flat against the grass then walked them out and held a plank before reversing the motion and standing again.

"So you're meeting the parents today, huh?"

I looked at Dan standing across from me.

"Yep." I chuckled. "There's a first time for everything, right?"

"Just be grateful her father isn't *Mac Flynn*. I know that's just a character my father-in-law plays but Aaran still made my balls retreat when he warned me to be good to Hannah, leaving the *or else* unsaid." Jack gave an exaggerated shiver.

"There is that," I said. "But I'm actually looking forward to meeting them. It means our relationship is moving forward."

"With you married and you in a committed relationship, I'm convinced hell has frozen over," Dan said looking at us in turn.

"My first date with Karen was four months ago today."

I know I have a sappy smile on my face but I don't even care if they bust my ass about it. I'm too happy to care.

We finished stretching and headed toward the dugout. Karen had told me they might not make it for the start of the game so I didn't get concerned when the first pitch was thrown and I still didn't see them in the stands.

Our first three batters got out so I grabbed my glove and ran out to first base and shifted my focus to the game. Rusty took the mound and after getting ahead with two quick strikes, gave up a little excuse-me hit that rolled so slow, no matter how fast Jimmy Chavez charged it or how hard he fired it to me, the runner was safe.

The next batter hit a one hopper right to me. I snagged it then pivoted and tossed the ball to second then got out of the way as Jack threw the ball to Rusty, who ran over to cover first base for a 3-6-1 double play. The next batter struck out to end the first inning. As I ran off the field, I spotted Karen and Jeremy and a man and woman I assume to be her parents sitting in the stands. I smiled up at them and waved before stepping into the dugout.

I stood in the on-deck circle and looked up at Karen

and her family. Her father looked happy listening to Jeremy animatedly talk about something. But her mother looked less than thrilled to be here. Whether that's because she's not a fan of baseball or not a fan of me I'm not sure, but either way, I can't worry about it now. I have a game to concentrate on.

We're behind by two runs here in the seventh and we need to start making things happen. After Riddle struck out, Kasprzyk went deep into the count then managed to sneak a ground ball between short and third for a single.

I stepped up to the plate and took a called first strike. The next pitch came right at my shoulder and I couldn't get totally out of the way. It got me in my upper arm and I took my base. I have no idea what's going on but the precedent was set in spring training and I continue to get hit by pitches. It's insane. But it gives us runners on first and second with one out so I can't complain.

After the pitcher settled onto the mound, I took a step and a half toward second. Kasprzyk took a few steps toward third. I caught sight of Karen's mother staring down at me and shook my head to tune her out. I don't want to get picked off because I'm not focusing.

Thankfully I'd gotten my head back in the game because Chavez hit a line drive over the third baseman's head. They stopped Kasprzyk at third, not willing to test the left-fielder's arm, so that stopped me at second.

Shawn Riggs stepped up to the plate and fouled off the first two pitches. After that, he took two balls in the dirt. The next pitch was a hanging curveball. Riggs timed it perfectly and sent a no-doubt-about-it shot out into the left field stands for a grand slam.

As I rounded third, I saw Karen and Jeremy on their feet cheering. I'm still not totally used to the warm feeling they trigger in my chest and I rubbed my hand over it then smiled up at them as I crossed the plate.

I ran out to my position in the bottom of the ninth, thankful this game is almost over. We've managed to hold onto the two-run lead Riggs's homerun had given us. And thankfully our closer, Malik Walters was throwing triple digits. Tampa's hitters just couldn't catch up. He struck three batters out with nine pitches.

So we're walking out of here with another win on the books. Now I just have to get cleaned up and meet Karen's parents so hopefully I can score a win there, too.

KAREN

DALE HAD BOOKED a table in one of the private alcoves at Gianni's.

Jeremy and I rode with my parents and he's meeting us here. Then we'll get a ride home with him.

The waitress had just filled our water glasses when Dale arrived.

"Sorry I'm late." He leaned down and gave me a quick kiss then hugged Jeremy.

Walking around the table, held out his hand to shake my mother's then my father's. "It's nice to meet you, Mrs. Jenkins, Mr. Jenkins."

My mother just offered a small smile in return. I have no idea what her issue is but I've warned her through the whole game that she better behave during this dinner. She doesn't have to love Dale like I do, but she does have to be polite.

"It's nice to meet you, too." My father stood and shook

his hand. "I've certainly heard a lot about you from Jeremy. He's definitely a fan of yours."

"I'm a fan of his, too."

Dale smiled at Jeremy as he sat between us.

My mother watched their interaction, her lips in a thin straight line. I've told him that my mother isn't quite sure about us dating. Hopefully he'll charm her the way he did me.

The waitress came back to recite the specials and placed two baskets of bread in the middle of the table along with the seasoned olive oil. Dale looked at me, then my mom and dad.

"Do you want to order a bunch of appetizers for the table? They're all delicious and we'll be able to sample them all."

"That sounds like a great plan," my dad said.

Dale rattled off a list of appetizers without looking at the menu.

When the waitress left, he tilted his head toward Jeremy and said, "One of those fried mozarellas is for you. I know how much you like it."

"Thanks Monte."

"And this bread is amazing."

Picking up the basket, Dale held it out toward Jeremy and me to take a slice before he took one. My father followed his lead picking up the basket and holding it out to my mother but she shook her head. He shrugged and took a slice before placing the basket back on the table.

"How's your shoulder, Monte?" Jeremy asked.

"It's a little sore right now but it'll be better tomorrow. You know how it is. You've been hit by pitches before."

"I've never been hit with a ninety-eight-mile-an-hour fastball." Jeremy laughed. "Is there a bruise yet? Can you see the stitches?"

Dale pulled up the sleeve of his polo shirt revealing a bright purple bruise on the top of his arm and the curve of his shoulder. And yes, you can see the stitches.

My mother's eyes widened. "Will you be able to play with that?"

I think they're the first words she said directly to Dale up to this point.

He nodded. "It's just a bruise. The trainer made me put ice on it right after the game so that helped control some of the swelling. That's what took me so long to get here. I had to keep the ice pack on for fifteen minutes."

"It looks so painful," she added.

"I think it looks worse than it feels. That or I'm just getting used to it. For some reason, I keep getting hit this season."

That led to Jeremy telling my parents about all the times Dale has been hit by the ball this season.

After the waitress brought out the appetizers and took our orders, Dale said, "Okay, enough talk about me." He looked at my father. "Mr. Jenkins, Jeremy tells me you're a great golfer," Dale said. "Maybe you can tell me your secret because my game is pretty pathetic."

I enjoyed a sampling of the food while my father, Jeremy, and Dale discussed golf. My dad was thrilled when Jeremy showed interest in the game because neither my brother nor I like to play. Jason used to fill in if my dad needed a fourth player, but it wasn't his favorite game either. But so far Jeremy likes it so my dad takes him out either to the driving range or to play a round whenever he can.

Once there was a break in the conversation, my mother pounced.

"So Dale, do you have any children?"

"Nope, no children."

"Have you ever been married?"

"No."

"A man your age must have had some serious relationships through the years."

I shot my mother a warning look but she ignored me. Dale squeezed my hand, letting me know it was okay.

"Not really," he said. "I never met anyone I wanted a serious relationship with until now."

My mother is very computer literate and I have no doubt she's Googled Dale and knows all about his dating history. Hell, she probably knows his social security number, blood type, and mother's maiden name.

She raised her eyebrows before taking a drink. I took the opportunity to ask Jeremy about his plans with Chloe the next weekend. While my mom isn't a huge fan of Chloe's, she knows Jeremy is so she won't say anything derogatory about her.

The waitress came and cleared our appetizer plates, refilled the water, and took additional drink orders. Jeremy excused himself to go to the bathroom. Without him at the table, my stomach twisted as I wondered what embarrassing question my mother would ask next. But Dale decided to take things into his own hands instead of waiting for her to attack.

"Mrs. Jenkins, I totally understand if you're concerned about me dating Karen and spending time with Jeremy. But let me assure you that while this relationship thing is relatively new to me, my feelings for Karen are very real."

He looked at me and smiled. "When I saw her for the first time two years ago, I knew she was special. She was standing at the wall at Victory Park and I was all the way across the infield but there was a connection between us I couldn't ignore."

Turning back to face my mom, he said around a

chuckle, "Trust me, I tried because she turned me down every time I asked her out for two years." Turning serious, he added, "Once she agreed to that first date, I swore I would do everything and anything to keep her in my life and make her happy. And that includes Jeremy. I love them both and I'm here for as long as they'll have me."

Chapter Thirty

KAREN

"SO WHAT ARE you doing tomorrow night?" Chloe asked.

She's taking Jeremy to a wall climbing gym then he's spending the night at her place.

"Catch up on laundry and clean the house. Then I'm getting a mani/pedi at three o'clock, but after that I'm not sure. Watch the game. Read a book. Relax."

It's been a long week. I've been busy at work, Jeremy has had practice every night except for Wednesday, when we went out to dinner with my parents. Which, I have to say, went well.

"It's too bad Dale is on the road again or you could have had some alone time." She bobbed her eyebrows. "Speaking of, I want more details about your dinner with the parents. You said he managed to charm Marge?"

"It seemed like it. Her judgy stare wasn't so bad by the end of the night."

"Then I'll have to talk to Dale and ask him how it's

done. It's two decades later and I'm still seeing that stare. Which is mind boggling because she loved Jason."

"She did, but you know it took time. And even though she liked him, she still wasn't happy we stayed together all those years. She told me I was going to regret not 'exploring the world.'" I used air quotes around those last three words. "But you know she and my dad didn't get married until she was thirty and they started dating two years before that. She had a whole life and career before they even met." I shrugged. "I guess she felt I was missing out by being 'tied down' to Jason all those years, but I never felt that way. We were happy together so why go *exploring*?"

"All true points. You're not really an exploring kind of gal."

"I can't imagine dating the way you and Hope used to. It exhausted me just listening to your stories. And the one girl in my office is always entertaining us with her tales of online dating. It's at the point where she meets these guys and expects the dates to be bad. So what's the point?" I shook my head. "I'd rather be alone."

"I agree and there's no way I'd do what I used to. It was fun back in my twenties, but I'm much more discerning now."

"But back to Wednesday's dinner. I'd warned her to behave and with Jeremy sitting right there, she didn't say anything. But she can't control her face." I chuckled. "The first time that pissy look disappeared was when Jeremy asked Dale how his arm was feeling after getting hit by a pitch. When he showed us his swollen, purple arm, she looked shocked instead of disapproving. Then the inquisition started. I seriously thought she was going to ask about his intentions toward me."

"But you said Dale cut her off."

She looked so excited by that fact.

"He basically told her that it took him two years to convince me to go out with him and he'll do anything to keep me and Jeremy in his life."

"You know, I'll admit when I first nudged you to go out with him, I just wanted you to get out and have fun with a hot guy. But Dale has surpassed my lack of expectation and you two are really great together."

"Things with him definitely turned out to be more than I expected."

"You love him."

That wasn't a question.

"And he loves you."

Neither was that.

"We actually exchanged the words in Myrtle Beach." I shook my head and laughed. "This is all still surreal to me but I'm not doubting or questioning it anymore. Dale has let me know how he feels in every way possible and more than that, he makes me happy."

"He's definitely a keeper."

DALE

"YOU OWE ME FOR THIS," I said to Dan as I spotted Monica Blair across the room.

She was one of the see-and-be-seen women I spent time with through the years and the architect of the new children's wing at our local hospital. Dan has always been involved here, making donations, attending fundraisers, and more importantly, regularly visiting the children.

Through the years, he's gotten Jack, Cal, and me

involved along with a few other teammates. But the four of us are the ones here today for the ribbon cutting.

"That woman is a shark," Jack said. "I don't know why you ever spent any time with her."

"I could tell you but you might blush," I said. "But seriously, she was just someone to spend time with when I was in town and she didn't want more than that either. So it worked out well for a while."

"She strutted you around town like a prize pony and used your name to open doors for her."

Jack has a point, but I honestly didn't care at the time. But once I met Karen and decided I wanted more out of a relationship, I stopped seeing her. She wasn't happy because of the reason Jack mentioned, but eventually stopped calling.

And now she's here and I do kind of feel like she's circling me. She's been talking to the heads of the hospital, but her attention has most definitely been on me.

The photographer asked us for a photo so Dan, Jack, Cal, and I posed. That spurred Monica into action and she rushed across the lobby to my side.

"Can you get a photo of the five of us?" She'd placed her arm on the photographer's arm to stop his departure. And even though what she'd said was phrased as a question, it definitely wasn't one.

She plastered herself against my side, wrapping her arm around my waist. Logic would dictate that she should be in the middle. She's a foot shorter than the four of us and with her on the end, I imagine the photo is going to look lopsided. But honestly, I don't really care. I just want the guy to hurry up and snap the picture so I can peel Monica off my side.

Just before the guy snapped the photo, I felt her hand slide down to my ass and squeeze. I looked down at her but she just gave me a big smile before turning her attention toward the camera again. I moved out of her grasp and stepped away as soon as the guy had his shots.

She gave me a saucy smile over her shoulder as she walked away.

The guys and I did our thing there and then, since we have a few hours before we have to be at the stadium, decided to go to lunch.

"Thanks for today, guys," Dan said. "I owe you one."

"Yes you do. Monica grabbed my ass while we were taking that picture. And I swear that perfume she douses herself in is embedded in my jacket. I need to send it to get dry cleaned."

I'll admit that same scent used to be like an aphrodisiac, but now it just turns my stomach.

The waitress brought our burgers and refilled our drinks. We dug into the food, putting a good dent in it before speaking again.

"So Hannah said Karen and Jeremy might be coming up again."

I nodded and finished chewing, then swallowed and took a drink.

"It's not definite yet, but it's looking good."

We're home for the next couple days, then in Ohio and Texas, followed by a ten-day stretch on the west coast. Then we're home for nine days. If all goes well, Karen and Jeremy will come stay for at least those nine days.

"You know my wife is taking full credit for your relationship."

"I'm aware," I said around a chuckle. "And since she's the one who convinced Karen to come to my birthday party, I'll let her take it."

"If they do come down, you should bring Jeremy to the academy," Cal said, referring to the *Next Step Baseball*

Academy he and Dan opened last year. "He can work out and get familiar with the place. Maybe convince his mom it's where he wants to train."

"I'm sure he'd love it and I'll bring him with no ulterior motive."

But I'll admit, life would be much easier if Karen and Jeremy lived in Myrtle Beach. I can't ask her to uproot her whole life just to be with me at this point. Once we get through the season, instead of heading to my ranch in Aspen, I plan on heading down to Clearwater instead. I'll have the whole winter plus spring training to devote to our relationship. After we celebrate our one year anniversary, we can figure out what we'll do going forward.

Chapter Thirty-One

DALE

"CALL HANNAH as soon as you can," Jack said as I got out of the shower.

I didn't like the look on his face, but instead of grilling him, I went to my locker and grabbed my phone and called Hannah.

"What's wrong?" I asked as soon as she answered.

"Relax, it's nothing too awful, but it's definitely something you should know."

I'm not totally reassured when she says it's not *totally awful* because Hannah has had to deal with some horrible shit through the years. So her idea of awful and mine probably aren't the same.

"There's a picture of you and Monica Blair looking pretty chummy circling the internet."

"It has to be from years ago."

"It's from the ribbon cutting at the hospital last week

and the headline and copy suggest that the two of you have rekindled your relationship."

"Mother fucker!" I yelled at the top of my lungs. Dragging my fingers through my wet hair, I squeezed the back of my neck instead of punching the wall like I'm dying to do.

"Right now, it's just on local sites, but you know how things explode once they get on the internet. I figured I'd let you know so you can give Karen a head's up."

"I appreciate it, Hannah. Thank you."

Honestly, if she didn't tell me about the picture, I probably wouldn't have known. I stopped reading stories about me a long time ago.

We hung up and I got dressed in record time. I need to talk to Karen as soon as possible. Jack had obviously filled Dan in on the details because he didn't look surprised when I told them I was heading to the hotel instead of out to dinner with them like I'd originally planned.

I texted Karen as I waited for my Uber to arrive, asking her if she was available to FaceTime in about a half hour. She said yes with a smiley face emoji so I'm guessing she hasn't seen the pictures.

As soon as I got to my room, I dialed her number. Normally I use my Mac when we FaceTime so I can get comfortable, but I don't want to take the extra time to power it up.

Her beautiful, smiling face filled my phone screen.

"Hi there," she said. "You have great timing. We just got home." I'd been trying to control the sense of panic I've been feeling since speaking to Hannah, but obviously haven't been successful. "What's wrong? Are you okay?"

"I'm fine. Physically anyway." I dragged my fingers through my hair. "Hannah just told me that there's a picture on the internet of me and a woman I used to see with headlines suggesting we're back together."

"Oh."

She looked down and started nibbling her bottom lip like she does when she's nervous or uncertain. I don't ever want to make her feel either of those things.

"I want you to know that it's total bullshit. She's the architect for the children's wing of the hospital so she attended the ribbon cutting I was at last week with Dan, Jack, and Cal. I haven't seen the picture, but honestly the only contact I had with her at the event was during a photo opp and the guys were in it too, so I'm not sure how anyone could come to the conclusion that we're together." She continued to look down and bite her lip. "Please say something. Anything. I need to know what you're thinking."

Her gaze met mine through the screen.

"So you're saying there's nothing happening with this woman?"

"No, nothing. I haven't laid eyes on her in nearly two years and we were in each other's company for less than five minutes at that event."

Karen knows I wasn't a saint before I met her, but it's still embarrassing admitting how shallow I kept my relationships. But despite my discomfort, I told her about Monica and explained that she liked spending time with me because of how my name increased her profile in a male-dominated field. I got no-strings sex out of the deal, but thankfully Karen didn't make me spell that out.

"I realize that most of what's on the internet is fake but I'm still glad you let me know. It would have been a shock to see the picture without warning."

I blinked. "So we're okay?"

"Yeah, we're okay. Unless there's something more."

I stared into her eyes and my mouth curled up into a smile.

"Have I told you how much I love you?"

She flashed a sexy smirk. "I think you've mentioned it once or twice. But you can tell me again. I don't mind."

KAREN

I FLIPPED through the *Netflix* menu, trying to find something to binge watch that will numb my brain enough so I can't think. In the past week, more pictures of Dale and that woman have appeared on the internet, each with a sexy are-they-back-on headline. He swears they're not, but at this point, I have to wonder if I'm just being a fool.

After dropping Jeremy off at school this morning, I headed back home and curled up on the couch instead of going into the office like usual. While I haven't officially announced to anyone there that Dale and I are dating, they found out. I can't face the looks of pity or deal with hearing the whispers today.

Before I could settle on something to watch, my phone rang. I held my breath until I saw Chloe's name on the screen. I'm sure Dale will call as soon as he sees the latest picture and I can't handle talking to him right now. My thoughts and feelings are just too jumbled.

I swiped my finger and Chloe's face filled my screen. A second later Hope appeared.

"I just saw the latest. How are you?" Chloe asked.

There's no way I can answer that, so I just shook my head.

"Sorry but I'm behind on this," Hope said. "I'm looking up the picture now." Her face fell. "Oh shit."

"Well said." My chuckle held no humor.

The latest picture shows Dale and Monica lying on the beach facing each other, him in board shorts and her in a tiny bikini. His hand is resting on her hip and hers is on his chest.

"What are you thinking?" Chloe asked.

"I don't know *what* to think. He swears he's had no contact with her in two years and I bought that after the first picture. But this is what, the eighth one? I want to believe him, but at this point, I'm afraid I'm just being gullible."

"Have you talked to anyone else? Hannah?" Hope asked.

I shook my head. "It's not a good sign if I have to check what Dale is telling me with someone else, is it?"

"I guess not," she said.

"Are you still going up there in a couple weeks?" Chloe asked

"I hate to disappoint Jeremy but I don't know how I can go if this continues." Dale's name flashed on my phone. "He's calling right now," I said, then hit the *decline* button. "I need to get my thoughts together before I talk to him."

"I know you didn't ask for my opinion, but I'm going to give it anyway," Chloe said.

"Now there's something new." I rolled my eyes.

"I believe him. What he told you about that woman using their relationship to further her career makes sense. I did a little digging and rumor has it, she's starting her own firm. I'm sure she's behind the articles. And he said they were involved which explains the pictures."

"See that makes sense," Hope said.

"It does, but I still need some time to process all this. I mean, if this Monica person is doing this, who else is going to pop out of the woodwork with their own stories?"

"So you're breaking it off with him?" Chloe asked.

I blinked back the tears thoughts of that brought on and swallowed.

"I think we need to take a break."

My phone buzzed and Dale's name popped up on my screen again. Instead of declining this time, I said, "That's him again. I better go tell him what I'm thinking."

Chapter Thirty-Two

DALE

THIS FUCKING break is driving me insane. And I swear, Monica Blair better hope I don't see her because I won't be responsible for my actions.

My teammates have given me a wide berth and I can't blame them. I've been miserable. I haven't spoken to Karen in a week and it seems like forever.

After getting my shoulders rubbed down, I took an extra-long shower, turning the water as hot as I could stand it. I've been so tense lately, my back and neck feel like they're made out of cement. Plus I have a headache I can't shake.

The good thing is that the locker room is mostly empty by the time I get out of the shower. I dried off and stepped into my boxer briefs and pants.

"You coming to dinner?" Jack asked.

I turned to look at him as I slipped into my shirt and buttoned it.

"No, but thanks."

He leaned against the locker, put his hands in his pock-ets, and just stared at me.

"Did you draw the short straw and get stuck having to talk to me?" I asked.

"Something like that," he said, not moving or changing position. "I've been where you're at. Not for the same reason, but if you'll remember, Hannah told me she wanted a break and I felt like someone stuck a fist into my chest and ripped my heart out."

"So then you understand."

"I do."

I put on my shoes, stood, and looked him in the eye.

"It just sucks the big hairy meatball."

The corner of his mouth kicked up.

"Yeah it does," he said. "Is she still coming up when we get back?"

Tomorrow is our last night in Texas and then we head out to the west coast. Hannah and Jeremy are supposed to be coming to Myrtle Beach when I get there for the nine-day home stretch.

"She hasn't canceled their plane reservations or told Jeremy about our *break*, so that gives me a spark of hope," I said. "I just spoke to him last night. He sent me game video of him throwing the circle change I showed him and said he's excited about the trip. I can't imagine she'd disap-point him at the last minute. But at this point, I don't know."

"Why don't you come out to dinner? You know we can handle your pissy mood and it's better than sitting alone in your room and obsessing about it."

Jack followed when I started walking toward the door.

"Thanks but I'm beat. I'll probably fall right to sleep."

He didn't look convinced, but didn't push. Like he said, he's been there.

Dan stood just inside the door leading out to the parking lot talking on the phone. He looked at Jack, who shook his head, then said something else and ended the call.

"You know how to reach us if you need us."

I followed them outside, the heavy door slammed behind us.

They said goodbye and hopped into the car that had been idling at the curb.

I opened my app and requested my own car.

For the millionth time, I brought up Karen's name on my phone and thought about calling her, or at least texting. But she asked for space and I promised I'd give it to her.

Still, maybe a text just to let her know I'm thinking of her would be okay.

I don't know.

My car pulled up and I got into the back seat. The driver confirmed my destination then drove through the parking lot and out onto the road. Resting my head back, I looked up at the pattern on the headliner thinking about this situation with Karen.

I understand her need to take some time but it really is driving me nuts. As we merged onto the highway, I looked out the window, seeing my miserable reflection in the glass. Looking at my phone again, I brought up Karen's name and before I could second-guess myself typed a message.

> Just wanted you to know that I'm thinking of you. I miss you and love you. xoxo

Some of the tension left my shoulders as I hit send. It makes me feel better to have some sort of communication with her.

I held my phone in my hand. If she messages back, I don't want to miss it.

Out of nowhere, bright lights stabbed my eyes and I looked out the window to see their source.

"Shit!" I heard from the front seat as the driver echoed my thoughts. "Hold on."

He swerved to the right, but couldn't get out of the way of the car that had hopped the barrier from the other side of the highway and was coming right at us.

I heard a loud crash and felt my head slam against the window then everything went black.

KAREN

I LOOKED at Dale's text for the hundredth time in the past half hour, trying to decide if I should message him back. It's been a week since we've spoken and I'll admit, it's been awful. If it wasn't for Jeremy, I probably would have spent all seven days wallowing in bed.

He has no idea that we've taken a break. If things end up working out, it's no use upsetting him over nothing. And if they don't...well, then he'll find out later.

My mother has been chattering in my ear, leaving the "I told you so" unsaid but I've heard it loud and clear. The stories have been limited to small internet sites and media local to Myrtle Beach but since she set up a Google alert on Dale, she saw every one of them. She even came back down to Clearwater to "support" me through this.

If anything, her interference has made me want to run back to Dale. I've missed him so much and maybe I'm a fool, but I believe everything he's told me. I just want to take the time I asked for to make sure I can handle it if it happens again.

Rolling over, I plugged in my phone and placed it on the nightstand. I grabbed the remote and turned on the TV and clicked on *The Office*, picking up the series where I'd left off last night. Ironically, the episode playing is the one Dale told me is his favorite. Andy had just punched a hole in the wall when my phone rang.

Shifting over, I picked it up and saw Hannah's number on the screen. I thought I would have heard from her before now, pleading Dale's case. She's supposedly trying to find the source of the articles, but since I've broken contact, I haven't heard if that's happened.

But if she was calling to discuss either of those things, she probably wouldn't have waited until nearly midnight.

"Hi Hannah," I said.

"Karen."

I sat up and whipped the blankets off.

"What's wrong?"

"Dale's been in a car accident."

"Oh my God!"

I jumped out of bed and started running around the room, grabbing clothes.

"Relax, he's at the hospital and in stable condition. They're running tests to rule out internal injuries."

"I have to see him," I said then put the phone on speaker and dropped it onto the bed. After ripping off Dale's Waves T-shirt, I put on my bra and pulled on my own shirt. "Can you text me his details? I need to go see him."

"Karen, I know how upsetting this is for you but you have to try to relax. You don't want to get into an accident rushing off."

Her calm words slowed down my manic behavior. I sat on the bed and dragged my hands through my hair.

"Okay," I said. "I'm okay now."

"I have you booked on the first flight to Houston in the morning. A car will pick you up at seven and another one will meet you at the airport and take you to the hospital to see Dale. I didn't think you'd want to take Jeremy, but I can add him if you decide you want to."

"No I'd better go myself. And thank you Hannah. For calling, calming me down, and booking the arrangements."

"He's going to be okay, Karen. It's not like—" She paused. "Let me know when you get there, okay?"

"I will, and thanks again."

As soon as we hung up, I called my mother.

"Hello." Her sleepy voice answered on the second ring.

"Mom, I'm sorry to call so late, but I need a favor. Could you come over around six-thirty in the morning and stay with Jeremy for a couple days?"

"Is everything all right?"

"Dale was in a car accident. He's in the hospital in Houston and I'm going to see him."

"But I thought—"

"Mom, we were just taking some time apart. We didn't break up. I love him and I want to be with him," I said. "If you can't stay with Jeremy, I'll take him with me."

"No, I can come over." She paused. "I just want you to be happy Karen."

"I know Mom and thank you. I'll see you in the morning."

Chapter Thirty-Three

KAREN

THE FLIGHT TOOK JUST a little over two hours but I shifted and fidgeted in my seat the entire time. I felt sorry for the woman sitting next to me.

I'm doing the same thing in the car but at least I'm by myself. I sent Hannah a quick text to let her know I landed and am on my way to the hospital.

I'd only managed to sleep a couple hours last night, and I'm surprised I got that much. For hours, every time I closed my eyes, I pictured Dale hurt so I fought to keep them open. But I drifted off at some point and woke to my buzzing alarm.

I got dressed, packed a bag, and waited until the last minute to tell Jeremy what's going on. He asked to come but I reassured him that Dale is all right and there was no reason for him to miss baseball. He was asleep again by the time my mom got to the house.

Thankfully she didn't lecture me before I left. She actually seemed more concerned about me considering my late husband died in a car accident and now the man I love was just in one.

We only had a few minutes before the car arrived but I explained everything to her one last time. I even included what Chloe said about Monica Blair opening her own firm and that she's probably looking to drum up media attention.

She didn't seem totally convinced but told me she'd support me in whatever I decide to do. Since I was rushing off to Houston to see Dale, I think that's pretty obvious.

Finally we pulled up to the hospital. I was out of the car before the driver got out to open my door. I thanked him, hiked my bag over my shoulder, and ran through the sliding doors.

Hannah had given me his room number and assured me no one would stop me from seeing him even though we're not family.

I followed the signs to the elevator and thankfully one came almost immediately. The short ride to the third floor seemed to take forever and the doors were barely open when I ran out and down the hallway.

After turning the wrong way, I righted my direction and slowed in the busier space. A man was exiting the room as I approached.

"Can I help you?"

"I'm here to see Dale." I looked over his shoulder as though I'd be able to see through the door. "My name is Karen."

He narrowed his eyes and studied me then smiled and reached out his hand to shake mine.

"So you're the famous Karen," he said. "I'm Travis Pearce, Dale's agent."

"It's nice to meet you." I glanced at the door again. "Can I see him?"

"I think he'd fire me if I kept you away any longer."

He reached behind him and opened the door then stepped aside so I could enter.

"See you later, buddy," he said and walked away.

Dale's gaze never left mine as I slowly walked into the room. The whole right side of his face is bruised and he has a bandage over his eye. But he's alive and breathing and I want to launch myself at him. I just don't want to hurt him.

Standing at the side of the bed, I blinked back tears.

"I'm so happy you're okay."

Placing my hand over my mouth, I covered a sob.

"Oh baby, don't cry."

He held out his left hand and I went to that side of the bed and sat next to him.

"I was so worried."

"How'd you find out?"

"Hannah called me. Didn't she tell you?"

"No I haven't spoken to her. My phone was crushed in the accident."

"How did she find out then?"

"The car service let someone in the organization know. They called Travis and obviously Hannah called you. The only person I was able to talk to was Penny."

"Is she coming?"

"I told her not to. She's at camp now and I'm banged up but I'll be out of here tomorrow if not later tonight. By the time she got permission to leave, I'll be on my way home." He studied my face then met my gaze again. "I'm so glad you're here. I've missed you so much."

"I've missed you too. I'm so sorry."

I wiped away the tears that had escaped.

"Don't be sorry. You're here now and that's all that matters."

He pulled me closer for a kiss but I stopped before our lips touched.

"I don't want to hurt you," I said.

"Right now, not touching you hurts."

I pressed my mouth to his carefully making sure to keep my hands off his chest and splinted wrist. He groaned and wrapped his hand around the back of my head, holding me in place when I started to pull back. Moving his mouth back and forth over mine, he kissed me slow and sweet.

We pulled apart like guilty children when a nurse walked into the room.

"Sorry to interrupt," she said. "I just want to check your vitals and change that bandage."

Dale held on to my hand when I stood. The nurse smiled.

"I'm guessing you don't want me to ask her to leave," she said.

Dale kissed my hand. "Absolutely not."

She nodded and wrapped her hand around his wrist to check his pulse.

"Is there any word on the driver?" he asked her.

"I can't tell you anything other than he's in stable condition. But I'll tell his nurse to let him know you're asking about him."

She finished her physical assessment and reached up to remove the bandage over his right eye. I cringed when I saw the stitches and the full extent of the bruising. After disappearing into the bathroom, she returned with a basin of soapy water.

"You're very lucky you weren't sitting on the other side

of the car." She wet a piece of gauze and pressed it over the stitches, cleaning away the dried blood.

"I know. My agent showed me the pictures. It looks like the back half of the driver's side took most of the impact."

She dried off the stitches, applied an ointment, then covered them with another piece of gauze, securing it in place with tape.

"Do you think I'll be released today?" he asked.

"That depends on what the rest of the tests say. You have a concussion but as long as you have someone to keep an eye on you, you'll be okay to go." She glanced at me and smiled again. "And I'm assuming you do."

"Absolutely," I said.

"It looks like you're in good hands here," she said. "I'll see what's holding up those results.

DALE

THANKFULLY ALL MY tests came back negative and other than the concussion and a sprained wrist, I received a clean bill of health. The doctor released me around dinner time and Karen and I took a car to my hotel.

She kept fussing and seemed afraid to touch me but I guess that's to be expected. I know I look like shit and I also know it's gonna be even worse tomorrow. But no amount of pain or bruising will stop me from wanting to hold her and have her touch me.

We ordered room service and after eating, I made use of the new phone Hannah had sent to the hotel to make some calls. Penny and Jeremy were at the top of my list and I also texted the guys to let them know I was released and that I have a phone. Then I called Hannah and thanked her for said phone as well as for calling Karen and getting her by my side.

After all that was done, I pulled Karen against me on the bed and switched on the game.

The announcers talked about my accident and wished me well. Theo Bowman will be playing first for the next couple weeks. He's a utility player who can pretty much fill in anywhere on the field, aside from pitcher and catcher. His bat isn't great but he's strong defensively.

As if reading my mind, Karen asked, "How long will you be out?"

"Ten days, maybe two weeks." She shifted back to look at me. "What?"

"You just look so awful. I can't imagine you playing again so soon."

"Awful? Gee thanks."

She laughed at that.

"Those bruises look so painful and all those little cuts must hurt like hell." She kissed my cheek. "But your face is still as handsome as ever. And you know you'll probably have a scar on your forehead that's just going to up your sexiness factor even more. The girls won't be able to resist you."

I know she's being playful, but I need to know that she understands that none of that matters.

"Hey, are we okay?"

She blinked and her smile slowly faded, then she nodded.

"Yeah, we're okay."

"I need you to look me in the eye and tell me that you know none of that stuff printed about Monica Blair and me is true."

"I know," she said. "It's not that I totally believed the

stories but I needed to process everything and make sure I could deal with it all."

"And?"

"I'm here, aren't I?" She kissed my chest before meeting my gaze again. "Dale, I trust you and I promise you that I'm here for the long haul. We were only apart a week and I missed you so much I physically hurt."

"It was horrible." I pulled her close for a quick kiss. "Hopefully by the time my stint on the IL is over, my teammates will forget what an insufferable shit I was while we were apart." That made her giggle. "You think I'm kidding?"

"Well I'm here and I'm not going anywhere again."

I pulled her back against my chest and held her tight thanking the universe for bringing this woman into my life.

Chapter Thirty-Four

KAREN

A MONTH HAS PASSED since Dale's car accident and he's back on the field, playing as good as ever. Two days after he got out of the hospital, we flew back to Clearwater and he spent most of his time on the IL there with Jeremy and me. He returned to Myrtle Beach and after being cleared, joined the team in New York.

The team is heading back home after the game tonight for a seven-day stretch and Jeremy and I are traveling up again to be with Dale.

We're about halfway through the flight and Jeremy pulled out his earbuds and looked over at me.

"Mom, if you and Monte get married, will we be moving up here?"

I shifted in my seat to look at him.

"We're not quite ready to discuss marriage," I said.

"But if you keep going out, it'll probably happen eventually, right?"

"I'm not sure," I said, because honestly, I'm not.

Dale and I have discussed a lot of things but marriage isn't one of them. Since we got together, we've been focused on making it work and besides our little bump with Dale's ex, we have been.

"But you have to know I'd never just agree to up and move us without talking to you. We're a team, right?" I leaned over and bumped my shoulder against his. He nodded and smiled.

"His house is really cool though so it wouldn't be so bad if we did move in with him."

After dropping that bomb, he put in his earbuds and went back to playing his game.

The conversation bounced around my head for the rest of the flight and once we arrived at Dale's house. He won't get home until much later so at least I have time to push it from my thoughts before he arrives.

Instead of making plans with Sabrina, Hannah, and Barbara, Jeremy and I decided to have a quiet night together. We dropped the top on the Mercedes and went out for an early dinner. After filling up on seafood, we took the long way home, enjoying the ride.

I'll admit that the thought of driving the luxury car initially freaked me out but Dale had insisted and it only took one ride for me to get over my fear.

The garage door opened as I approached then closed behind me. After putting the top up, I turned off the car and joined Jeremy inside. He was already perched on the couch flipping through the channels to find the game. Dale has every sports channel known to man so there's no chance we won't be able to watch.

I sat on the other end of the couch just as he found the right channel. Grabbing a pillow, I curled up to watch as Boston took the field.

It still amazes me how comfortable I feel in Dale's home even when he's not here. But it's definitely better when he is. Thankfully it won't take him too long to fly home after the game.

DALE

I WALKED through the garage and into the lower level and stopped short. Karen and Jeremy asleep on the couch is the sweetest thing I've ever seen. I closed the door behind me and rubbed at the warmth in my chest.

After going to my room to change, I went back downstairs and placed a blanket over Jeremy. He snuggled further into the couch sound asleep.

After turning off the overhead light, I walked to the other side of the couch, leaned down, and scooped Karen up in my arms. I thought about taking her to my room but we haven't discussed that, so I brought her into the guest room. I flipped back the blankets and set her down on the bed and covered her. The corners of her mouth curled up into a small smile as she snuggled into the pillow.

I kissed her forehead and left while I still have some will power.

The next morning, I found Karen out on the deck with a mug of coffee. She's wearing cotton shorts and a Waves T-shirt and with her hair in a ponytail, she could pass for a teenager.

"Good morning."

She turned from the railing and smiled. "Good morning. I'm sorry I missed you last night. You should have woken me up."

"If I'd woken you, you wouldn't have gotten any sleep at all."

I leaned down and kissed her, then wrapped my arms around her from behind. She rested back against me and I breathed in her sweet scent.

"It was nice having you here when I got home last night."

"It was nice being here." She set her mug on the railing and settled further against me.

"I'm glad." I kissed the top of her head. "I told you last time you were here that I want you and Jeremy to stay whenever you can and consider it your home." She stiffened after I said that. "What?"

She shook her head. "Nothing."

Placing my hands on her waist, I turned her in my arms to face me.

"We need to be honest with each other for this to work between us. If there's something you don't like here, you need to let me know."

"No, I love it here."

"Then what is it?"

She looked into my eyes and let out a sigh then took my hand and led me to the couch.

"You'll probably want to be sitting down for this conversation."

We sat next to each other and I shifted to face her.

"Karen, you're killing me here. Please tell me what's wrong."

"I'm sorry, nothing is wrong. You can relax." I raised my brow. "Seriously. There's just something I wanted to tell you in case Jeremy brings it up to you." She took in a deep breath and let it out. "On the plane ride down here, Jeremy asked me if we're going to be getting married. Then he asked if we'll be moving here if we do."

"And what did you tell him?"

"I said it was kind of soon to be talking about marriage and that I wouldn't make a decision to move anywhere without discussing it with him first."

I took her hand in mine and kissed in the middle of her palm, then placed her open hand over my heart and looked into her eyes.

"I love you, Karen. I've never said that to another woman. Ever. I know that you're it for me." She blinked but didn't say anything so I continued. "I'd be thrilled if you and Jeremy wanted to move up here. But you're absolutely right, that's something that needs to be discussed. As far as getting married, I'd be lying if I said I haven't thought about it. But I don't want to rush this or you by asking a question you're not ready for." I leaned forward and kissed her. "We've made it this far. The season will be over in a couple months then we have the whole winter and spring training to spend together." She was still listening so I decided to swing for the fence. "And maybe by then, you'll be ready for me to ask that question."

A lone tear traced down her cheek and I wiped it away with my thumb.

"I know I just dumped a ton of stuff on you just now but please say something," I said around a nervous chuckle, wondering if I'd gone too far with that last sentence. "I'm dying here."

"I love you, too." She wiped at the other tears that had escaped. "And everything you said is perfect. I do think we need some more time together, preferably in the same city." Placing her hand on my cheek, she added, "But you need to know that even though I'm not ready to answer that question, you're it for me, too."

I pulled her into my arms and crushed my mouth against hers. As our breath mingled and our tongues tangled, I knew I'd hit a home run with that swing. Slowly ending the kiss, I looked down at her and smiled.

"Come on, let's go cook breakfast." I stood and held out my hand. "If we're gonna plan the rest of our lives together, we'll need a full stomach."

Are you ready for Trey's story?

Chapter 1

Trey

A black Toyota Camry pulled up and I grabbed my bags and walked toward it. The driver popped the trunk and stepped out of the car.

"Trey Youngman?"

"Yep."

He took my bags and dropped them in the trunk and smiled over at me as he slammed the lid shut.

"I'm Joe," he said, and I shook his extended hand. "Holy hell, Trey Youngman in my

car."

He opened the back passenger-side door.

"It's nice to meet you," I said and settled into the back seat.

After slamming my door shut, he jogged around the front of the car and got behind the wheel. I looked out the window as we pulled away from the extended stay hotel that's been my home for the past few weeks, glad to be moving onward and upward.

"I don't normally take such a long fare, but when I saw the name and where this one was going, I couldn't pass it up," Joe said. I nodded in response when he glanced at me through the rearview mirror. "I've followed your career since you started playing for New York. I thought they sent you down too soon. Sure you had some control issues, but nothing you wouldn't have worked out in time." He shrugged and smiled back at me. "But now it looks like you're getting another shot. Good for you."

Again I nodded and as the car merged onto the high-way, I shifted further into the seat and rested my head back. Staring at the ceiling, I prayed for patience. If this guy keeps chattering like this for the whole two-hour drive, I'm gonna need it. The Waves are all about being fan friendly. This is a perfect opportunity for me to practice.

I made sure to keep both my face and voice neutral as I

answered his questions about my former teammates and baseball in general.

"Seriously though," Joe said. "They never gave you enough credit. Maybe it's because

you were in New York. Things are always tougher there." He shrugged. "I don't know, but I've never seen anyone paint the corners like you. You are a true artist on the mound."

"Thanks, I appreciate that."

It's about time someone besides me realizes that. Yes, I grew up with every advantage and was lucky enough to play on elite teams and have lessons with the best instructors but when it came down to it, I had to do the work. I'm the one who has to deliver when I'm standing on that mound alone. But people always lead with the fact that I was born with a silver spoon in my mouth and overlook those things.

Joe was about to say something else when his phone beeped.

"Sorry, I need to check this." After easing over to the side of the road, he put the car in park. "What the hell are the chances?" he said more to himself than me. Then he turned and looked over the seat. "There's someone else going to Myrtle Beach. Would you mind sharing your ride?"

I opened my mouth to give a resounding *hell no* but reconsidered before the words came out. Maybe another person in the car will take Joe's attention off me. Because if I have to put up with two hours of polite conversation, I'm seriously going to lose my shit. And I know that won't go over well with my new team.

"Nope, I don't mind."

He tapped his screen, then shifted the car into drive and pulled back onto the highway. I listened with half an ear as he continued to talk. This ride, more than losing my license, is my punishment for the collection of speeding tickets I accumulated in New York last year.

Of course, my father could have taken care of those tickets with one phone call, but he decided to be a prick instead. So the judge took away my license for six months. Which pissed me off, but wasn't the worst thing in the world when I was living in Manhattan and could just step out of my apartment and hail a cab. But I'd been sent down to Triple-A in Scranton a few months before the sentencing then got traded to Fayetteville shortly after, and not being able to drive in those cities really sucked.

My first instinct was to hire a private car service, but the therapist I'd started seeing in an attempt to become a better person made me realize that wasn't the best move. It was just me using money to avoid the consequences of my actions. In both places, my hotel was only a few blocks away from the stadium and since I wasn't going out every night—or any night for that matter—it wasn't necessary to have a car at my beck and call.

Which is why, after last night's game when I got called up to the Waves, I had to figure out a way to make the hundred-mile trip. I hoped someone from Fayetteville's staff would be able to take me, but supposedly no one was available. So a ride share was my only option.

I'll be paying for Joe's round trip and of course, I'll give him a big tip as long as he gets me to First Allegiant Bank Park in time. Which might be throwing money at the problem, but it's definitely for a good cause.

The last thing I want to do is fuck up this opportunity because I was late getting to the stadium, or because I was rude to my driver. Both of those things seem like a stretch, but it's hard to shake a reputation like the one I cultivated in New York so I know I'm going to be on a short leash with my new team. It wouldn't take much for the Waves to send me back down.

As if he read my thoughts, he said, "Our other passenger is just off this exit, then we'll head right to the stadium so you get there safe and sound in time for tonight's game."

"Thanks."

"You two can split the fare on the app."

"That's fine. I got it."

He turned right then pulled over to the curb and put the car in park.

"That's something you and the lady can discuss," he said, before getting out of the car.

I leaned my elbow against the door and rubbed my eyes. It's been a long day and it's not even noon. Taking in a few deep breaths, I focused on happy thoughts like my therapist always suggests. This ride will be over in a couple hours and I'll be back in the major leagues where I belong.

The door opened and the scent of cinnamon filled the car as the other passenger settled in next to me.

"Thanks for letting me ride along. My car broke down and I need to get back for a three o'clock meeting."

Opening my eyes, I looked over at the woman on the other side of the seat and blinked. Twice.

Her husky voice didn't prepare me for its pixie-like owner.

"No problem," I said, taking in her petite form and bright pink hair before looking into her violet eyes.

"I'm Nori."

She held out her hand and surprised me with her firm grip as I shook it.

"Trey."

Joe got back behind the wheel, started the car, and pulled out into traffic.

"Sit back folks, I'll get you where you need to go in no time."

"You're a lifesaver, Joe," Nori said as she released my hand and wiggled into her seat.

Frowning, I rubbed my hand against my thigh, trying to stop the tingling her touch had caused. I studied the woman next to me, trying to figure out what that's all about. She's definitely not my usual type. Tiny women with pink hair and tattoos who smell like dessert are nowhere on my list.

Nori

I don't know what the deal is with the guy sitting next to me but he's been staring for ten minutes straight. He's pretending to have his eyes closed, but I can feel him watching. At least I'm not sensing disapproval, which is what I'd expect from someone who looks like him.

I mentally shook that last thought away. I don't want people judging me at a glance, so I shouldn't do it either. Even if he is a clone of every prep school, upper-crust guy I grew up with, not to mention my ex-fiancé.

"So you gonna be pitching tonight?" Joe asked.

Trey's whiskey-colored eyes fully opened, sweeping over me before turning toward the front seat.

"They stressed that they wanted me there today so we'll see."

Apparently the guy is a baseball player. That wouldn't have been my first guess for his profession. I would have figured finance or some sort of fancy corporate job. Although, with his straight nose and symmetrical features, he could definitely be a model. Not to mention his eyes.

Their color is amazing, but contrasted with his raven hair, it's truly spectacular and give him a unique look.

My fingers twitched and without thinking, I reached into my purse and pulled out my sketchbook and pencil. With a few quick strokes, I had the outline of his square jaw and perfectly-shaped head. After adding his nose and eyes I paused, my pencil poised over the paper, and shifted my eyes to look at his mouth. His lips are plump and nicely-shaped and I drew them as I imagined they'd look if they weren't set in such a grim line.

But I have to give the guy credit. If I didn't have such a good bullshit meter, I wouldn't even be able to tell he's annoyed by Joe's constant talking. He's being very polite, but I grew up surrounded by people who showed one thing on the surface while something very different was going on inside.

I'd just put the finishing touches on my sketch when Trey shifted in his seat and leaned his head against the window. The light hit his profile perfectly and I flipped to a clean sheet to capture it. I worked quickly, the scratches of my pencil the only sound in the now-quiet car.

It didn't take long for a decent profile to take shape. With quick flicks, I added his hair and smiled to myself. The short messy style looks tousled and carefree but I'd bet my entire last commission it's the result of a $200 haircut and $50 worth of product.

I added some shading to his jaw and smoothed it out with my pinky then my thumb. After adding in a few more details, I looked over at him to check my work and found him watching me. Crossing my legs, I rested my sketchpad against my knee, hopefully blocking his view of the page.

As I felt his eyes on me I continued working, even though all I wanted to do was snap the book closed to ensure he couldn't see. While adding dimension to the black-and-white sketch, I kept picturing those eyes in my mind. The amazing color would be challenging to duplicate in graphite, but I think I could capture them in acrylic or oil. It would take just the right mix of reds, yellows, and blues and a lot of trial and error to get an exact match but it would be worth it.

I glanced over at Trey and was surprised to meet his gaze. His eyes widened just a bit, then shifted toward my purse before meeting mine again.

"Are you an artist?" he asked, I'm assuming in an attempt to distract me from the fact he'd been blatantly staring.

"I am."

"Portraits?"

"Sort of." I tilted my head from side to side. "Portraits are my first love, but I make my living painting murals."

"Like on the side of buildings?"

"No. I mean, I have done that, but now, I mostly do them in people's homes." His brows drew together and I turned my phone so he could see. It's much easier than trying to explain. "This is what I drew for my meeting today. The client wants a fairy garden painted in her daughter's playroom."

"Nice."

"Thanks."

He turned back toward the window and I figured the polite chit-chat was over, but I was wrong.

"How long does it take you to actually paint something like that?"

"This design will take about two weeks since it's pretty large and there's a lot of detail," I said. "Thankfully it's close to home so if I get the job I won't have to travel far."

"Is that how long most of your jobs take?"

"No. This last one in Fayetteville just took the weekend, but it was a pretty simple design."

"What was it?"

"My client's husband is a huge Penn State fan so I transformed his man cave into his own

little Happy Valley. It was her anniversary gift to him."

"Nice gift."

"He seemed to like it."

"Do you have a picture?"

I flipped through my gallery and pulled up the panoramic photo I'd taken then handed him my phone.

His fingertips brushed against the screen as he moved the picture left to right and back again before nodding and handing the phone back to me.

"That doesn't look simple to me."

"Compared to some things, it is."

"Do you have a card?"

"Like a business card?"

The corners of his mouth curled slightly as he nodded. That was such a stupid question. What other kind of card would he be asking for? My cheeks were probably as pink as my hair as I reached into the side pocket of my purse, pulled out a card, and handed it to him.

He studied it before tucking it into his shirt pocket, then shocked the hell out of me by asking about my process and then my favorite project. I'd just finished showing him pictures of the latter when Joe spoke, pulling my attention to the front seat.

"I'm gonna drop Trey off at the stadium first then circle back around to drop you off."

I glanced at my watch, surprised we've been on the road for just about two hours.

"That sounds good." I looked at Trey. "My email

address is on my business card if you want to pop into the app so we can split the cost."

"No worries," he said. "I got it."

"I can't let you do that."

"Sure you can. I was going this way anyway."

"If you're using that logic, so was I."

He smiled at that. Not a slight curling of the lips, but a full-blown, dimple-popping smile that transformed his face from amazing into something truly spectacular. I took a mental picture so I could sketch it later. Like as soon as he stepped out of the car.

"That's true," he said. "But seriously, I got it."

"Well, thank you. I appreciate it."

I fought the urge to fidget or obsessively tuck my hair behind my ear, or bite my fingernails like I would have done years ago.

Joe turned off the interstate and we moved in stops and starts through traffic. Before long we pulled up in front of First Allegiant Bank Park.

"Is there another entrance where I should drop you?" Joe asked.

Trey glanced out the window and looked around.

"This is fine." He looked at me and patted his pocket. "I'll be in touch when I buy a house."

That said, both he and Joe stepped out of the car. I heard the trunk pop open and glanced out the back window. Trey was mostly hidden by the trunk lid, but his ass peeked out just enough for me to appreciate. Which I did.

I jumped in my seat when they slammed the trunk shut. Shifting to face forward, I watched through the rearview mirror as Trey shook Joe's hand, picked up his bags, and walked toward the stadium entrance.

Joe got back behind the wheel and smiled at me over his shoulder.

"We'll get you to your destination in no time," he said.

"Thanks Joe, you're a prince."

I reached into my purse for my pencil and sketchbook, but instead of flipping the book open, I placed it back in my purse and rested my head against the window.

The image of Trey's smiling face is burned into my mind and I'm sure it won't go away any time soon. And when I draw it, I want to take my time and savor every single pencil stroke.

* 9 7 8 1 9 6 1 5 3 9 1 5 0 *